Heartsong

By
Lynn Ames

HEARTSONG
© 2010 BY LYNN AMES

ISBN: 978-0-9840521-3-4

This trade paperback original is published by

PHOENIX RISING PRESS
PHOENIX, ARIZONA
www.phoenixrisingpress.com

First Printing: October 2007

CREDITS
EXECUTIVE EDITOR: LINDA LORENZO
COVER PHOTOS: JUDY FRANCESCONI, PAM LAMBROS
AUTHOR PHOTO: JUDY FRANCESCONI
COVER DESIGN BY: PAM LAMBROS,
WWW.HANDSONGRAPHICDESIGN.COM

Visual Epilogue™ is a registered trademark of Judy Francesconi, and used with permission for this publication.

Dedication

For those who truly believe in that one great love.

Other Books in Print by Lynn Ames

Outsiders

What happens when you take five beloved, powerhouse authors, each with a unique voice and style, give them one word to work with, and put them between the sheets together, no holds barred?

Magic!!

Brisk Press presents Lynn Ames, Georgia Beers, JD Glass, Susan X. Meagher and Susan Smith, all together under the same cover with the aim to satisfy your every literary taste. This incredible combination offers something for everyone — a smorgasbord of fiction unlike anything you'll find anywhere else.

A Native American raised on the Reservation ventures outside the comfort and familiarity of her own world to help a lost soul embrace the gifts that set her apart. * A reluctantly wealthy woman uses all of her resources anonymously to help those who cannot help themselves. * Three individuals, three aspects of the self, combine to create balance and harmony at last for a popular trio of characters. * Two nomadic women from very different walks of life discover common ground — and a lot more — during a blackout in New York City. * A traditional, old school butch must confront her community and her own belief system when she falls for a much younger transman.

Five authors — five novellas. *Outsiders* — one remarkable book.

One ~ Love, (formerly The Flip Side of Desire)

Trystan Lightfoot allowed herself to love once in her life; the experience broke her heart and strengthened her resolve never to fall in love again. At forty, however, she still longs for the comfort of a woman's arms. She finds temporary solace in meaningless, albeit adventuresome encounters, burying her pain and her emotions deep inside where no one can reach. No one, that is, until she meets C.J. Winslow.

C.J. Winslow is the model-pretty-but-aging professional tennis star the Women's Tennis Federation is counting on to dispel the image that all great female tennis players are lesbians. And her lesbianism isn't the only secret she's hiding. A traumatic event from her childhood is taking its toll both on and off the court.

Together Trystan and C.J. must find a way beyond their pasts to discover lasting love.

The Kate and Jay Trilogy

The Price of Fame
When local television news anchor Katherine Kyle is thrust into the national spotlight, it sets in motion a chain of events that will change her life forever. Jamison "Jay" Parker is an intensely career-driven Time magazine reporter. The first time she saw Kate, she fell in love. The last time she saw her, Kate was rescuing her. That was five years earlier, and she never expected to see her again. Then circumstances and an assignment bring them back together.

Kate and Jay's lives intertwine, leading them on a journey to love and happiness, until fate and fame threaten to tear them apart. What is the price of fame? For Kate, the cost just might be everything. For Jay, it could be the other half of her soul.

The Cost of Commitment
Kate and Jay want nothing more than to focus on their love. But as Kate settles into a new profession, she and Jay are caught in the middle of a deadly scheme and find themselves pawns in a larger game in which the stakes are nothing less than control of the country.

In her novel of corruption, greed, romance, and danger, Lynn Ames takes us on an unforgettable journey of harrowing conspiracy—and establishes herself as a mistress of suspense.

The Cost of Commitment—it could be everything...

The Value of Valor
Katherine Kyle is the press secretary to the president of the United States. Her lover, Jamison Parker, is a respected writer for Time magazine. Separated by unthinkable tragedy, the two must struggle to survive against impossible odds...

A powerful, shadowy organization wants to advance its own global agenda. To succeed, the president must be eliminated. Only one person knows the truth and can put a stop to the scheme.

It will take every ounce of courage and strength Kate possesses to stay alive long enough to expose the plot. Meanwhile, Jay must cheat death and race across continents to be by her lover's side...

This hair-raising thriller will grip you from the start and won't let you go until the ride is over.

The Value of Valor—it's priceless.

CHAPTER ONE

The sound, eerily similar to a gunshot, reverberated off the mountain's ominous face.

"Avalanche! Down!" she screamed into her walkie-talkie as a wall of white spiraled downward at an alarming pace. Four figures on the ice above her scrambled to find cover. She took a second to check their positions, key on her beacon, and grab the ice ax from the holster on her harness. Her heart hammered in her chest. Instinct drove her to the ground, where she threw one hand over her head and gripped the ice ax tightly with the other. She stabbed the tool into the ice in front of her and held on for dear life.

The deafening noise drowned out the sound of her thundering heart. Almost immediately, her world went terrifyingly silent save for the wheezing noise that she recognized as her own shallow breathing. Tendrils of fear licked at the edges of her mind as she slowly became aware of her predicament.

She tried to inhale. Snow clogged her airway and she gagged. Her heart pounded against her rib cage. A searing pain sliced through her torso. Tears froze on her face and she struggled not to panic. The need to breathe was overwhelming. Her diaphragm contracted, sending a renewed jolt of agony through her. She gritted her teeth. Melting snow trickled into the back of her throat and she swallowed hard. Almost at once, the pressure of the snow in her airway eased.

Experimentally, she rocked her hips. On the third try, she was able to create enough space to roll onto her side. Intense pain ripped through her arm and up to the shoulder that gripped the ice ax. A scream burst forth, wrenched from a place deep inside her. It was muffled by the snowy tomb. Furious at her body's limitations, she wiggled the fingers still clutching the ice ax.

She allowed herself one deep breath, then yanked as hard as she could on the handle. The ice ax broke free. *Thank God.* Tears of pain and relief leaked from the corners of her eyes. Seconds seemed like hours as she laboriously chipped away at the walls of her prison. Sweat dripped into her eyes. Each small stroke of the ax sent spears of agony shooting through her. A wave of nausea swamped her.

Knock, knock, knock.

"Room service."

Knock, knock, knock.

"Room service."

Danica Warren blinked once, and the hotel room came back into focus, even as the pulse continued to hammer in her neck. "Coming," she called out. She moved away from the window overlooking the Washington, D.C. skyline and walked to the door on shaky legs, steadying her breathing as she went.

"Thank you," she said to the young man as he set the breakfast tray on the small table near the window. She slipped him a five-dollar bill before dismissing him.

Danica had been famished when she'd ordered the bacon and eggs. That had been before her memories had intruded. She swallowed the lingering taste of nausea, pushed the food around the plate, and finally gave up. She checked her watch—enough time for a quick run.

The route was familiar and Danica easily settled into a rhythm. She mentally reviewed the background information she'd received on the Credit Union National Association. In her opinion, too many speakers ignored their audience and stuck strictly to their stock speech. Danica liked to connect with people on a more personal level, to let them know that they weren't just another stop on her tour. She tailored every speech so that the issues she addressed were pertinent to that particular audience. By the time she turned the corner five miles later and re-entered the hotel lobby, she knew what she would say.

෯෯

"Who's the keynote speaker again?"

"Chase Crosley, do you ever pay attention to what I tell you?"

"Yep. About once every fifth sentence." Chase winked affectionately at Jane Beezer, her friend and long-time director of governmental affairs.

"No kidding, I swear you never listen." Jane shook her head in disgust. "Danica Warren."

"Who?"

"Danica Warren. She's major."

Chase shrugged. "Never heard of her."

"The woman saved three other climbers' lives in an avalanche a few years ago. Her memoir's been on the *New York Times* Best Sellers list for more than a year. They made a huge movie out of it called *Thirty Seconds to Eternity*. Didn't you see it?"

"I haven't been to the movies in months."

"You're pathetic, you know that?"

"So I've been told." Chase stopped short. A shadow momentarily crossed her face. "Listen, I'll be back in a minute. I forgot something in my room."

"You have a reserved seat right up front with the rest of the board. Don't be late—it's rude."

"I'll do my best," Chase said as she jogged away toward the bank of elevators.

∽∾∽

Danica kept her eyes on the back of the security person in front of her. Two others flanked her sides and one followed behind as she walked down the corridor. Reporters crowded around and shouted questions at her.

"Danica! How does it feel to be back in Washington?"

"Any chance you'll be coming back here full time?"

"Are you surprised at the success of your book?"

"What did you think of Anka Lynch's performance as you in the movie?"

"Have you kept in touch with the other climbers?"

"How are they doing?"

Danica blinked and clenched her jaw but kept moving determinedly forward.

"The one who died, what was her name? Do you ever hear from her family?"

Danica's nostrils flared. She stopped abruptly and turned in the direction of the haranguer. "Her name was Sandy Isaacs." Danica spoke deliberately to keep her voice from shaking. "She was a brilliant, talented woman. I live with her loss every day. The world is a dimmer place without her."

"Danica…"

"I have to go." Danica walked away at a brisk pace. Mercifully, the staging room was only a few yards in front of her.

A security guard opened the door and escorted her inside where she was greeted immediately by a familiar figure.

"Ms. Warren, it's lovely to see you again." She accepted the kiss on her cheek. "Can I get you anything?"

"No, thank you. I'm fine." Danica subtly rolled her shoulders, placing her anguish and guilt over Sandy's death in a remote corner of her brain. "And if you call me Ms. Warren one more time, I may come down with a sudden case of laryngitis."

Mike Nestor, the smooth-talking CEO of the Credit Union National Association held up his hands, palms out to indicate surrender. "Point taken."

"You're getting soft, Mike. You never used to cave so easily." Danica smiled as he spluttered. She had first met Mike when they were both freshmen United States senators. She had been delighted when the speakers' bureau had e-mailed that Mike wanted her to be the main speaker at his organization's signature conference.

"I hope you don't mind. We've got a little surprise for you this morning," Mike said as he led Danica to a comfortable chair.

Danica raised an eyebrow. "As long as it doesn't involve being crammed into a small space or accosted by more reporters, I'm intrigued."

"No small spaces, I promise. As for the media, I'll do my best." Mike squeezed her shoulder and turned as one of his staff members whispered something in his ear. "Excellent. You ready?"

"As I'll ever be." Danica tilted her head from side to side, trying to loosen the tension in her neck. She felt the usual butterflies take up residence in her stomach. The moments before she stepped out on stage, those few seconds when the adrenaline started to flow, were always the most anxiety producing. She rose from the chair and followed Mike's retreating form.

"Wait right here. Don't move," Mike said when they'd reached the stage's side curtain. He adjusted his already perfectly tied tie, checked to be sure that his lapel microphone was working, winked at her, and strode onto the stage.

"Good morning, everyone, and welcome to our annual invasion of Capitol Hill."

The audience laughed and clapped.

"God, the man has presence," Danica muttered.

"This morning, we have an incredible program for you. Our keynote speaker, Danica Warren, is one of the most amazing human beings I've ever met. I'd say more, but if you'd never seen her in action yourselves, you probably wouldn't believe me. So I've taken the liberty of having a little video montage put together for you to experience, firsthand, the force that is Danica."

Mike pointed toward two massive video screens on either side of the stage. "Ladies and gentlemen, here's a special look at the incredible Danica Warren."

A buzz rippled through the ballroom as the lights dimmed and an image of a stunning, trim, immaculately dressed blonde dominated the screen. She was standing on the floor of the United States Senate.

"I may be the youngest woman ever elected to this august body, but I was not born yesterday. The U.S. Constitution imbues us with great powers, and it balances those powers with awesome responsibilities. Each and every day I step into this chamber, I remind myself of the oath I took when I became a U.S. senator. I humbly suggest you all do the same." She pointed at a row of white-haired senators to her right. *"We have a duty to the people of this great country. I will not be a party to using the Constitution, the very foundation upon which our democracy is built, for the purposes of disenfranchising a segment of our society."*

The crowd in the ballroom cheered. The picture on the video screens shifted to a breathtaking scene of a massive sheer rock face against a bright blue sky. The camera zoomed in on a lone woman, her arm muscles standing out in sharp relief, her powerful fingers gripping a tiny ledge, one foot perched precariously in a crevice, the other on another miniscule ledge. The smile on her face was enormous, the joy in her eyes infectious.

The scene shifted again to a snow-covered mountain range. Five individuals posed together with the summit of a glacier as a backdrop. They were laden with ropes, harnesses, and backpacks. Their body language suggested they were ready to conquer the world.

From her vantage point in the wings, Danica struggled to keep her composure. Her breath came in short gasps. She turned away and reached blindly for a nearby wooden support. It was the last picture of them before...*Don't think about it.*

The next image on the screens was one of a battered climber, her short blond hair and the right side of her face streaked with blood, supporting the weight of one of her fellow mountaineers as she helped her into a waiting helicopter. Her face was a picture of grief. The audience gasped.

Offstage, Danica closed her eyes tightly and threaded her fingers together to keep her hands from shaking. *Not now. You can't fall apart here.*

The montage shifted to a television studio. Danica, her left arm in a sling, a bandage covering a portion of her forehead and eyebrow, was sitting across from an interviewer. The CNN logo was in the background.

"The world is hailing you as a hero. The experts say you defied all the odds by being able to save the lives of three other climbers after digging yourself out."

"I'm not a hero."

"You had three broken ribs, a dislocated shoulder, a large gash on your head, and a concussion. With all that, you unburied yourself and three others, administered CPR to one, and called for help. I think that would be considered heroic by any definition."

The lights came up as the crowd clapped enthusiastically. Danica turned around again to face the stage. She blinked as her eyes readjusted to the light. *Sandy died up there. I couldn't save her.* Danica hung her head and fought back tears of heartache. *You'll have a lifetime to live with that. Right now you have a job to do.* She focused all her attention on Mike, who was walking to the middle of the stage.

"When I came to Washington as a wet-behind-the-ears freshman senator from middle America, one of the first people I met was Danica Warren. I was blown away. Here she was, the youngest woman ever elected to the U.S. Senate—a maverick, a lightning rod as an out lesbian. In the stodgy halls of the Capitol! I was in awe of her graciousness and class. But it was more than that.

"Apart from being one of the brightest people I've ever known, Danica is the finest political strategist in the country. Period. If that isn't enough, in a field perhaps best known for being nasty and cutthroat, Danica is as genuine, as honest, and as kind as they come.

"I spoke to Danica shortly before she went to New Zealand to climb Mount Cook. She was so excited about getting to take her first real vacation in years. I laughed with her and joked that I wished I could go, but I would have to live vicariously through her."

Mike's expression turned somber.

"I never dreamed Danica's trip would end in such tragedy. I have wished more than once that I could rewind the clock for her. When I heard that she had rescued three of the four other climbers, I was not surprised. That Danica would do something heroic is completely within character. That she was more concerned with saving the other members of her party than with her own safety and well-being tells you all you need to know about Danica Warren.

"Everything I've learned about courage and bravery, I've learned from her. Ladies and gentlemen, it is my distinct honor to introduce to you my hero, my friend, Danica Warren."

Danica again took a deep, steadying breath and stepped out onto the stage. She was greeted by a thunderous ovation.

Mike met her halfway and enveloped her in a warm hug. Mindful of the audience, he put a hand over both of their microphones. "I hope you didn't mind that," he whispered in her ear. "I didn't realize until I saw it myself how hard that might be for you."

"It was very classy." The last thing Danica wanted was to make Mike feel bad when he'd been trying to do something nice for her.

"You okay?"

"I'm fine."

Mike pulled back and gave Danica a long, measured look. "Why don't I believe you?"

"I'm okay, really."

"You never were a good liar."

"You were one of the few people who could see through me," Danica said.

"Knock 'em dead." Mike kissed her cheek, waved to the crowd, and walked off stage, leaving Danica alone in the spotlight.

∝৩∽

Chase hurried to the side door of the ballroom, intent on getting to her seat before the speech began. As she stepped into the auditorium, however, the room went pitch black. *Damn.* It wouldn't do to trip over her colleagues in the dark.

She paused just inside the door, deciding on a course of action. The video screens filled with a commanding presence, and Chase stopped thinking and watched, mesmerized.

The videotape ended and Chase was still rooted to the spot, her heart breaking for the woman on the screen. Then Mike was talking and it was too late for Chase to move. By the time she regained her wits, the woman from the videotape was striding onto the stage.

Chase's breath stalled halfway between her lungs and her mouth. *Wow.*

"Chase," someone whispered nearby. It was Jane.

"What?"

"You better get up there and sit down before she starts talking."

"Right," Chase said absently. She negotiated the rows of bodies, barely taking her eyes off the stage as Mike embraced the speaker. *Wow.*

∝৩∽

"Thank you. Thank you very much," Danica said. "Please, sit down." The audience reluctantly complied. "How about that? It's not every day I get rock star treatment and my very own promotional video. Normally that would be quite an honor, and—

14

don't get me wrong—I'm tickled pink. But a lead-in like that tends to raise expectations. Now I suppose I'm going to have to live up to them. Darn. Talk about performance anxiety."

"We love you, Danica," someone shouted from the back of the ballroom.

"Ah, I see my father is here," Danica said without missing a beat. The crowd roared.

Danica opened her mouth to launch into her speech and stopped dead as a woman made her way to a seat in the center of the second row. She was tall and lean, her brown hair cascading in soft waves down to her shoulders. Danica's heart stuttered, lurched, and assumed a rhythm slightly faster than its normal pace. *I know you. Where do I know you from?*

It occurred to Danica that she should be saying something, although for the life of her she couldn't remember what it was. *Snap out of it.* She strolled to the left side of the stage, away from the distraction. "I know that you folks in the credit union movement don't know anything about having to overcome long odds to succeed."

The audience chuckled.

"I mean, it's not as though the banks are trying to put you out of business or anything, right? It's not as if they've outspent you eight to one lobbying Congress, right?"

Laughter.

Danica moved back to center stage and tried hard not to stare at the woman in the second row. She failed. *You have a beautiful smile.* Danica shifted her line of vision. *Focus on the speech.* "Sounds like a fair fight to me. Not! So let's talk about what it takes to overcome all the odds."

For Chase, the world narrowed to one face, one voice, one woman as her eyes tracked Danica's movements back and forth across the stage. It could've been a minute that passed; it could've been an hour. She wasn't sure, and she didn't care. She was riveted.

"Life isn't always fair," Danica was concluding. "Too often, we are faced with situations and circumstances far beyond our control. Think about your own life. I'm willing to bet that you can come up with at least one moment when you've experienced exactly what I'm talking about."

Chase felt her skin prickle with electricity as Danica came to stand directly in front of her. Danica's eyes locked on hers, and Chase had the distinct feeling that somehow Danica could see deep inside her.

"Life is seldom as we plan it. What we do—how we act and react in those unscripted moments—that, in my opinion, is what defines who we are. Who are you? And who will you be when your moment comes? Looking at all of you, I have faith that you'll be the kind of people I'd be honored to have standing beside me. Thank you very much." Danica waved and stepped back from the edge of the stage.

Chase rose to her feet, clapping and whistling along with the rest of the audience. She smiled, utterly charmed that Danica seemed embarrassed by the group's reaction.

"Come on."

"What?" Chase resisted the tug on her sleeve.

"Come on, we've got to hurry to make sure they don't run out of books."

"What are you talking about?" Chase was still watching Danica on stage.

"Danica is signing copies of her book after this. The line's going to be out the door. You do want a copy of her book, don't you?"

Danica left the stage and Chase finally turned to face Anita, a colleague and fellow board member. "Yeah, I do." *Boy, do I.*

"Let's go then. Show some hustle. It was a great speech, wasn't it? The hour just flew by."

"Yeah, it was." It was all Chase could manage to say as her brain tried to process what she'd just seen and, more importantly, what she'd felt.

By the time Chase reached the front of the line, she estimated Danica had signed more than one hundred autographs. She'd had a chance to observe without being watched herself, and she was secretly pleased at that.

With each passing second, her admiration for Danica grew. No matter how ridiculous the request or question, Danica smiled and had a kind word for every single person who wanted her attention. When her turn came, Chase hesitated. Her palms were sweating. *You're not some school girl with a crush. Just ask her to sign the book. Geez.*

"Hi."

Chase swallowed hard, momentarily drowning in the shimmering depths of Danica's eyes. "I'm sorry to bother you," Chase stammered, trying to recover her equilibrium. "You must be exhausted by now."

"No worries, I'm just getting warmed up. Who would you like me to make this out to?"

"Huh?"

"To whom would you like the book autographed?"

"Oh."

Danica smiled, and Chase felt her insides melt. "Chase."

"That's a beautiful name. It reminds me of something exotic and elusive. It's nice to meet you, Chase."

As Chase reached for the autographed book, the official photographer stepped forward. "Why don't I get a picture of you two together?"

"I'm sure Ms. Warren..." Chase started to hold up her free hand, but Danica reached forward and covered it with her own.

"That would be great." Danica stood and stepped out from behind the table. "Gives me an excuse to stretch my legs," she stage-whispered to Chase.

"Well, who am I to stand in the way of a good stretch."

Chase's heart skipped a beat when Danica drew close to her and slid an arm around her waist. Chase returned the gesture.

"Thanks. That's great. One more. Smile. Perfect." The photographer stepped away.

"Thank you for that. I know you have so many people waiting." Chase reluctantly retreated from Danica's personal space.

"My pleasure. I hope you enjoy the book, Chase."

"I know I will." *I can't wait to learn more about you.* Chase ran her fingers over the embossed printing on the front cover of the book. She imagined she could still feel the warmth of Danica's hand covering hers. *I know I will.*

CHAPTER TWO

As soon as she got back to her room, Chase threw her briefcase on the bed and kicked off her shoes. She looked down again at the face smiling up at her from the back cover of the book in her left hand. *I want to know everything about you, Danica Warren.* "Damn." Chase put the book down as if it were radioactive. She brought a hand to her head and grabbed a handful of hair. There was no denying the instantaneous attraction she'd felt, nor the way her heartbeat accelerated when Danica made eye contact with her. It was as if they had been the only two people in the room.

"This is insane. This stuff doesn't happen in real life."

Chase looked at her watch. Time to go back downstairs for the next session. "Damn." She sighed. All she really wanted to do was to prop herself up on some pillows and read. "You and I have a date later," she said to the book. Reluctantly, she hunted down her discarded shoes and headed for the door.

"Danica, that was fantastic. I can't thank you enough."

"My pleasure, Mike. Audiences aren't always as responsive and involved as yours. Nice group." Danica accepted a hand up, rose from her chair behind the autograph table, and joined Mike as he walked down the corridor toward the elevators.

"Most of them really are true believers. They make it their mission to make their members' lives better."

"Must be a refreshing change from the Capitol."

19

Mike laughed. "You've got that right. Not nearly as much self-interest or cynicism in this bunch. Believe it or not, they occasionally do things just because it's the right thing to do."

Danica stared at him in mock horror. "Say it ain't so."

"It's so."

"I'm glad you've found yourself a great spot, Mike."

"Yeah, me too."

Neither Danica nor Mike was willing to bring up the last election. The Republican Party had targeted Mike's seat and instigated a full-scale attack, replete with hideous lies about Mike's personal life. In the end, he hadn't been able to overcome the smear campaign. It had left him devastated.

"Well," Mike said as they reached the bank of elevators leading to the lobby. "I've got to tend to the masses. I'll see you tonight at the dinner?"

"I said I'd be there, didn't I?"

"You did, indeed. I can't think of any better surprise to spring on the members."

"Happy to make you look good, big guy. But, Mike, black tie?" Danica made a face showing her distaste. "I didn't come prepared for that."

"You'll look beautiful as ever, I know."

"You're such a charmer."

"I just tell it like it is." He squeezed her arm. "See you later."

Danica punched the button for the lobby. In truth, she wasn't really sure how she'd gotten talked into attending the dinner dance. She normally shunned such events, especially in the last few years. Worse still, the fact that formal wear was required meant that she'd have to take a trip across town. She'd been studiously avoiding that. *You could always go out and buy a new dress instead.*

❧

Chase tried her hardest to focus on the presenter. She'd been looking forward to this session for weeks. *Damn it all to hell.* All she could see was Danica's face. All she could hear was Danica's voice. All she could feel was the warmth of Danica's hand on hers.

A thought struck Chase suddenly and her stomach dropped. She might never see Danica again. *Jesus.* Chase chewed her lip. "This is ridiculous. You don't even know this woman," she muttered.

"What?"

"Nothing." Chase clamped her jaw shut and shoved any errant thoughts of Danica Warren aside.

The rest of the day dragged on interminably for Chase. When the last session had ended for the afternoon, she breathed a sigh of relief and made a beeline for the elevator.

"Hey, Chase. Where's the fire?" Tisha Sterling, one of Chase's best friends, was hustling toward her. "Join me for a drink."

"Can't. I need to get ready for tonight." Chase was glad she was still far enough away that Tisha couldn't see her face. She had no doubt that Tisha would have seen through the lie immediately.

"You've got two hours. Surely even you can't take that long to get ready." Tisha came up alongside.

"Where've you been all day?" Chase asked, trying to change the subject.

"I've been around."

"I haven't seen you."

"I saw you. Sneaking in late, as usual. Some things never change."

"I wouldn't want to disappoint you."

"I'll have you know I was insanely jealous of your seat. Man, I would've given anything to be on the board this morning just to sit that close to Danica Warren. Phewy, what a hottie!"

"Down, girl," Chase said.

"Tell me you didn't notice."

For reasons she couldn't explain and wasn't ready to admit, Chase felt a swell of anger rise up. Somehow talking about Danica as if she were something to be ogled felt wrong to her. "What I noticed was that she was an extraordinary woman. Bright, articulate, strong, and engaging."

"Whoa, sister. What brought that on?"

Chase pinched the bridge of her nose. "Sorry. I'm just worn out. I think I need to disappear for a little while before the dinner, okay? Regroup, you know."

"Fine, if it means you'll be in a better mood the next time I see you."

"Promise," Chase said, stepping into the elevator.

"I'm going to hold you to that. And see if you can't be on time for once in your life," Tisha called after her.

∞∞

Danica took a deep breath and tried to insert the key in the lock. *You just need to get the dress and get out. It's been long enough. You can do this.* Her hand shook violently. She dropped it to her side and sat heavily on the front stoop. Once seated, she clenched her hands together until her knuckles turned white. "Maybe this wasn't such a good idea."

"Danica Warren? Is that really you, girlfriend?"

Danica swore under her breath, glanced up, then away. She rubbed her hands on her slacks, tried to compose herself and, failing that, feigned nonchalance.

"As I live and breathe, it is you. I'd given up hope of seeing you around these parts. Thought I'd have to kidnap you and drag you down here."

"Fish man. How the heck are you?"

"Better'n you, I'd say from the looks of it. What's going on? What *are* you doing here, anyway? And why didn't you tell me you were coming?"

Danica sighed. She and Sandy had been close to their neighbors, Ted and Ronnie. The four of them had been nearly inseparable, in fact. Sandy had dubbed Ted "Fish man" because his last name was Fisher. Danica should've known she couldn't fool him.

"I needed a dress for tonight," she said, as if that explained everything.

"Well, shit, girl, I've got one in my closet you can wear."

They both laughed, and Ted sat down next to Danica, hip-butting her to make her move over.

"Rough, huh?" Ted asked.

Afraid she would lose what little composure she had, Danica merely nodded.

"Want me to go in with you?"

"That's incredibly sweet."

Ted inclined his head to look at her. "When was the last time you stepped foot in the place?"

"Three years ago," Danica mumbled.

"Ah. I've always wondered why you didn't sell. I mean…" Ted stopped talking.

Danica put a hand on his arm. "I know." She shrugged. "Every time I thought about it, I just couldn't bring myself to do it. It's…it was home for her, you know?"

"Yeah, I think I do." Ted put his arm around Danica's shoulders.

"Pathetic, huh?"

"Not at all. I don't blame you one bit. If I'd been you and it had been Ronnie, I'm sure I'd feel the same way."

"I'm glad you don't have to find out," Danica said, standing up and brushing off the seat of her pants. "Time to face the music."

"I meant what I said, girlfriend. I'll come in with you if you want," Ted said, standing as well.

"I know you did." Danica stood on her tiptoes and kissed Ted on the cheek. "And I think you're the sweetest man for it. This is just something I have to do myself."

"I get that. I'll be right next door if you need anything."

"Thanks. I really appreciate that."

"Hey, stop over on your way out. Doodles really misses you."

"And I miss her."

"You wouldn't disappoint the queen of canines, would you?"

"Never. See you in a bit."

Ted grasped Danica by the shoulders. "I'll be right here. It's not cowardly to ask for support. Honest."

"I hear you."

"Yes, but are you listening?"

"To you? Have I ever?" Danica tried to lighten the mood.

"You have a point there." Ted took the key from Danica and fitted it into the lock. "Here you go, honey."

⋘⋙

The first thing Danica noticed was the smell—mustiness of disuse mixed with a hint of Sandy's perfume. How could her scent still be in the air after all this time? Danica barely made it to the bathroom before she threw up.

For a long while, she simply sat on the bathroom floor. The tile was cool and smooth. She rested her hot cheek against it. *You can't hide in the bathroom, Nick.* Danica could almost hear Sandy's voice. *You can do this. Pull yourself together.*

Danica stood and found a new toothbrush in a drawer. She rummaged through the medicine cabinet and located an old tube of toothpaste—the end was curled up and the cap was crusted firmly in place. It took her several frustrating moments before she managed to pry the tube open. The paste felt gritty against her teeth, but the minty flavor was a pleasant counterpoint to the stale taste in her mouth.

"You *can* do this," she told herself resolutely, blowing out a breath and squaring her shoulders. She exited the bathroom, her quick, powerful strides in sharp contrast to the emotions swirling within.

"You can do this," she repeated, her voice faltering a little as she arrived in the bedroom she and Sandy had shared. Nothing had changed in the three years since she'd been gone. The place was cleaned periodically and maintenance was kept up on it; she saw to that. Friends and colleagues had suggested she rent the townhouse out, but she'd never been able to bring herself to let someone else live there. It was the last place she and Sandy had lived. It was, in Danica's mind, her last tangible tie to Sandy.

Enough of that. Danica wiped some stray moisture from her eyes and opened the door to a spacious walk-in closet. When they'd renovated the place five years earlier, Sandy had insisted on incorporating hers and hers closets into the design to house both of their extensive wardrobes.

Danica thumbed through a series of dresses until she came to a black cocktail-length dress. "Simple, yet elegant." She turned the dress and examined it from all sides. "That'll work."

She strode out of the bedroom, ignoring the personal mementos and family pictures that graced the dressers and night tables. Her footsteps echoed on the earth-toned slate tile in the hallway and foyer, the sound in keeping with the emptiness in Danica's heart. She fixed her gaze directly in front of her. One more look around the place that was her and Sandy's last real home would have been her undoing; she was certain of it.

∽୬୨∾

When she emerged back out on the front stoop, Danica took a huge gulp of air. She hadn't even realized she'd been holding her breath. Suddenly, her legs felt rubbery, and she grasped the porch railing for support. The dress dangled over the edge of the wrought iron. Danica stared at it. What she saw wasn't a piece of material, it was the fabric of a life she no longer had and a partner forever gone. She burst into tears. *Sandy. I miss you so much.*

Briefly she considered not going next door, but that wasn't fair to Ted, and Danica did miss him. Before she could chicken out, the door to Ted and Ronnie's place opened and a huge black streak bolted out.

"Doodles." Danica laughed, wiping her eyes with the heel of her hand as the big Rottweiler bounded at her, stood up on her hind legs to place a paw on either of Danica's shoulders, and gave her an enthusiastic kiss. "I missed you too, sweetheart."

"I don't know what to do with her," Ted said in exasperation. "You're the only one she ever listened to. Just look at those manners. Appalling."

"Ignore him, Doodles. He's just sore that you always loved me best."

"You're too right there. Get in here, Doodles, and bring your girlfriend with you."

The dog cocked her head inquisitively at Ted but didn't budge.

"Come on, D. Better do as he says." Danica pointed toward the open front door.

Immediately the dog trotted back into the house.

"See what I mean?"

"It just takes a woman's touch, dear," Danica said.

"Well, if that's the case," Ted said dramatically, "I shouldn't have any trouble getting her to listen and obey."

Danica threaded her arm through his. "Let's go, drama queen."

∽୬୨∾

Ted made a show of fixing tea for both of them. "You really shouldn't isolate yourself the way you do, Dani. It's not healthy."

"I'm not isolated. I'm surrounded by people most of the time."

"That's when you're traveling. You burrow up in that little cabin of yours in the middle of nowhere. You barely have phone service, for goodness sake."

"I have satellite, high-speed Internet access, a cell phone."

"What you don't have is contact with humans. *In person* contact," he added when Danica arched an eyebrow.

"The cabin is what I need right now," Danica said.

"You're too young to hide yourself away, Dani."

"I'm not hiding."

"You're not living, either." Ted covered his mouth with his hand.

An uncomfortable silence ensued.

"I'm sorry, Dani. I had no right—"

"Don't apologize, Ted." Danica gazed inward. Was he right? She tried to look at it objectively. When was the last time she had called any of her old friends? When was the last time she'd gone out to be social or done anything that wasn't required of her to fulfill a work-related obligation? "You're right," she whispered. "I've been so busy existing that I haven't made any time for living."

"I didn't mean—"

"Yes, you did. It's okay." Danica turned tear-filled eyes toward him. "It's just…I don't feel like I really deserve to have a life, if that makes any sense to you."

"Of course you do, honey."

"No." Danica shook her head. "What life does Sandy have?" Her voice cracked. "It's not like she can go to a movie or out to dinner and a concert. It's not like I gave her any of those choices." Danica buried her face in her hands.

"Oh, Dani." Ted pulled Danica up from her chair and into his lap. He lowered her hands and cradled her head between his neck and shoulder. "It wasn't your fault, doll."

"It was. It was my fault." Danica began to cry huge, round tears. They dripped down her face and onto Ted's shirt. "I made a decision. If I'd made a different one, she'd be alive today." Her words were almost indistinguishable through her sobs.

Ted rocked her and rubbed her back. "You can't be sure of that. If you'd made a different decision, five people could be dead instead of one. You've got to know that." He looked at her beseechingly. "You have to."

Danica shook her head and dried the tears on her shirt sleeve. Ted put two fingers under her chin and tipped her head up. "Every expert has told you the same thing. I know they have." "They weren't there," she said miserably.

"Some of them were." He said it gently.

Danica thought of Petra, Ann, and Val. "They couldn't see. They were hurt. They couldn't assess the situation." Fresh tears pooled in her eyes, clouding her vision. "It was mine to do. The responsibility rests with me."

"It was an avalanche, Dani. A freak act of nature. You did everything you could."

"I didn't. I didn't," she repeated, shaking her head again. "I didn't." This time more softly, "I didn't," she whispered.

"You did," Ted said resolutely. "Somewhere inside, you know that. Dig deep and find that place. I know you. You're a fighter, Danica Warren. Sandy would be royally pissed if she could see you like this. She'd want you to pick yourself up and get back in the game."

Danica sniffed. She wanted to argue with Ted, wanted to make him see that she was right. But there was no denying that he was right about what Sandy would think of how she'd been behaving.

"See?" Ted ducked his head to force eye contact. "You know exactly what I'm talking about. Dani, sweetheart, what happened was awful. It was horrific. There's no denying that. No one should have to make the choices you did. But that's not a reason to give up on life. And whether you want to admit it or not, that's what you've been doing."

Danica accepted the handful of Kleenex Ted offered her. She blew her nose and dabbed at her eyes. "Remind me why I used to like you?"

"Used to? I'm deeply wounded." Ted held his hand over his heart dramatically.

"Oh my God," Danica said, spying the clock on the wall. "I've got to get going. I'll be late."

Ted leaned back and wiggled his eyebrows. "Got a date already? Maybe I underestimated you."

"Very funny, Fish man. I promised to attend a formal dinner tonight for the group I spoke to today. It's a favor for an old friend."

"Well, you've got to start somewhere. Maybe there'll be a cute chickie at the ball."

Danica thought of the woman from the second row. Chase, her name was. Mortified at the direction her thoughts had taken in light of the conversation she and Ted had been having, she blushed.

"Did I hit a nerve?"

"No," she said too quickly, getting up from Ted's lap and straightening her slacks. Doodles sprang up from her bed nearby and whined.

"Sorry about the shirt." Danica pointed to the wet spot near Ted's collarbone.

"It's only water, sugar."

She leaned down and scratched the dog's head. "You behave yourself, young lady. Pretend to listen once in a while, okay?" The dog wagged its stump of a tail and licked Danica's hand.

Ted walked Danica to the front door. "No more of this incommunicado stuff, right?" When she didn't answer, Ted put a restraining hand on her arm. "Right?"

"Have I ever told you you're a pain in the ass?"

"No doubt. But I'm still charming and the most handsome guy you know. Besides, you love me."

"Sadly, that's too true," Danica said, then kissed Ted on the cheek and retreated down the steps to the sidewalk.

≈❦❧≈

Chase turned another page. She was sitting on the bed in her hotel room, her bare feet crossed at the ankles, her lips moving silently as she read. So intent was she on the story that the ring of the telephone barely registered in her mind.

"Hello," she said distractedly when she finally picked up.

"This is your friendly neighborhood reminder that you have less than half an hour to get ready for dinner."

"Hi, Tisha."

"You sound like you're a million miles away. Did I wake you?"

"Huh? No. Listen to this."

"Chase, did you hear me say you've got less than half an hour to be ready and downstairs?"

"Yeah, yeah. 'From the time I was old enough to understand what a voting booth was—and that was about eight years old—I knew I wanted to be a politician. My father would ask me why. I would tell him it was because I wanted to make a difference in the world. I wanted to make the world a better place. He would laugh and ruffle my hair and tell me never to change. I don't think I have.'"

"What are you reading from?"

"Danica Warren's autobiography. Did you have any idea what you wanted to be at eight?"

Tisha laughed. "I hadn't a clue. All I knew was that I wanted to climb the tree next door."

"Yeah, that's about how I felt."

"There's more. 'By my eighteenth birthday, I ran for my first office—mayor of tiny little Hanover, New Hampshire. I was a freshman at Dartmouth and I thought I owned the universe. Everyone but me was shocked when I won. I guess it never occurred to me that I wouldn't.'"

"Very cool. Now will you get ready? I'm picking you up in twenty minutes, and you'd better be dressed and waiting outside."

"One more—"

"No. No, Chase. You can read later. You're a member of the board, for Christ's sake. You're expected to set an example. Not only that, but you're sitting at the head table. It was bad enough that you had to climb over twenty people in the middle of this morning's session."

"Okay, okay. I get the point."

"Good, now get ready."

"Yes, mother," Chase said, hanging up. She crossed to the bathroom, where she had hung her suit earlier. "But I'd really rather stay here and spend the night with you, Danica."

CHAPTER THREE

Y ou clean up nice," Tisha said as she surveyed Chase
from her vantage point in the doorway.
"You say that as though I normally look like crap."
"It's not that, it's just that I don't often get to see a woman who
can wear a tux and manage to make it look so damn feminine."
"Nice save. I'll let it pass for now," Chase said, breezing past
Tisha and practically shutting the door on her nose. "By the way,
you don't look too shabby, yourself. Nice dress. Coral is definitely
your color."
"Thanks."
The two women walked along in companionable silence
toward the elevators.
"So you're really getting into the book, huh?" When Chase
didn't answer, Tisha persisted, "Yoo-hoo. Earth to Chase, come in,
please."
"What?" Chase pushed the down arrow. "Those speakers, do
you figure they just fly right back out when they're done?"
"You mean like Danica Warren?" Tisha asked, watching her
friend appraisingly. "You were really taken with her, weren't
you?"
"She's a very impressive woman. And you didn't answer the
question."
"I don't know. They probably whisk them away as soon as
their obligation is over."
"She must live here though, right? In D.C.? I mean, she's a
senator."
"Used to be a senator," Tisha corrected. "I would guess she
probably had a place here. Most senators have a D.C. base and a
house in their home districts."

31

"She's not a senator anymore?"

"No. Didn't you read her bio in the program? It said, 'former senator.' She dropped her re-election bid after the accident."

"Oh."

"What did you think about the other sessions today?"

"Huh? Oh, they were okay."

"What is it with you, Chase? It's like you're completely fixated on Danica Warren."

Chase shrugged. "I'm not. I just—"

"Chase, Tisha, wait up."

Chase and Tisha groaned simultaneously. Jack Newton was one of the most obnoxiously chauvinistic men they knew. Behind his back they tended to call him "Jack-ass."

"Hi, Jack."

"Hello, ladies. You both look ravishing. The only thing you're missing is a male to escort you into the ballroom. Good thing I came along when I did." He held out an elbow for each of them to thread her arm through.

Reluctantly, Chase and Tisha allowed Jack to walk them into the dinner. Once through the door, Chase gave Tisha a mischievous look. "I'd love to stay and chat, Jack, but I have to be at the head table. Bye, Tisha. See you later."

Tisha favored her with a murderous glare.

Danica ran her fingers through her hair once more and squared her shoulders. *Show time.* All thoughts of Sandy, the accident, and her difficult afternoon faded into the background as Danica crossed the threshold into the ballroom. She was chagrined to note that everyone already was seated; she would have to walk through virtually all of them to get to the head table. "That'll teach you to be late," she muttered to herself.

She did her best to be inconspicuous, but she might just as well have worn a neon sign. The buzz began before she'd made it past the first table.

"It's Danica."

"That's her, I know it is."

"She's so much shorter than she looked on stage."

Danica let her retort to the last remark die before it reached her mouth, but she couldn't resist smiling.

By the time she'd reached the second table, people were craning their necks to get a look at her. Before she'd passed the third table the crowd was on its feet, clapping.

The blush began at the base of Danica's neck and quickly covered her cheeks until she was bright red. "I certainly didn't intend to make such an entrance," she said when she arrived by Mike's side at the head table.

"Sure you didn't," Mike said, kissing Danica on the cheek and pulling out the chair next to him for her.

"I swear, I didn't. It's more than a little embarrassing." Out of the corner of her eye, Danica caught a glimpse of a familiar face. The color in her cheeks, which had just begun to fade, intensified. *You look incredible, Chase.*

"Well," Mike said, "you shouldn't be embarrassed. You look fabulous."

Danica recovered her focus with difficulty. "Thanks."

"Now sit down so I can say more things to make you blush."

"Good Lord. And here I was, doing you a favor."

Mike gave her a playful shove into the seat and pushed it in. "Ladies and gentlemen, I'm so pleased and proud to introduce tonight's very special guest. I had to use every bit of charm and cunning to convince Danica to join us." Mike paused. "I told her what the dessert was."

The crowd laughed.

"All kidding aside, I know you all were every bit as impressed with Danica as I was this morning. It's no wonder she made *People* magazine's list of twenty-five most fascinating people last year."

"Enough of that," Danica said, rising to her feet. She was aware of Chase's eyes on her and the knowledge made her stomach do a small flip. "Mike is just looking to get back at me for a certain birthday present I sent him a while back." She turned to Mike. "Sit."

He did and the audience clapped in delight.

"You all got to hear plenty about me today. But I didn't get a chance to say anything about your fearless leader." Danica glanced at Mike fondly.

"I can't tell you how lucky you are to have a man like Mike Nestor at the helm of your organization. There is no person more respected in Washington, no more effective lobbyist, no more capable CEO.

"When I first came to D.C., I kept hearing about this hotshot young senator from Minnesota. I thought, 'There's no way anyone can live up to that kind of hype.' Then I met Mike. Let me tell you, he was everything they said, and more. I've been proud to call myself his friend ever since. Likewise, any friend of Mike's is a friend of mine, so I'm happy to be among so many friends tonight. Thank you for having me. Now please, sit and eat before your salad gets warm."

Applause and laughter warred as Danica sat. Mike leaned over and whispered in her ear, "You didn't have to do that. It's not why I asked you to come."

"I know. But they should know how fortunate they really are."

"Let me make some introductions before it gets any deeper in here." Mike turned his attention to the people seated around the table. "Danica Warren, I'd like you to meet the members of my board of directors. Glen Herman, Lou Carducci, Anita Hathaway, Carly Stern, Alan Cert, Nancy Termin, and Chase Crosley."

Danica stood and shook hands with all of them. "It's a pleasure to meet you." When she got to Chase, Danica's smile brightened. "Hello there. Thanks again for letting me stretch these incredibly long legs during the autograph session."

"It was a tall order, but I was glad I was up to it." Chase winked.

"Pfft. *Tall* order. Good one. I'll get you back for that."

"I'm sure you will."

The dinner passed in pleasant conversation with discussions among the group of everything from politics to the pitiful state of original television programming. Danica found herself wishing she was sitting closer to Chase. Try as she might, Danica was finding it impossible not to steal glances at her. *What is it about you?*

When the dessert was served, a live band began enticing people onto the dance floor. Danica watched as a good-looking man approached Chase and bowed gallantly.

"May I have this dance?"

34

Chase fidgeted with her napkin and glanced briefly in Danica's direction before facing her would-be dance partner. "Not right now, thanks."

The man walked away, obviously disappointed.

I'd be disappointed too. Danica shook her head slightly, as if to clear her mind. *Where did that come from? What the hell's wrong with me?* She rose abruptly. *I've got to get out of here.* "I'm sorry to be a party-pooper, folks, but I've got an early flight in the morning. Again, it was a pleasure to meet all of you." The words came out more clipped than Danica had intended.

"Are you okay?" Mike asked sotto voce.

"Of course."

"Are you sure?"

Because she could see the concern in his eyes, Danica made an effort to soften her expression. "Positive. I'm just tired, that's all. It's been a long day."

"Yes, it has. It was good to see you, Danica. Thanks for getting the conference off to a great start."

"Always happy to help out the good guys. Take care of yourself, Mike."

"You too. Call me anytime you're in D.C."

"You bet." With a final wave to the table's occupants, Danica was gone.

Chase chewed her lip as she watched Danica go. Why had she left so suddenly? Chase couldn't answer that; all she knew was that the room seemed somehow empty without her.

Chase hesitated only a moment before excusing herself, ostensibly to go to the bathroom. She scanned the nearly empty atrium area outside the ballroom. Danica was nowhere to be seen. A check of the bathroom and the elevator banks also failed to turn up any sign of her.

She pushed the button to summon the elevator. Maybe Danica was still in the lobby. *What are you going to do if you find her, genius?* Chase didn't have any idea, but it didn't stop her from pushing the button impatiently a second time.

"Leaving so soon, beautiful?"

Chase tightened her hands into fists and tried to clamp down on her irritation. Jack Newton had to be the single most annoying individual on the face of the planet. "I'm coming right back. I just need to ask the concierge a question," she lied.

"Now? The fun's just getting started, baby. Come back inside and let Jack show you some of his moves."

It was the last straw. "Some other time, Jack. Like maybe in your next lifetime." Chase gave up on the elevator and started walking down the hall toward the stairs. She didn't look back. Dealing with Jack had cost her precious minutes. Danica could be anywhere by now.

Indeed, a search of the lobby proved fruitless. Chase started back down the stairs, then thought better of it. "I said I had a date with Danica tonight, and so I will." Resolutely, she headed for her room and a few hours of uninterrupted time with Danica's memoir. It would be a pale imitation of the real thing, but Chase couldn't summon any enthusiasm for returning to the party.

Washington's fabled monuments stood sentinel over the city, basking in artificial light, awash in the glow of history. Danica, having shed her formal wear in exchange for a pair of jeans and a sweatshirt, strolled along the Mall. Walking like this through the pillars of the past had been one of her favorite things to do when she'd been a senator. It helped her remember what she'd come to the nation's capital to do. Back then, she'd been driven by a sense of purpose—a deep and abiding need to champion the cause of the people.

Why had she come to this spot at this moment? When she'd started out from the hotel, she hadn't had any clear idea where she was going. Perhaps it was the reassurance of familiarity that she sought.

The water of the reflecting pool at the base of the Lincoln Memorial winked at Danica, the ripples gently lapping against the side walls. The calm of the scene belied the turbulence of her thoughts. A vision of Chase played across her mind's eye, and her pulse quickened.

Her reaction to Chase had been unequivocal and instantaneous. Although she could try to explain it away, she couldn't deny the immediate attraction she'd felt. Danica searched her memory. What had happened the first time she'd met Sandy?

She had been swimming. Danica frequented the pool every morning that summer as part of her training regimen for a triathlon to benefit breast cancer research. She'd finished her laps and was just boosting herself out of the water. She squinted up into the sun to see a friend of hers standing on the deck.

"Hey, Dani. I want you to meet somebody."

Danica lifted herself out of the pool.

"Dani, this is my friend Sandy Isaacs. Sandy, this is Danica Warren."

There weren't any fireworks. In fact, Danica didn't think of Sandy at all after that initial introduction. If they hadn't bumped into each other again at the conclusion of the triathlon several weeks later, they might never have been more than passing acquaintances.

Their courtship was slow, comfortable, and easy. *Like our relationship,* Danica thought. It was a bond of friendship and love built over time, a partnership forged from shared interests and mutual respect.

Again, an image of Chase flitted across Danica's consciousness. There was nothing slow or comfortable about the way Danica's stomach had flipped at the first sight of Chase, a slight halo from the stage lights outlining her lithe form. Nor was there anything pedestrian about the way her heart raced when they'd stood together for the picture at the autograph session. And that white tuxedo... *Stop! It's just the conversation you had with Ted, that's all. The power of suggestion. Tomorrow you'll be gone, so will she, and life will go on as usual.*

Danica turned and headed back toward the hotel.

∽♡∾

"www.google.com...Sandy...Isaacs...S-a-n-d-y...I-s-a-a-c-s." Chase's fingers flew over her laptop keyboard as she mumbled to herself. "She had a girlfriend, fool. Of course she had a girlfriend. How could anybody as attractive as Danica Warren not be attached? Moron." Chase continued to chastise herself as she waited for the Web site to finish loading. Danica's memoir was resting on her lap, propped open against her chest. As much as she didn't want to know, she felt compelled to investigate this woman who had been such an integral part of Danica's life.

"Ten thousand two hundred matches. Holy cow." Chase clicked on the first link and began to read.

"An avalanche on Mount Cook, the highest peak in New Zealand, claimed the life of forty-three-year-old American Sandy Isaacs yesterday. Isaacs and four other climbers, including U.S. Senator Danica Warren, were attempting to negotiate the Summit Rocks via Linda Glacier when a massive avalanche overtook them.

"Warren, an accomplished mountaineer, was able to unbury herself and three of her companions but was unable, despite heroic efforts, to reach Isaacs, who was lead climber at the time. She was buried alive on the rock face. Her body was recovered several hours after the slide. Isaacs was Warren's partner of eighteen years. Although badly injured herself, Warren refused to leave the scene until Isaacs had been found."

"Eighteen years." Chase's hand flew to her mouth. "Oh, Danica. I can't even imagine how awful that must've been." She tried to put herself in Danica's place. How would she feel if she lost her long-time lover while saving the lives of others? It was incomprehensible. She hit the back button and returned to the Google page. The next ten entries were news stories rehashing the accident.

Chase yawned. 11:45 p.m. According to the schedule, the next morning's session would start at 8:30. *Better get some sleep.* Unwilling to let go of the book completely, Chase took it with her as she crawled under the covers. She told herself that it was just in case she woke up in the middle of the night with an urge to read. *Of course it is.*

❦

Chase opened one eye and squinted at the clock on the nightstand. 2:36 a.m. *Shit.* She rolled onto her back and sucked in a quick breath as a bolt of pain shot through her right eye. For a few moments, she stayed perfectly still, taking in air through her nose and blowing it out through her mouth. *This will pass; it always does.* Eventually, the viselike pressure eased enough for Chase to stand. She made her way into the bathroom, where she fished a prescription bottle out of her travel kit. Her fingers fumbled with the cap before she managed to release the childproof catch and shake two pills out into her hand. She swallowed them down with a glass of water.

On the way back to bed, she felt around on the desk for her personal digital assistant. *What did I ever do before the Treo?* She accessed her calendar while sliding back under the cool sheets; her next doctor's appointment wasn't for another month. *Damn. Better think about moving it up a few weeks.* Doctor Hugo Frankel had served with Chase on the Chamber of Commerce board several years earlier. He was one of the finest neurologists in the area, and Chase knew that if she asked, he would make every effort to fit her in earlier.

The silver lettering on the book cover lying next to her on the bed glinted in the dim light from the PDA. Another chapter sounded great, but Chase knew she'd never be able to focus. Instead, she twisted the knob for the light over her head, illuminating the bed with a soft glow. She turned the book over and traced her finger across the picture of Danica on the back. There was something so alive, so sexy, and yet so comforting about her. *She belongs to someone else. Belong-ed,* she corrected herself. Past tense. *Wonder what her story is now.* Without permission, Chase's eyelids began to droop. She imagined herself lying in Danica's arms. Her headache released and she drifted into a peaceful slumber.

When Danica emerged from the elevator with her suitcase, the lobby was crowded with tourists and conventioneers. She was glad she'd opted for the in-room quick checkout. She hurried across the marble floor, zigging and zagging to avoid other bodies in motion. Most of them were headed for the escalators leading down to the ballrooms where that morning's sessions were no doubt about to get under way. Danica did a double take as a flash of red caught her eye. Chase. For a fleeting second, Danica thought about going after her. Instead, she quickened her pace and strode in the opposite direction, past the front desk, and out onto the street where a car was waiting to take her to the airport. *Goodbye, Chase.*

CHAPTER FOUR

N o." Chase listened for a moment more, the phone cradled between her ear and shoulder. "Absolutely not." Another pause. "What part of no don't you understand? Is it the *n*, or the *o*?" She pressed her thumb and forefinger to the bridge of her nose. "I don't care. Get it done. I want it on my desk by tomorrow morning. No excuses." She slammed down the phone.

"Boss?"

"What?" Chase snapped without looking up. "Well, what is it?"

Lena, Chase's executive assistant, stood uncertainly in the doorway. "You said you wanted the list of attendees for Congressman Tighe's fundraising dinner."

"Right." Chase straightened in her chair and held out her hand for the list. "Please tell me there are more than fifteen names on it. We need a big turnout. These yahoos have no idea how the political process works. The banks are out there raising millions of dollars in contributions, greasing palms all over the place, and we look like backwater idiots handing over rumpled dollar bills from our allowance."

"Twenty-seven so far, and I'm still waiting to hear from another twelve."

"How the hell do these neophytes expect to be taken seriously in D.C.? We have to do better than this." Chase smacked her palm on the desk for emphasis.

Lena shifted uncomfortably from foot to foot. "I'm still making phone calls. Maybe we could send out another e-mail blast."

"I'm tired of holding these people's hands."

Lena started to say something but stopped when Jane came to stand beside her in the doorway. Under her breath she muttered, "She's in a mood."

"I know. I could hear her all the way down the hall."

"There's nothing wrong with my hearing, ladies. Don't talk about me like I'm not in the room."

Jane cocked her head at Lena and motioned toward the outer office. Lena gratefully slipped away as Jane stepped the rest of the way into Chase's office and closed the door.

"What?" Chase asked again, when Jane didn't say anything.

"You tell me."

"I don't have the patience for this right now," Chase said, fixing Jane with a withering look.

"I can see that. So can everyone else in the building. What's wrong, Chase? This isn't like you. You've been on a rampage all day."

Chase clenched her jaw shut. She closed her eyes against the harsh office lighting and rubbed her temples. *She's right and you know it.*

"Listen, I'll take care of the list." Jane gently removed the pages Chase still held loosely in her fingers as she dropped into one of the two visitor chairs facing the desk. "Are you still getting headaches?"

Chase didn't answer.

"What did the doctor say?"

"My appointment is this afternoon."

"Good. Ask him about mood swings while you're at it."

"Mood swings," Chase scoffed.

Jane gave her a meaningful look. "Yeah, mood swings. I want to know what happened to my always smiling, always genial, always patient boss and friend."

"Nothing happened."

"Tell it to someone who believes you." Jane touched Chase's hand. "C'mon. This has been going on for a week. One minute you're fine, and the next you're taking someone's head off. It's not like you. You've got everyone walking on eggshells around here, and I'm worried sick about you. It's not good."

"Fine. If it makes you happy, I'll ask him why I've turned into the bitch from Hades."

"I mean it, Chase. Something's not right."

"I said I'd ask him, didn't I?"

"So you did." Jane took her leave without uttering another word.

"Shit," Chase muttered, her fingers going to her temples again.

৵৩৵

The auditorium was packed as Danica stepped onto the stage. She waited for the applause to die down.

"I understand you all had a rocking time down on Sixth Street last night, so I'll try to talk softly." The last she stage-whispered as the audience laughed. "I didn't realize accountants were such a wild bunch—makes me look at debits and credits in a whole different light."

A figure crossed Danica's line of sight, distracting her. Someone tall and slender. She squinted into the lights. Could it be? The figure resolved itself into an older woman with graying hair, and a sliver of disappointment crept into Danica's heart. Although she'd tried hard, she hadn't been able to put Chase completely out of her mind. She'd given three speeches since the D.C. engagement, and at each stop she'd found herself looking for her.

Danica finished giving the speech by rote, signed the requisite autographs, and retreated to her hotel room, where she called her agent.

"Listen, Toni, I'm exhausted. I want to go home for a while, okay?"

"We've got requests up the wazzoo for you. We need to strike while the iron is hot."

"At $50,000 a pop, I'm not hurting for money…"

"You need to stay in the public eye."

"The movie did gangbusters for months, the book is number one on the *New York Times* Best Sellers list for the thirty-second week in a row. I don't think I'm in any danger of falling off the radar screen if I take a couple of weeks off."

There was a pause on the other end of the line, and Danica could hear the clicking of a keyboard.

"Okay. Here's the thing. I'll give you your two weeks—"

"Thank you."

"I wasn't finished yet. I'll give you your two weeks if you let me say 'yes' to *60 Minutes*. They want to do a segment on you."

Danica groaned.

"C'mon. They want to film it at your cabin. You wouldn't even have to leave home. They apparently already shot some tape of you at one of your recent gigs. Please, Danica. You've got to give me something here. I'm dying."

"Have you ever thought of going into acting? You're quite good, really, although you're a little over the top in the drama department."

"Yeah? I'll keep it in mind. And your answer is?"

"Okay, okay, already. But not this week."

"You're a saint. I'll set everything up and get back to you. Have a good trip home."

"Gee, thanks. See you, T. Oh, and you're coming up to the cabin for the *60 Minutes* thing too, right?"

"Of course. Wouldn't miss it for the world. Bye."

Danica hung up the phone. She was going home. She closed her eyes and breathed a sigh of relief.

❧

"Follow my finger." Doctor Frankel watched Chase's eyes intently as he moved his forefinger in an arc in front of her face. "How have the headaches been?"

"More consistent, longer in duration, and I've had a few wicked migraines."

"Have you been using the medication I prescribed?" The doctor rolled back a few feet on his stool.

"Yes."

"Does it help?"

"Some."

"Mmm. Touch your finger to your nose, please."

"The headaches aren't the only thing," Chase said, complying with the doctor's instruction.

"No? What else is going on?"

"I've been a little testy lately."

"We all get edgy at some time or another, Chase."

"No. It's more than that. I can go from happy to rage in zero point three seconds."

"Congratulations. That must be some kind of speed record."

"It's not like me. Three-quarters of my staff is about to mutiny. And that's not all. I keep forgetting things."

"What kind of things?"

"I don't know…stupid stuff, mostly. Like I leave the house and forget my briefcase. Or I can't remember where I put my keys, whether I put deodorant on, what I said fifteen minutes ago."

"Mmm. What day is it today?"

"Tuesday."

"Who plays Spider-Man in the *Spider-Man 3* movie that came out a few months ago?"

"Tobey Maguire."

The doctor stood and looked out the window. "Where did you park your car?"

"Outside your office."

"I meant which space."

"I don't know."

"That's okay. If I didn't have a designated spot, I'd never know where mine was, either." He winked and came to sit opposite her again. "Great book, isn't it?" he asked, picking up Danica's memoir from the chair where Chase had dropped it when he'd come into the examining room.

"Fascinating. I had a chance to meet her a few weeks ago. She's remarkable." *And I haven't been able to get her out of my mind since.*

"I imagine she would be." The doctor studied Chase appraisingly. "When's the last time you had a vacation?"

"Six months ago, I think."

"Look. I know all this is very disconcerting to you, and I promise we'll get to the bottom of it. Right now, I'm inclined to say you're a busy woman who's under a lot of stress. Stress can cause all of the symptoms you're experiencing."

"I've been under worse stress and I've never reacted like this."

"Mmm. How's your personal life?"

"What?"

"What are you doing outside of work? Any friends, romantic interests, recent breakups? Are you isolating yourself or getting out and doing things?"

"How is that relevant?"

"It's possible you're suffering from a bout of depression. Combine that with your stress level and it would explain a lot. Depression can cause memory lapses and mood swings."

"I'm not depressed," Chase said defensively.

"There's no shame in it, you know."

"Shame has nothing to do with it. I'm not depressed."

"Have you ever been to therapy?"

"No."

"I can give you the names of a few really good psychologists."

"I told you, I'm not depressed."

"Okay. Would you humor me so that we can rule it out as a possibility?"

"I can rule it out for you right now."

"I didn't realize you had a psychology degree." He smiled at Chase to lessen the tension. "All I want is to find scientific explanations for your symptoms. To do that, I have to look at all possibilities. Stress and depression are the most likely culprits. I should think that would make you happy since those diagnoses are also the least serious and most easily resolved."

"Can you see me jumping for joy here?"

"Just go once and let a qualified expert evaluate you. Please? If you're right that you're not clinically depressed, it shouldn't be any more painful than wasting an hour or two of your time."

Chase pursed her lips. It wasn't that she objected to psychology as a field or that she had a prejudice against people who really did need help. It was that she wasn't one of them. She weighed her options. "Fine. One session for evaluative purposes. That's it."

"Deal. I'll have the nurse give you some names."

"I'd prefer a female therapist. Preferably a lesbian."

"I'll see what I can do. I'm going to want to see you again next month—after I've received the report. In the meantime, I want you to concentrate on de-stressing your life and taking it easy."

"Right."

"I mean it, Chase. This is about your health. You want to feel better? Follow doctor's orders."

عحعی

Chase hadn't even reached the parking lot when her cell phone rang.

"Well, what did he say?"

"Most people start a conversation with, 'Hi, Chase, it's Tisha. How are you?'"

"That's why God created caller ID. So we can avoid all those time-wasting pleasantries."

"Oh, is that why."

"Well, what did he say?"

"He thinks I'm stressed and depressed. Can you believe it?" Chase fished the car keys out of her pocket and pushed the remote to unlock the doors.

Tisha was quiet on the other end of the phone. When she did speak, it was without her usual joviality. "He could be right, you know."

"Not you too." Chase moaned in exasperation.

"Listen, you've got a lot going on. It's not beyond the realm of possibility."

"The stress, sure. But I'm not depressed, damn it." Chase yanked on the seat belt and put the car in reverse.

"Okay. Okay. Whatever you say. So what does he want you to do next?"

"He's insisting that I go for at least one session with a psychologist."

"You agreed to it?"

"I really had no choice, did I? He won't consider other possibilities until I prove I'm not depressed. My word isn't good enough."

"What do you have against therapy? I've been going for years."

"Yeah, and look what it's done to you." Chase laughed for the first time in what felt like days. "Sorry. You walked into that one."

"I suppose I did."

"Therapy can be useful, Tish, I'm not disputing that. I just resent being shoved into it, especially when I know I'm not depressed. I know myself. I'm not."

"Okay, already. I hear you. Did you tell him you didn't want to go?"

"Believe me, he was well aware of my feelings."

"But?"

"He asked me to humor him."

"Which, of course, you were thrilled to do."

"Uh-huh," Chase said unenthusiastically.

"So find a different doctor."

"This guy has a great reputation. I know him and I trust him."

"Except that he's asking you to do something you don't want to do, something you don't think is necessary."

"Yes. But I don't want to start over with a new doctor. I'll see a damn therapist, if only to get this guy to rule depression out. I just feel like we're wasting time and not getting to the crux of the problem."

"Then make the therapy appointment sooner, rather than later."

"I will, believe me. I want it over with."

"Here's hoping the therapist is cute."

"Very funny," Chase said as she disconnected the call. She ran her thumb over Danica's picture on the back cover of the book as she picked it up off her lap and placed it on the passenger seat of her car. "Now if *you* were the therapist, I'd sign up for a lifetime of appointments."

⚬⚬⚬

Thwack, thwack.

The sound of the ax hitting solid wood echoed back off the cliff face. With a last mighty swing, Danica split the log clean through. She straightened up slowly and stretched her aching back and shoulder. The evidence of her handiwork lay at her feet and scattered for twenty feet in each direction—a full cord of wood, split and ready to stack. That would be a job for another day, she decided, glancing at the fading sunlight.

There was no question that she could afford to have already-split, dried wood delivered. But Danica enjoyed the exercise and the sense of satisfaction she got from having done the work herself. The cord of wood would likely last her through the spring and part of the summer, if the days were warm enough and the nights not too cold.

The vibration of the cell phone against her hip yanked Danica back from her musings. "Hello?"

"Are you ready?"

"Hi, Toni," Danica said dejectedly.

"If I didn't know any better, I'd say you didn't sound happy to hear from me. That could give a girl a complex, you know."

"I'm always overjoyed to hear from you, T. Especially when I'm busy enjoying the wonders of the great outdoors and the bliss of solitude." Danica plopped down on a tree stump.

"What's that supposed to mean?"

"In this case, it means you're about to ruin a perfectly good sunset."

"Sorry to interrupt your Grizzly Adams Utopian moment, but you do remember the *60 Minutes* crew is coming tomorrow, don't you?"

"I didn't, but I knew you'd remind me. And I distinctly remember you promising to come along for the ride."

"Yes, well, I was going to, really I was, but since I have an AWOL client holed up in the middle of nowhere, I can't swing it."

"Uh-huh." Danica watched as the sun dipped below the tree line.

"The masses are clamoring for your presence. I've been fighting them off with a stick."

"Likely story. Your cell phone will work just as well up here."

"No can do, Dani. I promise you I'll be there next time."

"You've said that the last three times I've invited you up here. I think I'm the one who's beginning to get a complex." Danica stood up and walked inside to sit on the couch and put her feet up.

"You know I love you. It's just the wilderness I hate. All those bears and bugs and things. Eww. They give me the willies."

"You city folk are such babies."

"Perhaps, but we're comfortable babies with all the amenities a big city offers."

"I assure you, I've got everything I need here." Danica looked around at her cozy living room with a view of the lake, a first-class entertainment system, and a fireplace.

"You scare me, Dani. I swear, you really do. Did I happen to mention that *60 Minutes* wants to see you in your 'natural' habitat?"

49

"We're already giving them that. They're coming up here, right?"

"Yes, but they want something more than that. They want to tape the interview while hiking. They pitched it as a walk in the wilderness with former Senator Warren."

"Wonderful alliteration, to be sure. They want to take a camera tramping through the woods?"

"So they say."

"The poor cameraman."

"No kidding. Sucks to be him, eh? Oh, and Dani?"

"Yes?"

"He's got control over how you look, so you might want to take pity on the guy and not drag him straight uphill."

"Sure, take away all my fun."

"I'm just looking out for your best interests."

"As you always do."

"Can we go over your schedule for a minute?"

Danica looked forlornly out the window at the darkening sky. "Since you've already wrecked the sunset, you might as well go for broke."

"Here's a flash for you—I'm told the sun sets every single day."

"That's only a rumor. It's perpetuated by city slickers who have no appreciation for the beauty of life and the sanctity of nature."

"Boy, is it getting deep in here. I've got you booked for a southeastern gig on Monday."

"You didn't waste any time, did you?"

"Hey, I gave you your two weeks. Stop complaining."

"Did I say I was complaining?" Danica decided to see what was in the refrigerator for dinner.

"It was implied. Or was that inferred? I don't know. I can never get those two right."

"Okay. Where am I flying to this time, Toni dearest?"

"You want the airport or the destination?"

"Surprise me."

"You'll like the destination better, so let's start with that."

"Chicken." Danica took the marinated chicken breast out of the fridge and chuckled to herself.

"Yes, I am. How does Longboat Key sound to you?"

"As in near Sarasota, Florida?"

"Yep. Beautiful beaches, swimming with the porpoises and dolphins..."

"Let me guess, I get to enjoy it all through a hotel window in the fifteen minutes before my next flight?" Danica walked back outside to start the gas grill.

"Wrong. I took pity on you and booked you for an entire four-day stay."

"Wow. Very generous of you."

"Don't say I never did anything for you. You've got an e-ticket for a 2:05 p.m. flight Sunday. The itinerary is in your e-mail inbox. Don't be late."

"Have I ever missed a flight yet?"

"There's always a first time."

"I'll be there...relax. And, Toni? Thanks."

"For what?"

"For indulging me."

"Of course. You're my meal ticket."

Danica laughed. "You do so like to eat."

"What can I say? It's a weakness. Good luck tomorrow, Dani, although I know you don't need it. I'll check in with you later in the day to see how it went."

"I promise not to leave them eating my trail dust."

"Glad to hear it."

"They will be too. Bye, T."

Danica terminated the connection and went inside to finish preparing the chicken for the grill. Four days at the beach didn't sound so bad.

CHAPTER FIVE

Thishis is a beautiful trail."

"Yes, it is, isn't it?" Danica walked side by side with Dustin Newbury, the newest addition to the *60 Minutes* team. He was young, handsome, and fit—the latter being the most likely reason he'd been chosen for the assignment. Danica pictured some of the other *60 Minutes* correspondents hiking with her to Round Pond and she almost laughed out loud.

"Is this one of your favorites?" He didn't mention the name of the trail or their destination on purpose. He and Danica had agreed the potential threat to her safety, given the remoteness of the location, was too great if some psychopath was of a mind to stalk her.

"I come this way often, yes. It's like being in a cocoon, sheltered by an umbrella of hundred-year-old pines, walking on a bed of maple leaves. Eventually, as you'll see shortly, you come to a break in the trees and a whole new world opens before you—a pristine lake, plenty of wildlife, and bursts of sunshine that enhance the color of the leaves and the moss on the rocks. It's magical."

"You certainly make it sound that way."

"Look out," Danica called, as she reached out a hand to steady the cameraman, who was walking backward in front of her. She caught him by the belt loop and yanked hard, ducking as he and the camera pitched toward her. She held her ground, stopping his forward progress by lowering her shoulder into his midsection.

"Whoa." The cameraman stumbled another step or two before catching his balance against the pressure of Danica's shoulder. "What the heck?"

Danica pointed behind him at a large log he'd been about to trip over.

"Ah. Thanks. Perils of the job."

"I've hiked this path a thousand times, and even I wouldn't want to do it walking backward."

"Well, if you'd prefer me to shoot your backside instead of your face, you just let me know." He gave Danica a winning smile.

"You've got a point there. I think the viewers would rather that you risked your life than have to stare at my derriere."

"I wouldn't be so sure…Anyway, thanks for saving my ass."

"You're welcome."

The cameraman stepped over the offending log and resumed his backward journey.

"You're pretty strong," Dustin said with obvious admiration once he was sure the camera was rolling again. "Was that the same shoulder you dislocated in the avalanche?"

"No, thank goodness. It was my left that was damaged, so it's a good thing I'm right-handed."

"No kidding. How is the bad shoulder feeling these days? Any residual physical effects from that and your other injuries?"

"I get aches and pains every now and then, and my range of motion in that left arm isn't all the way back yet. But other than that, I'm feeling fine."

"I imagine the emotional scars run far deeper, don't they?"

Danica's jaw muscle jumped. She hoped it was the only sign of her discomfort with the subject. "I think emotional scars are always harder to heal," she said guardedly.

"In this case, you lost your life partner of, what, eighteen years?"

"Yes. Sandy and I were celebrating our eighteenth anniversary with the trip to New Zealand."

"That's got to be devastating."

"Yes, it was." Danica forced herself to make eye contact with the reporter. She guessed she should've been used to talking about all this by now, but it simply never got easier, and it was not a subject she was planning on revisiting in depth. She hoped that much was obvious to Dustin.

54

"You've got a very successful career now—speaking engagements all over the country, a best-selling memoir, a movie based on your experiences."

"Mmm-hmm." *Points for you for reading your subject correctly and switching tactics.* "To all appearances, you've adjusted remarkably well for everything you've been through. And yet, in a sense, you've removed yourself from life."

A vein popped in Danica's neck and she counted to five to rein in her temper. "I have to disagree with you there, Dustin. I'm in the public eye all the time, I've spoken to dozens of audiences..."

Dustin swept his hand out in front of him to indicate the environment around them. "What you say is true, but you also live in a very isolated spot, far from the rest of humanity. Some might say you were hiding from life. It's been more than three years since Sandy's untimely death. You're a beautiful, intelligent young woman. I don't get the sense there's anyone special in your life at the moment..."

A vision of Chase in her white tuxedo flashed through Danica's mind, followed closely by a stab of guilt. Was it unfaithful to Sandy's memory that thoughts of another woman should intrude unbidden? *Another issue for another day. Stay on point. He's trying to get a rise out of you.* "I choose to spend my downtime surrounded by beauty and nature. I don't see anything odd or unusual about that."

"The silence is deafening, and it's nearly thirty miles to the closest grocery store."

Not knowing what to say to that, Danica shrugged.

"You got high marks from your constituents as a senator." Dustin shifted gears. "Any chance we'll see you in the political arena again?"

"I learned long ago never to say never, but at this point, I think it highly unlikely."

"Why?"

Because that life reminds me too much of what I lost. "Time moves on, priorities change. I think and hope I did a lot of good as a public servant, but I've found a new way to help people, one that, to my mind, is equally as important and valuable."

"No doubt."

"What do you think of the view?" Danica asked, relieved for the distraction as the trail widened out to reveal sparkling waters.

Before Dustin could answer, she put a hand up and shushed him. A moose stepped out of the forest some twenty yards away and waded into the pond to get a drink.

"Now you know why I live here," Danica whispered.

✍

"So, Chase, what brings you here?"

Chase sat across from Doctor Jackie Lund, a fifty-something handsome butch with a gravelly voice and spiked, graying hair. Doctor Lund, or Jack, as she informed Chase she preferred to be called, had come highly recommended by Chase's doctor and several friends she trusted. "This visit is a one-time deal. It's a prerequisite for proving there's something physical wrong with me, not mental."

"Ah, a hostile witness. Good. I love a challenge."

Chase sighed. "I'm not hostile. I'm sorry if I came across that way. It's just that I know myself, and I know my body. There's something physically wrong here."

"Okay. Why do you say that?"

"In the past few months, things have been changing. I've been having constant low-grade headaches and occasional migraines. I've never had anything like it before. On top of that, I've started forgetting things. At first, I thought I was just too busy and needed to slow down. But that's not it."

"What kind of things are you forgetting?"

"I'll walk out of the house and forget my briefcase. I'll forget something someone told me the day before or sometimes even the previous hour. I'll put my keys someplace where I won't forget them, and then I can't remember where they are."

"Can you give me some idea when you first noticed these problems?"

Chase chewed her lip in concentration. "Probably about four months ago."

"Anything change in your life around that time?"

"Such as?"

"New job responsibilities? A new girlfriend? A breakup with an old girlfriend? Financial troubles?"

"No, no, no, and no."

"Okay."

"There's one more thing..." Chase picked nervously at her cuticles.

"Chase, I can't make an accurate assessment without all the facts." Jack looked at her kindly. "Help me out here."

Chase took a deep breath and folded her hands in her lap. "There's something really strange going on lately. My mood goes from one extreme to another in a heartbeat and for no apparent reason. I can be laughing, having a good time, and all of a sudden I'm pissed as hell and I have no idea why. It's like I know it's happening and I can't do a thing about it."

"I bet that's damned inconvenient."

"No kidding."

"Any chance that you're pregnant?" Jack asked.

"Not unless it's the Immaculate Conception," Chase answered.

"Do the mood swings happen perhaps in conjunction with your period?"

"No."

"You look too young to me to be menopausal."

"You got that right," Chase agreed.

"Do you have any family history of mental illness, depression, manic depression, personality disorders?"

"Nope."

"Did the mood swings start four months ago, like the forgetfulness?"

"No. This is a lovely new addition in the last couple of weeks."

"I see. Anything change around that time?"

"No." Chase paused. "Wait, that's not true."

"Oh?"

"A week earlier I was at a national conference. The speaker was Danica Warren."

Jack whistled.

"Exactly." Chase nodded in agreement. "One look at her and I was a goner."

"You and half the lesbian nation."

"No. I don't mean it like that." Chase pursed her lips in frustration, trying to put into words feelings for which she had no frame of reference. For weeks, she'd been puzzling through what happened at that moment when she looked up to see Danica on the stage. Still, her feelings were so far removed from anything she'd ever experienced that she didn't know what to make of them. It wasn't something she would have shared with anyone else, but Jack was a complete stranger, a professional in the realm of emotions whom she likely would never see again. *What the hell.* "Have you ever met someone and it made your entire life up to that point seem irrelevant?"

Jack raised an eyebrow in response.

"I don't know how to explain it to you. It was like, I saw her, and something I didn't know I was missing clicked into place. I've been trying to put my finger on it. All I know is that I reacted to her in a way I've never reacted to anyone before."

"Ah, you've got it bad."

Chase nodded. "I do. But it's so much deeper than that. This isn't some silly adolescent crush…it's…different." Chase jumped up and began pacing around the room. She paused in mid-step and pivoted toward Jack. "I know that sounds so lame." She resumed her pacing.

"Not necessarily. Tell me a little bit about your relationships. Would you say you're someone who falls in love quickly?"

Chase considered for a moment. "No. I tend to be cautious with my heart. I'm not afraid to ask a woman out, but I have to get to know her before I decide to commit to anything more than having a good time. I mean, there's that initial physical attraction, which is what makes me ask her out in the first place, but I don't share much of myself until I see what else is there."

"But that's not the way you feel about Danica?"

"Not even close. It was like she already knew me. During her speech, there was a moment when she came to stand in front of me and it was like she looked right inside me." Chase's voice took on a note of wonder. "I felt completely naked, but safe, somehow. Does that make sense?"

"Did you actually meet her or just hear her speak?"

"I met her...twice in the same day. The first time was when she autographed my book, then again at the formal dinner that night. She sat across from me at the head table."

"Did you talk?"

"We didn't have much of an opportunity, but we had a couple of exchanges."

"Did you get the sense she was feeling something between you too?"

"I was so blown away by my own reaction I can't be sure." Chase closed her eyes in an attempt to recall. "I think it would be safe to say I made an impression on her. I mean, she remembered me at dinner from the autograph session, and she must've met literally a thousand or more people. I got a great smile from her and she joked with me when we were formally introduced at the dinner table too."

"Well, that's something. Are you in a relationship now?"

"No," Chase answered emphatically.

"Okay then." Jack feigned being shoved backward. "I take it the last one didn't go so well."

"You could say that. I knew something was going on. I called her on it several times."

"You thought she was cheating on you?"

"I was almost positive. I just couldn't prove it. Finally, she broke up with me in public, at happy hour, no less."

"Ouch. So, you were right about there being another woman?"

"Uh-huh."

"How long had you been together?"

"Six years."

"Double ouch." Jack made a sympathetic noise. "How long has it been since you broke up?"

"A little over two years."

"I gather you're not still on friendly terms?"

"Not a chance, although she'd probably like that. She's the only ex I don't keep in touch with."

"How many relationships have you had?"

"Four."

"Was that the longest one?"

"No. I had one that lasted eight and a half years."

"What happened there?"

"Different priorities." Chase shrugged. "We just grew apart. Finally, it became apparent that we made better friends than lovers."

"But you've stayed friends?"

"Yes. She moved to Boston. We still talk and e-mail often, and I see her and her girlfriend once or twice a year."

"Ah, she's resettled."

"Yes. About two years after we broke up. I like her girlfriend. She's sweet, and I'm glad to see them both happy."

"Nice when it all works out that way."

"Yeah, it is."

"What have you been doing in the last two years?"

"I've been dating a little bit."

"And nothing much has come of that?"

"No one has made my heart race, if that's what you're asking."

"And Danica? She makes your heart race?"

"Like I'm riding a horse in the Kentucky Derby."

"That's never happened in your experience before, even when you first met your girlfriends?"

"Never. Not like this."

"What are you going to do about it?"

"Do about it?" Chase threw up her hands. "What can I do about it? She's Danica Warren."

"Which means, what? She's not human?"

"No. But she's not exactly accessible, is she?"

"How do you know unless you try?" Jack checked her watch. "Wow, time flies when you're having fun. Just a few more questions. When you have these mood swings you've described, do they tend to happen while you're doing anything specific?"

"Not that I'm aware of."

"Do they always occur around the same time of day?"

"No. There really isn't any set pattern to them."

"Do they happen, say, when you're preoccupied with thoughts of Danica?"

"No, that just makes me smile and my heart pound." *Like now.*

Jack stood up and held her hand out. "It's been a pleasure meeting you, Chase."

"That's it?" Chase asked incredulously.

Jack laughed. "I'm sorry. You should see the look on your face. Yes, that's it."

"Well?"

"Well, what?"

"Did I pass the test?"

"There was no test here, Chase. But if you're asking me for a diagnosis, I'd have to say you're probably right. I don't think you are depressed, at least not in the clinically depressed sense. Sorry to disappoint you."

"Hardly. That's great news."

"Still, if you ever need me, I'll be here."

"Thanks. No offense, but I hope I'll never have to take you up on that offer."

"No offense taken. I suspect most of my patients feel the same way." Jack walked Chase to the door. "Good luck with Danica. If you feel as strongly as you seem to, you'll find a way to make something happen."

"I hope you're right."

"Send me an invitation to the wedding," Jack said, her eyes twinkling.

"Count on it," Chase concurred, laughing as she walked away.

The spray of the surf pounded against the hard sand as Danica strolled along the beach on Longboat Key. She was dressed comfortably in shorts and an untucked T-shirt, her bare feet leaving imprints everywhere she stepped as she slogged through the water at the shoreline.

Flashes of orange bounced off the surface of the water as the sun made its descent toward the western horizon, and Danica paused to admire the sunset. The transition to night would bring with it a chilling breeze, so she turned and retraced her steps to the resort.

Out of habit, she turned on the television in the room as she unpacked her suitcase. She'd barely bothered to hang her garment bag up before she'd changed from her travel clothes and jogged down to the beach.

Her head jerked up from the task at hand when she heard her own voice. It was the speech she'd given to the Credit Union National Association, the speech where she'd met Chase. Danica shoved blindly at the suitcase, making room to sit down on the bed. Her heart hammered as she recognized the moment that she'd given in to an overwhelming urge to talk directly to Chase.

"Life is seldom as we plan it. What we do—how we act and react in those unscripted moments—that, in my opinion, is what defines who we are. Who are you? And who will you be when your moment comes?"

She hadn't planned those words, and she didn't fully understand where they'd come from, or did she? Danica had wanted very much to know who Chase was and what defined her; in fact, she still did. The simple reality of that hit Danica like a fist in the chest. She swallowed hard as, on the screen, the camera zoomed in first on her face, then on the crowd, most especially, on Chase. Would it be as obvious to the rest of the world as it was to her? Had Chase seen that look in her eyes? It was as though there hadn't been anyone in the audience for her except Chase. Danica covered her face with her hands. *Oh, God.*

Chase sat riveted to the TV set. There was Danica, in fifty-two-inch LCD High Definition splendor on her wall, standing directly in front of her in the audience. Chase leaned forward, as if doing so would enable her to see more clearly into Danica's eyes. Jack's question echoed in her mind. *Had* Danica felt any of what she'd felt? There was no question that Danica was looking directly at her. Was that intentional? Were the questions meant especially for her? Or was that wishful thinking?

The telephone rang and Chase swore. *Not now.* She checked the caller ID and let it go to the answering machine.

"Chase? Don't know if you're near a television, but you're on *60 Minutes*. How cool is that? Anyway, give me a call when you get a chance. Oh, it's Melanie. Your ex. Remember me?" Melanie's laugh sounded tinny on the answering machine. "Bye."

When Chase returned her full attention to the screen, the scene had shifted to a beautiful wooded trail. Danica and the reporter were walking next to each other. By the time Chase heard the reporter questioning Danica about her solitude, she already had begun formulating a plan.

CHAPTER SIX

"Morning, sunshine."

Danica stretched and shifted the phone so that it was cradled between her shoulder and the pillow. Since her speech wasn't until the afternoon, she'd allowed herself the luxury of sleeping in. "Morning, Toni."

"I take it the accommodations are to your liking?"

"Absolutely. This place is fabulous. Thank you."

"See? I take good care of you."

"You always do," Danica answered slowly. To her ears, her agent sounded nervous. Toni was never nervous. It also dawned on Danica that Toni never called her at this hour. "I'm sure that's not why you called. What's going on?"

"So what did you think?"

"Of the *60 Minutes* piece?"

"No, of my new wallpaper," Toni answered, the sarcasm clear in her tone. "Yes, of the *60 Minutes* piece."

"I wasn't crazy about Dustin making me sound like I'm a recluse. On the whole, though, it could've been a lot worse."

"Agreed."

"Then why are you so nervous?"

"Me? Nervous?"

"Yes, nervous. You're talking too fast and you sound like you're jumping out of your skin. What the heck is going on with you?"

"Can't a girl call her client to discuss business?"

"Yes, but you're never this jittery when we talk about work. There's clearly something else. Spill it." She was fully awake now.

"You know I hate that you can tell that over the phone without even seeing my face."

"I spent too long in politics. There, if you don't learn to pay attention to all kinds of nuances, you're dead. Now stop stalling, please. The suspense is killing me."

"Fine."

Danica waited patiently through the lengthy pause on the other end of the phone.

"You know, Dani, that I would normally never bring something like this to you. I'd handle it myself."

"I don't know that until I know what 'it' is."

"You know I love you, right?"

"A-yeah."

"And you know I only want to see you happy."

"True. Toni, whatever this is, just say it and get it over with already. I'm not getting any younger, and I've got a speech to give in four hours."

"Okay. Here goes. There was a very attractive woman sitting in the audience at the speech *60 Minutes* highlighted," Toni said in a rush. "You stood directly in front of her when you were talking. They zoomed in on you, then on her."

Chase. "What of it?" Danica's heart was pounding for reasons she didn't fully understand.

"You know I never meddle in your personal life, right?"

"Yes, it's one of the many things I like about you. You respect my privacy."

"Yes. Yes, I do."

"And?"

"Like I said, normally I wouldn't even make you aware of something like this. I'd just deal with it on my own, but…"

"Deal. With. What?" Danica said, clipping off each word and over-enunciating the *t* to emphasize her growing frustration with Toni's seeming inability to get to the point.

"Her name is Chase Crosley. She seems to think you might remember her…"

Danica lost Toni's next few words to the sound of her pulse hammering in her ears.

"I'm sorry, what?" Danica bolted upright.

"I said, she e-mailed me last night. Then she called me at the office before I could even get my morning cup of coffee today. It's Monday morning, for heaven's sake. Is there no decency in the world anymore?"

"Apparently not," Danica managed to say, although the inconvenience of Toni's having had to answer the phone before being caffeinated was not what she was thinking about. *Chase called? She e-mailed?*

"People claim to have met you all the time and are always convinced you'd want to hear from them. Remember that guy from last year? And like I said, normally I would send a very polite 'Danica appreciates your interest but doesn't answer personal correspondence,' and I wouldn't bother you about it, but..."

"But what?" Danica asked, forcing herself to sound calmer than she felt.

"I don't know. There was something in the way you looked at her that made me think she wasn't just blowing smoke."

God. Everyone saw the way I looked at her. "What, exactly, did she say?"

"She said you shared some brief conversation and that she knew she was probably just one of many people who tried to get in touch with you, but she would really appreciate it if I would give you her contact information."

Danica opened her mouth to speak, but no words came out. Chase knew. Not only that, but she may have felt something too.

"Dani? Are you still there? Look, don't worry about it. I'll take care of it. I'm sorry to have bothe—"

"Forward me the e-mail she sent you. And include her contact information, please. Don't do anything else. I'll take care of it."

"Yes, ma'am. I'm sending it even as we speak."

Danica could hear the smile in Toni's voice, and it was her turn to be nervous. "I just want to see what she said."

"Uh-huh."

"Toni," Danica said, a warning clear in her tone.

"I'm agreeing with you. Absolutely."

Danica frowned. "I'm sorry bringing that to my attention made you so anxious. Am I that much of an ogre?"

Toni laughed. "You, an ogre? Get real. No. It's just that I didn't want to cross a line, and I wasn't sure whether or not you'd welcome me bringing the matter to your attention."

"You did good, Toni."

"Thanks."

"Toni?"

"Yeah?"

"Just what was it about the way I looked at her that made you think I might want her contact information?"

"Umm, I think I hear my mother calling. Gotta go."

"Your mother's been dead for ten years."

"So? Bye, Danica. You're going to be great today."

Danica listened to the dial tone for a moment before hanging up the phone. Chase was reaching out to her. Her heart skipped a beat. *Oh, God.*

✧

Chase stared at the stack of papers in front of her and read the same paragraph for the fifth time. *Give it up. You know you're never going to be able to concentrate.* The phone rang and she pounced on it. "Hello?"

"Chase? It's Mike Nestor."

"Hi, Mike." Chase tried not to sound as disappointed as she was not to hear Danica's voice on the other end of the line.

"Am I catching you at a bad time?"

"No, of course not. What can I do for you?"

"Not a thing today. I just wanted to make sure you caught *60 Minutes* last night. Your face was beamed into millions of homes across the country."

"I saw. It was a great free plug for CUNA too."

"Yep. You can't buy that kind of exposure. Remind me to send Danica a Christmas card."

"Don't be cheap. For that you should send her a present."

"I probably should at that."

"So, you and Danica cut your teeth in politics together, eh?" Chase bit her lip. She wasn't at all sure it was smart to express an interest in Danica to Mike. *He knows her well. You want insights. He may be able to give you some.*

"That we did. Everything I said about her is true, you know. She's a remarkable woman. And, my Lord, what a politician. She was the best—that's for sure. I'm sorry to see her on the sidelines, even though I understand why she left."

"Did you know her partner?"

"Sandy? Yep, I did. What a sweetheart she was, smart as a whip and a strong woman in her own right."

"What did she do for a living?"

"Sandy ran her own political consulting business. Every candidate who wanted to win hired Sandy to help figure out how to get it done. She had a remarkable success rate."

"I bet a lot of people miss her."

"That's an understatement. Hey, listen. I've got to run. I just wanted to make sure you'd seen yourself in lights. You're a star now. Not that you weren't one before, of course."

"Nice save, Mike." Chase hesitated. "You don't happen to have contact information for Danica, do you?"

"Not anything current. We got her for the conference through a speakers' bureau. Why?"

"Ah, that makes sense. Well, I'll let you go. Thanks for calling." Chase deliberately ignored the last question.

"You bet. Talk to you soon, Chase."

"I'll look forward to it. Bye."

"So much for Plan B," Chase mumbled to herself after she'd hung up the phone. She had hoped that if contacting Danica's agent didn't work, Mike might be able to help. *Looks like that's a dead end.*

Chase pushed the intercom button that connected her to her executive assistant. "Lena?"

"Right here, boss."

"Any call from someone named Danica?"

"Nope."

"If a call comes through from either Danica Warren or a woman named Toni, I want you to put it through."

"Okay."

"I don't care who I'm talking to or what I'm doing, you're to interrupt me."

"Got it."

"If I'm not here, forward the call to my cell."

"Check."

"Even if I'm away from my desk but still in the building. Whatever happens, I can't miss that phone call."

"Chase, I understand. It's important."

Chase paused just as she was about to emphasize the point again. *Deep breath, girl. Lena knows her job.* "I'm sorry. It's just that Danica is impossible to get hold of and I don't want to miss her call."

"This wouldn't have anything to do with a certain television news program, would it?"

"You saw it too?"

"Sure did. Bet you're glad you didn't fall asleep during the speech, aren't you? That could've been embarrassing."

"No chance of that. You saw a piece of Danica's speech. Could you have fallen asleep?"

"Probably. I can fall asleep anywhere. But I see your point. She was pretty dynamic. So you know her, huh?"

Not as well as I'd like to. "I met her," Chase answered carefully.

"That must've been intense."

You have no idea. "Mmm-hmm."

"Phone's ringing. Gotta answer that or the boss'll kill me."

"You're right about that." *Saved by the phone. Thank God.*

Danica focused on her breathing as she ran along the shoreline. It was hotter than she was used to and a lot more humid than she would've liked it to be, but she knew she needed the exercise to calm the butterflies in her stomach. Chase's phone numbers were already emblazoned on her mind. In fact, she'd started to dial twice and hung up before the call connected, resisting the desire simply to hear her voice.

What she needed was a game plan. *What do you want from me, Chase? No way to know that without making contact. What do I want from you? I want to understand why I react to you the way I do. I need to know what that is.*

But that wasn't all she wanted, and Danica knew it. She stopped running and pulled her copy of Chase's e-mail from her shorts pocket.

> I don't want to be presumptuous, and I know you must meet thousands of people on a weekly basis, but I hope you remember me. You signed a book for me at the Credit Union National Association conference, posed for a picture with me, and we ate dinner together at the head table.
>
> It's very unlike me to do this—in fact, I've never done this, period. But you said something so compelling in your speech that I find myself wanting to discuss it further with you.
>
> I can only imagine what the demands on your time must be like, but if you are so inclined, I'm including my contact information for you. I will, of course, understand if I don't hear from you, but I hope I will.
>
> Best regards, Chase Crosley

At that moment, Danica knew she wouldn't let another hour go by without answering Chase's e-mail. She glanced at her watch and began sprinting back toward the resort.

Sweat continued to drip down Danica's cleavage and back as she sat in front of her laptop in her running gear. She struggled with the words on the page, deleted a paragraph for the third time, and drummed her fingers on the desk. She sat that way for a good ten minutes, composing and re-composing in her head what she wanted to say.

"Chase, rest assured that I remember you. I'm flattered that my words touched you in some way, and I'd be happy to talk to you." Yeah, that would work. She began to type. When she'd finished the first paragraph, she paused again and bit her lip. Normally, she would never tell a stranger where she was. But this wasn't exactly a stranger; it was Chase.

After only a second's hesitation, Danica added the details of her location, her schedule, and the fact that she would call Chase as soon as time allowed. She finished the e-mail in a flourish and hit the send button before she could reconsider.

ৡৣৢ

Chase leaned over her computer screen and read the e-mail again. A bubble of giddy laughter rose up in her throat. Not only had Danica remembered her, but she was looking forward to talking to her. The feeling of euphoria was quickly replaced by a knot of anxiety. *Now that you've got her attention, smart girl, what are you going to say to her?* She checked the time. 4:23 p.m. She jumped up and began to pace. According to her e-mail, Danica had probably finished speaking and moved on to the autograph session by now. Chase tried to remember how long the autograph session in D.C. had lasted. She thought it was about an hour. Figuring in time to get back to her room and change clothes, it would likely be 5:00 before Danica called her.

Chase walked to the full-length glass wall in her office. It overlooked a serene duck pond, and she often sat gazing out at the scene to center herself and shake off the stress of the day. Several Canada geese and some mallard ducks were swimming around, and a mother goose and her progeny waddled in front of the window in formation. Chase took a deep breath in through her nose and let it out through her mouth to settle herself.

Danica is just a woman. She puts her pants on one leg at a time. What would you say to anyone you wanted to get to know better? "Hi. I'm Chase and you make me feel things I've never felt before." *No.* "I can't stop thinking about you and I want desperately to see you again? To hear your voice? To see your smile?" *That ought to scare her away in a hurry.*

The phone rang behind Chase and she rushed around the desk to answer it, knowing from the ring tone that it was Lena. "Yes?"

"I've got Danica Warren on the line for you."

Chase cleared her throat. "Put her through." 4:47. She was early.

"Hello. This is Chase Crosley."

"Hi, Chase, it's Danica Warren."

Chase closed her eyes as that mellifluous voice washed over her. "Thank you for answering my e-mail and for taking the time to call me." She sat down clumsily, not sure her legs would hold her upright.

"My pleasure."

"I'm sure you get plenty of overzealous fans wanting your attention." Chase leaned forward slightly in an open and sincere gesture, as if Danica were in the room.

"I certainly get my share, yes."

Chase swallowed hard. "I hope you don't think that's what this is."

Danica laughed, and Chase's heart fluttered.

"No. I'd like to think I'm a pretty good judge of character, Chase. It's safe to say I'm not worried about needing protection from you."

"I'm glad." Chase smiled into the phone, her tight shoulder muscles loosening ever so slightly. "You couldn't be any safer. How was your speech today?"

"You'd be better off asking the audience, I think. From my standpoint I can always do better."

"You're a perfectionist. Simply shocking," Chase deadpanned.

"I know. I'm sure there's a twelve-step program out there for me somewhere. Perfectionists Anonymous. I can see it now. 'Do you always strive to do better? Are you never satisfied with your performance? We can help.'"

Chase chuckled and relaxed back into her chair. "I think I could keep you company there."

"We could both critique what we could've said better after each meeting."

"Perfect." *You have a marvelous sense of humor.*

There was a pause on the line.

Think of something else to say, smart girl. "I saw the *60 Minutes* piece last night."

"Mmm. Nice shot of you in the audience."

She remembers what I look like. "Thanks. That was unexpected."

"I bet you're glad you weren't sleeping."

"My executive assistant said the same thing this morning. I could never have slept through that. You were magnificent."

"You're making me blush."

"Points for me then." When Danica didn't say anything else, Chase pushed ahead. "The excerpt of your remarks *60 Minutes* showed—it was so powerful. That was exactly the piece of the speech I've been thinking about since I left D.C. I agree with you about unplanned events. You're absolutely right."

"I am? That must be a first."

Chase smiled again, utterly charmed. *She's modest.* "No, I mean it. Life is about the unscripted moments and how we choose to handle them. I hadn't thought about it much until you said that. But it makes so much sense." *And I haven't been able to stop thinking about it since I met you.*

"Well, it's certainly been my experience."

"I hope I'm not keeping you from anything. I know you've had a long day and you must be tired." *Please say no. Please say no.*

"I'm enjoying the conversation. Chase, it's not every day someone manages to find my agent, badger her before she's had her morning coffee, and convince her that she should pass the message along to me. I'm impressed. Usually nobody gets past Toni."

Chase blushed. "I feel truly lucky then." *Make a move now or you'll lose her.* "You're in Sarasota?"

"Yes."

"My grandparents used to live on Longboat Key. I vacationed there many times as a child. I loved to play on the beach and watch the porpoises. I still do." Chase held her breath, waiting to see what Danica would do with that information.

"Ah, I should wish you were here then. Toni's scheduled it so I have a few extra days on Longboat Key."

Chase's heart tripped. "That's a coincidence. My doctor thinks I need a vacation. I've been ignoring him, but I know he's right. A couple of days at the beach in the middle of the week might be just what the doctor ordered." She bit her lip nervously. *Did you really just suggest joining Danica Warren for a midweek stay at the ocean? Have you lost your mind?*

The silence on the other end of the line hung in the air, and Chase closed her eyes tightly. *There it is. You blew it.*

Finally, Danica said, "If you can swing it, I'd love the company."

"Tell me where you're staying. I'll book a room and be there tonight." *Oh, that was smooth, smart girl.* Chase smacked herself in the forehead. *Could you be any more obvious?*

"No one could say you weren't efficient."

It was clear from her tone of voice that Danica was smiling, and Chase breathed a huge sigh of relief. She jotted furiously on her desk blotter as Danica provided the details of her accommodations.

"I'll ring your room in the morning, if that's okay."

"That's more than okay. I'll look forward to my personally guided tour of the Key. Travel safely."

"See you tomorrow," Chase said, gently placing the phone in the cradle. "I can't wait."

CHAPTER SEVEN

D anica's hair stood on end where she'd been running her fingers through it for the previous hour while walking in circles on the deserted beach. *It's official. You've lost what little was left of your mind.* The tension in her back was so great she actually considered getting a professional massage for the first time in her life.

This is crazy. You don't even know this woman. You don't know the first thing about her. What if she's a nut case? What if she's got expectations? You don't just invite a stranger to spend two days with you at the beach and think she won't get the wrong idea.

Danica stopped short. It occurred to her that there wasn't any wrong idea for Chase to have. Before she could examine that notion any further, the phone on her hip vibrated.

She pushed the button on her wireless headset. "Hello?"

"Hi, sugar. It's Ted returning your call. To what do I owe the pleasure? Not that I'm not always pleased to hear from you."

"I think I just made a huge mistake."

"Uh-oh. You sound uptight. Tell the Fish man all about it. By the way, lovely story on *60 Minutes* last night. You were fabulous, as always."

"You saw that? Good. Did you happen to see the excerpt of my speech?"

"Of course. It was inspired."

Danica huffed in exasperation. "Did you notice anything unusual about it?"

"No." There was silence for a beat. "Wait a minute," Ted continued, a thought obviously dawning on him. "You're upset that they showed the way you looked at the beautiful dish in the audience, right? Oo-la-la, she's a hot one, honey. No shame there."

Danica groaned. "She's on her way here to spend a couple of days with me at the beach." She winced as Ted let out a loud whoop in her ear.

"That's fantastic. Oh, I am so proud of you. That's marvelous. You sly devil."

"Ted, you don't seem to understand."

"What's to understand? You saw a gorgeous babe at a conference, and you asked her out. Good for you."

"I didn't ask her out." Danica plunked herself down on a beach chair. "At least, I don't think I did. I don't know what the hell happened." Ted's laughter only fueled Danica's agitation. "It's not funny."

"I'm sorry, Dani. I'm not laughing at you, really. But how can you not know if you asked a woman out or not?"

"I don't know. She tracked me down through my agent. I called her back. A conversation ensued, and the next thing I know she's offering to fly down here for a couple of days."

"So she made the move then, not you."

"Yes. No. I don't know." Danica slapped her palm against her thigh. "Doesn't it count as making a move if I encourage her? Especially if I know, or at least suspect, where she wants the conversation to go?"

"Not necessarily. Does it matter who led and who followed, sugar?"

"It does to me. I'm not like that. I've never done anything remotely like that in my life."

"What was it you said in the speech about unscripted moments defining you?"

"I hate when my words come back to bite me." Danica sighed. "That seems to be a very popular line today."

"Take your own advice, Dani. Look at this as an unscripted moment. What does it say about you?"

"That I'm unfaithful?" A blanket of misery enveloped her.

"Aw, honey. To what? To Sandy's memory? You know she wouldn't agree. We've talked about this before. She would be jumping up and down for joy if she were here."

"I can't help it, Fish man. It doesn't feel right."

"News flash. You didn't die with Sandy, sugar."

The words hit Danica like a punch in the gut. "What?" she asked.

"I'm sorry, but that's the way you've been behaving. I know you lost a part of yourself when Sandy died, but you're still here and you've got to live. Like it or not, life goes on. It's wrong to deny yourself happiness and joy if you can find it. If this woman—and I want to know everything about her, by the way— gives you those things, you've got to grab her with both hands. Carpe diem, carpe woman, and all that jazz."

"You really think so?"

"I really think that the look you gave her in the middle of that speech spoke volumes. Even a blind man could see the sparks there, honey. There's no harm in digging a little deeper and seeing what that's about. For heaven's sake, you didn't ask her to marry you, did you?"

That surprised a laugh out of Danica. "Of course not."

"Right. Spend a couple of days taking romantic walks on the beach and talking. Open yourself up to the possibilities. You owe it to yourself and to Sandy. If nothing comes of it, then nothing ventured, nothing lost or gained, to mangle a phrase. Right?"

Danica pursed her lips and considered.

"Right, sugar?"

"Right," she agreed reluctantly.

"Call me if you need me. The Fish man is always here for you. Otherwise, I want every dirty detail when you get home and don't leave anything out."

"I didn't pick you for someone who lives vicariously through others."

"Oh, honey, you don't know the half of it."

◈◈◈

The pain gripped Chase's head like a vise, making even unpacking a daunting task. She checked her watch again, wondering why the pills hadn't kicked in yet. *Lie down. I just need to lie down for a few minutes.*

Chase didn't bother to disrobe or even to turn down the bed. The coolness of the pillowcase felt wonderful against her hot cheek, and she gratefully closed her eyes, willing the pain to go away.

When she opened them cautiously again, it took her several seconds to get her bearings. *Hotel. Longboat Key. Danica. Mmm.* She rolled over experimentally, heartened when the movement didn't cause her head to throb. The unfamiliar clock on the nightstand said 4:54 a.m. "Some few minutes." She thought about getting undressed and sliding under the covers, but she knew from experience that she'd never be able to go back to sleep.

Idly, she considered her options. It was far too early to call Danica. *Holy cow.* Her eyes popped open wide. This morning she would have breakfast with Danica. Her stomach did a nervous flip, and she considered pinching herself to prove it wasn't a dream.

If she didn't do something to ward off the butterflies, it would be a long few hours. What she needed, Chase decided, was the comfort of something familiar. The sun would be coming up soon; watching the sunrise with her grandfather had always been magical. She got up, finished unpacking, and changed into shorts and a sweatshirt.

By 5:15, Chase was strolling along the marina, watching the fishermen bait their hooks and the early morning boaters prepare to head out for the day. She remembered a game she played with her grandfather. He would challenge her imagination by asking her to guess which fisherman would catch the most fish that day, then explain her choice. She would studiously observe each man, paying attention to whether he was using live bait or a lure, whether he was clean shaven or scruffy, and what type of footwear he had on. Then she would turn to her grandfather and solemnly declare the winner. He would nod sagely and listen to her lengthy and serious dissertation on all the many reasons why that particular fisherman would win.

Afterward, grandfather and granddaughter would sit and watch the sunrise, their feet dangling off the dock. When the sun had cleared the horizon, they would amble back to the condominium where grandma had prepared a breakfast feast.

Chase smiled at the memory, picked out the winning fisherman of the day, and found herself the perfect spot to watch the sunrise. *This one's for you, Grandpa.*

Wide awake, Danica stared at the clock. It was barely dawn. She'd slept fitfully, her mind too preoccupied with Chase and her emotions in too much turmoil to allow for anything else. She threw on her gear and headed for the beach. Perhaps a run would settle her nerves, which seemed to be on hyper drive. The rhythmic pounding of her sneakers on the hard sand provided a soothing counterpoint to her tumultuous thoughts. Chase would be calling her in a matter of hours and she still wasn't sure how she felt about it. "You could've avoided contact, and you didn't. You could've sent a simple e-mail and left it at that. You didn't. You could've had the phone conversation and left it at that. You didn't. There must be a reason for that, Dani. You've never been a chicken in your life. Now's not the time to start. Fish man is right. It's not as if you're asking her to marry you. Just enjoy her company."

By the time she'd returned to her suite, Danica was feeling much calmer. She stripped and showered, allowing the hot water to beat a tattoo against her tight muscles. It would be nice, she mused, to enjoy the company of an intelligent, attractive woman.

Chase picked up the phone, started to dial, and dropped it back in the cradle. Her palms were sweating. "She's expecting your call. It's not like she's not going to take it." She gripped the receiver firmly and dialed.

"Hello?"

The sound of Danica's voice was like a tonic. It made Chase want to weep, and all she'd said was "hello."

"Hi. It's Chase."

"Good morning. I hope you got at least a little sleep. How late did you get in last night?"

"Somewhere around midnight, I think."

"Good Lord. What are you doing up at eight?"

Chase laughed, relaxed a bit, and sat down on the bed. It was amazing that just talking to Danica had such a calming effect on her. Whatever anxiety she had felt moments earlier simply melted away. "Actually, I've been up for a few hours. I watched the sunrise over the cut. I used to do that with my grandfather when I was little."

"That sounds like a lovely tradition. There wasn't much to see on my run, although I was out there about the same time."

"You must've been on the beach. It faces west."

"Yes. Great for sunsets, not so much for sunrises."

Without thinking, Chase said, "We'll have to be sure to catch the sunset tonight then. Can't have you missing something that beautiful on both ends of the day."

"Indeed."

"Umm, have you had breakfast yet?"

"No. I was waiting to hear from you."

"Great. I have just the place. I could pick you up at your room, or," Chase rushed on, "if you're not comfortable with that, I could meet you in the lobby."

"You can pick me up here, Chase," Danica said quietly. "I'm in twelve twenty-three."

"Okay. Can you be ready in half an hour?"

"Sure. Do I need to wear or bring anything special?"

"Wear something comfortable. A bathing suit and shorts would be appropriate."

"I think I can manage that. See you in a bit."

"Yes, you will." It wasn't until Chase hung up the phone that her hand began to tremble.

୭ୁ୬

Although she'd been expecting it—had, in fact, been sitting on the edge of the couch in the suite's living room waiting for it—when the knock came, Danica jumped. Her heart was beating so hard she was sure Chase could hear it through the door.

She took three quick strides and stopped just shy of the threshold to collect herself. *This is just about getting to know her. It isn't a big deal.*

When she opened the door to see Chase standing there, Danica froze. Her heart stuttered and she stopped breathing for what seemed like minutes, until her body demanded air. She blinked hard. *No big deal. Right.* "Hi," she managed meekly.

"Hi," Chase answered, her voice huskier than Danica remembered. "You look great."

"So do you." Chase was dressed in a pair of casual shorts that accentuated her long legs and a tight tank top that outlined small, high breasts. Her broad, muscular shoulders were bare and she carried a backpack slung over one shoulder. Danica licked her lips unconsciously.

"We should get going," Chase said, although she didn't appear to be in any hurry.

"Am I okay the way I am?" Danica asked, feeling a bit self-conscious.

Chase's eyes roamed over her body. "Oh, yes."

Danica felt the blood rush to her cheeks, then directly to her groin. She tried to remember if anyone, even Sandy, had ever looked at her that way or elicited such a visceral reaction from her. *Oh, boy.* "D-do I need a sweatshirt?"

"You might want to bring one along. It could get chilly." Chase continued to look at her in a way that made Danica want to squirm.

"Okay. I'll just be a sec. Come in, if you want," Danica called over her shoulder as she sprinted through the living room to the bedroom. She leaned on the table in the corner of the room, out of sight of the living room, trying to make sense of what was going on inside her. Her arms were shaking, her legs felt like Jell-O, and her heart was beating like a racing freight train. "Get a grip."

"Did you say something?" Chase called.

"No. I'm just trying to remember where I put the dang thing," Danica lied. With one deep, steadying breath she pushed off from the table, snatched the sweatshirt off the bed, and returned to the living room.

Chase was standing at the window, her back to Danica. When she turned around, her effervescent smile melted any reservations Danica might have had.

"Ready?"

"You bet. Where are we going, by the way?"

"You'll see."

"A mystery? This early in the morning?"

Chase made a show of checking her watch. "Seems to me we've both been up long enough that this is almost midday."

"Nine a.m., the new noon. I like it."

Chase's laughter warmed Danica to the core. They walked east out of the resort toward the marina in companionable silence.

"You don't get seasick, do you?" Chase asked.

"No. I love the water."

"Whew." Chase made a show of wiping her brow. "And you can swim, right?"

Danica laughed. "Are you planning on pushing me in?"

"Hmm, now there's a thought." Chase winked at her. "No. But you might get hot later and touching the bottom won't be an option."

Chase made a right turn down one of the walkways, and Danica's eyes widened. "We're having breakfast at sea?"

"No. Actually, we're having breakfast on the ocean," Chase corrected.

"Picky, picky. Let me rephrase. We're eating out on the water?"

"Yep." Chase bit her lip. "Is that okay with you?"

"Okay? It's fantastic." Danica squeezed Chase's hand and started when Chase interlaced their fingers. It felt so natural, so right. A wave of panic washed over her and Danica quickly disentangled their hands.

"I'm sorry. I didn't mean to make you uncomfortable."

Danica saw the look of contrition and confusion on Chase's face and scolded herself. "You didn't do anything wrong. Really. It's fine." When Chase refused to look at her, Danica pulled on her belt loop playfully. The last thing she wanted was for Chase to feel as though she had to edit every move she made. "Honestly. It just caught me off-guard, that's all."

"It was presumptuous. I apologize."

"No apology necessary, Chase. I don't want you to walk on eggshells around me." Danica struggled for words. "It's just that there hasn't been anybody since…"

"I was insensitive." The self-recrimination was obvious in Chase's voice.

"No. Please." Danica put a hand on Chase's arm to stop their forward progress. "What I'm saying is that it's an adjustment for me." She closed her eyes momentarily in an effort to settle her raging emotions. "I'm a little nervous and jumpy, and I apologize for that."

"I want you to be comfortable with me and have a good time. I understand and respect where you are—and where you're not. It's okay."

Danica blew out a frustrated breath. "Then you know more than me." She turned Chase to face her. "I'm confused." She searched Chase's eyes. "I know that I want more than anything to be here with you right now, enjoying a glorious day."

"But there's a part of you that believes you shouldn't be, right? Because of Sandy?"

The words were said quietly, gently, compassionately, and Danica wanted to weep. *How did you know?* She swallowed the lump in her throat and nodded, afraid her voice would fail her. Chase gathered her in her arms in a comforting embrace.

"I understand, Danica. I won't push you, I promise."

Chase's breath was soft on her hair, and Danica leaned into the embrace. For the first time in more than three years, she felt a sense of peace. More than that, she had the unmistakable sensation that her heart had found its home. It was a feeling unlike anything she'd ever known.

❧

"Are you enjoying yourself?" Chase had to shout to be heard over the wind. She watched as Danica arched backward, her eyes closed and a relaxed smile on her face. Although she had an overwhelming urge to wrap her arms around her, Chase stayed where she was, several feet away with her hands on the rail.

Danica opened her eyes. "Oh, yes. The smell of the ocean, the feel of the boat pounding against the waves, an endless horizon. It's perfect."

Danica's eyes were alive and bright, and Chase found herself falling into them.

"I can't believe you did this."

Chase shrugged nonchalantly, even as she secretly congratulated herself. "It seemed like a good plan."

"It was a fantastic plan. Tell me again whose boat this is?"

"It belongs to a friend of the family. He used to fish with my grandfather. Fortunately for me, he travels quite often and was happy to loan me the use of the boat and his captain. Are you hungry? We'll be there soon."

"I have no idea where 'there' is, but I'm famished."

"Okay, I'll be right back." Chase climbed the steps to where the captain stood at the helm. "How much longer, Jake?" Chase had known Jake Astor all her life. She'd spent countless days out on the water fishing with her grandfather and his best friend, Clyde. Jake was always along as captain. She cherished the time she spent with Jake, especially when he let her steer or help with the navigation.

"Hey, squirt. You didn't used to be so impatient."

"We're starving."

Jake made a show of looking Chase up and down. "You don't look like you're in danger of malnourishment to me."

"Very funny."

"About five minutes, give or take. And before you say it, don't worry, I'll be disappearing around the far side of the island. Fishing's better over there."

Chase gave him a kiss on the cheek. "You're the best."

"I know." He winked at her. "Now go keep your lady friend company before she gets too lonely."

"We can't have that now, can we?" Chase bounded down the steps. She skidded to a halt when she caught sight of Danica pulling her shirt over her head to reveal a black bikini top and rippling abdominal muscles. Chase's mouth went dry. *Oh, God, am I in trouble.* "Almost there," she croaked, looking Danica in the face with great effort. She wasn't sure, but she thought she saw a hint of knowing laughter in Danica's eyes.

CHAPTER EIGHT

The mid-morning sun sparkled off the waves as they gently lapped against the side of the boat. Chase and Danica sat in the stern at a small patio table, eating scrambled eggs and pancakes.

"Delicious, Chase."

"How would you know?" Chase smiled. "You're shoveling so fast I'm surprised you can taste anything."

Danica sat back, clearly chagrined. "I told you I was hungry."

"I can see that, now."

"Hey, I'm a growing girl."

"You wish," Chase said, poking Danica in the side. Her skin was warm to the touch and soft, and Chase fought a powerful desire to trail her fingers across to Danica's abdomen. Instead, she settled for conversation. "That path you were walking on in the *60 Minutes* story was beautiful."

"Yeah, it is. That's the trail to Round Pond. In the winter it's great for snowshoeing or cross-country skiing, and in the spring and summer it's perfect for hiking."

"What part of the country is that?"

"It's in the Adirondack Mountains. Upstate New York."

"You're kidding, right?" Chase felt a flush of excitement. It was too good to be true.

"No, why?"

"Is that where you live?"

"Yes."

Chase thought she saw a hint of unease. "I'm sorry. I'm sure you guard your privacy jealously, as you should."

"That's okay. It's just habit to be circumspect. Less than a handful of people know where I live these days, and that's intentional. But I feel safe with you," Danica said, laying a hand on top of Chase's to emphasize the point.

"I'm very glad," Chase said softly, savoring the feeling of Danica's hand on hers. "I only asked because we're practically neighbors."

"We are?"

"Uh-huh. I live in Saratoga Springs, about thirty miles south of the Adirondack State Park."

"I know where Saratoga is," Danica said. "It's a beautiful little city."

"I think so."

A gull circled overhead and they followed its progress.

"Do you work in Saratoga too?"

"No," Chase said. "My office is about half an hour farther south."

"I know you work in the credit union business. What exactly do you do?"

"I'm the president and CEO of the trade association that represents all the credit unions in New York state."

The boat rocked gently as a breeze rippled the water.

"And you sit on the national association's board?"

"Yes. I've been on the board for the past two years."

"That explains it."

"Explains what?" Chase asked, perplexed.

"I knew that if you'd ever been in my Senate office to lobby me, I would've remembered you."

"You would have?"

"Absolutely," Danica answered, her voice pitched low.

"Oh." Chase's breath hitched as Danica held her gaze.

"Should we go for a swim?" Danica asked, breaking the spell. She removed her hand from on top of Chase's and stood to clear the table.

Chase easily recognized the telltale signs of discomfort. *Let her dictate the pace. Otherwise she'll bolt.* "A swim sounds great." Chase stood also and cleared her own place. "Does this mean we get to ignore my grandmother's rule?"

"What rule is that?"

"No swimming until at least a half hour after eating."

"Did your grandmother know that it actually takes six hours to digest food?"

"Thank God she didn't." Chase laughed.

∽✧∽

"Woo." Danica let out a yell when she came up from her dive.

"That's freezing."

"Don't be a wuss," Chase said, looking down from the deck of the boat.

"Get in here and say that, tough girl."

"I'm coming."

Danica feasted her eyes as Chase stripped off her shorts and tank top. Underneath, she wore a white tankini with a plunging v-neck line. Despite the chill of the water, Danica suddenly felt warm. When Chase emerged from the water next to her, she had to make a conscious effort not to stare at the material as it clung to every curve.

"Nothing to it," Chase said, treading water.

"Then why are your lips blue?"

"They are not," Chase argued, diving under the surface, yanking Danica's legs, and pulling her under.

Danica wriggled free and swam away, with Chase in close pursuit. Just as Chase reached out to grab her, Danica veered off, twisting down and away until she was behind Chase. She wrapped her arms around Chase's midsection and tugged. For a brief instant, their bodies came in contact all along their lengths, Danica's front molded to Chase's back. Despite the differences in their size, the fit was perfect.

Danica pushed away and swam to the surface, breathing heavily, her emotions jumbled. She kicked hard, reached the stairs to the deck, and hauled herself up quickly. When she glanced back at the water, Chase was looking up at her, hurt and concern evident in her expression.

She didn't do anything wrong, Dani, and you're hurting her.
Not for the first time, Danica questioned her decision to invite Chase to come to Longboat Key. *Maybe this was a mistake.*

"Don't run," Chase said. "Please." She hurried up the ladder.

Is it that obvious? Danica backed up a step, even as part of her wanted desperately to hold her ground.

"Danica."

"I'm sorry, Chase. I'm sending you mixed signals all over the place."

"I know this isn't easy for you. I understand that you must be conflicted. When someone so vital to your life is ripped away, it leaves a hole that you think can never be repaired."

The compassion in Chase's eyes touched Danica deep inside, in a place she hadn't even known existed. She tucked the feeling away for later examination.

"All I'm asking for is a chance for both of us to explore new possibilities." Chase held out her hands in supplication. "I've never experienced loss on the level that you have as an adult, so perhaps I'm not qualified to say anything. But I know that you make me feel things I've never felt before. I can't explain it. I just know that it's the most powerful pull I've ever known." She dropped her hands to her sides. "Now I've probably succeeded in scaring you even more."

"No. You haven't." Danica took several steps forward until she was directly in front of Chase. "I feel it too. If I didn't, I wouldn't be here. But you're braver than I am, Chase."

Chase's head shot up, a look of incredulity on her face.

Danica gave a shy shrug. "I'm afraid. What I feel for you is attraction, yes, but it goes far beyond that and that's hard for me to reconcile." She bit her lip in consternation. "I loved Sandy. She was my life for a very long time." Despite her best efforts, Danica's voice cracked with emotion.

"I know," Chase said quietly, drawing Danica to her. "It's okay."

"Let me finish." Danica put a hand on Chase's chest and created a modicum of distance between them. She couldn't think clearly when she was in Chase's arms. "But I don't ever remember feeling for Sandy anything close to the intensity of what I feel for you, and I don't even know you. How am I supposed to live with that?"

"Guilt is a wasted emotion," Chase said. "It doesn't change anything, it doesn't solve anything. It only weighs you down and holds you back. You loved Sandy. That's very clear. She knows that. I know that too."

The words were measured and without rancor, and Danica willed herself not to pull away as Chase took her hands. "I don't want to compete with what you and Sandy had together. I can't." Chase shook her head. "Every relationship is different. The dynamics are different, the personalities are different, the circumstances are different." She held up their linked hands where they could both see them. "There's a connection I feel with you that I can't ignore, and I can't explain it away. I felt it the first time I saw you."

"I felt it too," Danica said around the lump in her throat. "And it terrified me."

"Join the crowd. But if we don't take the time and make the effort to find out what this is," Chase indicated their hands, "we'll always wonder. Life's too short and too precious. I don't want to look back and wonder, Danica."

Danica couldn't shrink away from Chase's penetrating gaze. What she saw in those eyes was tenderness, compassion, understanding, patience, and determination. "I guess this really is one of life's unscripted moments, huh?"

"I guess it is," Chase agreed.

Danica swallowed hard. "I can't tell you I'm not still scared out of my wits. But I've never been a coward before. I suppose it wouldn't do to become one now." She lifted her chin and looked Chase squarely in the eye.

"Good," Chase said, squeezing Danica's hands. "I know it won't be easy and I recognize that there will be some daunting challenges. All I ask is the chance for us to get to know each other better, to see what develops."

"Fair enough. Now about that dunking..." With a glint in her eye, Danica threw herself forward into Chase, carrying them both over the side and into the water.

"You are in so much trouble."

"You have to catch me first..."

❧

"You're where?" Tisha asked, her voice rising.

91

"I'm in Florida on vacation." Chase stood at the window in her hotel room, looking out at the water, the cell phone held against her ear.

"I got that from Lena, but I didn't believe her. She said you took off like a bat out of hell, shouting instructions over your shoulder on your way out the door last night."

"I had a plane to catch."

"Chase, this is me you're talking to. The last vacation you took was three years ago."

"Six months," Chase corrected.

"Three years, six months. It's all the same. The point is you aren't someone who just takes off on a whim. What gives?"

"Nothing 'gives.'" Chase could picture Tisha pacing around her office, gesticulating wildly.

"Bullshit. Where's the fire? You can't convince me that you suddenly had such an overwhelming urge to feel the sand between your toes that you junked everything in the middle of the night for a couple of days on the beach by yourself."

Chase knew that last line was a fishing expedition, but she wasn't ready to talk about Danica yet. She checked her watch. They were due to meet in the lobby in twenty minutes for a sunset stroll on the beach, followed by dinner. "It's called spontaneity, Tish. You ought to try it sometime."

"Chase Crosley…"

"Gotta run. I'll call you when I get back to New York."

"You are infuriating."

"It's part of my charm, remember?"

"Not so much right now." Tisha mumbled an expletive under her breath, as if something had just occurred to her. "It's not your health, is it? Are you feeling all right?"

"Fine, thanks for asking." Chase didn't want to talk about her health; she didn't want to think about it. Nor did she want to entertain any more of Tisha's speculations. *Better cut this short.* "I really do have to go. Bye, Tish." She hung up the phone and stretched out on the bed. For the first time in weeks, her head didn't hurt. In fact, she felt better than she had in months. *Thank you, Danica.*

Just the thought of her made Chase's pulse quicken. The day on the boat had been magical, and now she had the evening to look forward to. A vision of Danica in her black bikini, her hair slicked back, rivulets of water dripping down her cleavage, her nipples erect from the chill of the ocean, floated across Chase's mind. *A shower. I need a quick shower. A cold, quick shower.* Chase jumped up and stripped on her way to the bathroom.

అఖ

Danica examined herself critically in the bathroom mirror. Her skin was tanned from the day spent in the sun, her naturally blond hair had lightened a shade, and her face glowed with good health. She hardly recognized herself.

Since she had a few minutes before she had to be downstairs, Danica sat down on the couch in the living room. She could've invited Chase to pick her up at her suite again, but the setting felt too dangerous, too intimate, in her fragile emotional state.

Danica closed her eyes and thought about how the day had unfolded. Being on the water had been restorative, but it was more than that—much more, and she knew it. In addition to the conflict and confusion she had felt, there was a part of her that craved Chase in a way completely foreign to her. She had told the truth about the intensity of her feelings, although she still didn't fully understand them. The one thing she knew beyond a shadow of a doubt was that she was powerless to ignore the connection they clearly shared.

అఖ

"Shall we?" Chase asked, putting her hand on Danica's lower back and guiding her toward the front door.

"We shall, indeed." The feel of Chase's hand on her back sent a warm glow through Danica as they walked along comfortably together. "Thank you, again, for today. It was wonderful."

"Believe me, the pleasure was all mine," Chase said. "Not only that, but I did promise you a personally guided tour of the Key. No tour would be complete without the view from the water."

"Of course not." Danica paused when they reached the sand. "Oh, look." She pointed to a great blue heron that circled above the waves. "He's beautiful, isn't he?"

"He most certainly is," Chase agreed.

They stood watching for several minutes in silence. When the bird flew off toward the horizon, Danica kicked off her shoes and put them on a nearby beach chair. She waited for Chase to do the same, then surprised them both by slipping her hand in Chase's.

Danica's heart beat wildly as they strolled toward the shore, and yet it felt so natural, as if it had always been like this. "I'm so glad you were able to get away on such short notice."

"Benefits of being the boss." Chase laughed easily. "I'm sure you understand that."

"Ironically, I'm not really in control of my own time these days."

"No?"

Danica hopped over a large horseshoe crab. "I'm mostly a slave to the schedule."

"But surely you have some say over that?"

"Some, that's true. But on the whole, I leave it to Toni to manage the appearances."

"Has she been working with you long?"

"She was the one who helped me navigate through the sharks to secure the book deal and the movie. So I guess you could say she's been with me since the beginning of this phase of my life."

"How did you find her?"

"One of my friends in Hollywood was repped by her. Now I don't know what I'd do without her."

"Well, I know I'm grateful to her. If it hadn't been for her, I might've missed out on one of the best days of my life."

Danica squeezed Chase's hand. "That's incredibly sweet."

"It's just the truth."

"I feel the same way."

They walked a bit farther in silence, then, as if by some unspoken mutual agreement, sat down on the sand to watch the sunset. Their hands were still linked as they sat, shoulders touching, basking in the last glow of the day.

✎✎

As dusk fell and the sun slipped fully below the horizon, Chase felt Danica shiver next to her. "You cold?"

94

"A little chilly."

Chase unlinked their hands and put her arm around Danica's shoulders, rubbing a little to provide warmth.

"You're like a furnace." Danica laughed.

"So I'm told."

"Ah, so you put your arm around lots of women, eh?"

"No. I just mean..." Chase spluttered on until she saw the mischievous grin on Danica's face.

"I'm only kidding." Danica leaned into her shoulder. "I am wondering, though. How is it that a beautiful, lovely woman like you is available?"

"I haven't been all that lucky in love"—Chase shrugged—"so I've learned to be a lot more selective."

"I'm sorry."

"I was too, until now." Chase smiled.

Danica looked at her, a question in her eyes.

"I don't know about you, but I believe that everything happens for a reason. If my last girlfriend hadn't ripped my heart out, I might've stayed stuck in a bad relationship. Then I might not ever have met you."

"Mmm. True. Tell me if I'm out of line, Chase. I don't mean to put you on the spot."

"No, I don't mind. It was a long time ago, and I've made my peace with it. Mostly."

"Can I ask what happened?"

"She cheated." Chase tried to keep the bitterness out of her voice.

"I'm so sorry. Nobody deserves that."

Danica put a hand on her leg, and nothing that had happened in the past mattered to Chase anymore. "It's okay. The harder part was that she wouldn't admit it. Then she finally broke up with me...in a very public place."

"Oh, Chase. I hope you'll excuse me for saying so, and I don't know this woman so I probably shouldn't, but she's an ass. If I had a girlfriend like you, I'd never be tempted to look anywhere else."

"That's very sweet. Thank you." Chase pulled Danica a little closer. "As I said, it doesn't matter anymore."

"It obviously hurt you deeply, so it does matter," Danica disagreed, a note of indignation in her tone. "For the record, I have no patience for infidelity. Neither Sandy nor I were ever unfaithful."

Chase heard the hitch in Danica's voice at the mention of her dead lover's name. And when she looked at Danica's face, there was real pain in her eyes. "I'm sorry it still hurts so much." Chase paused, wondering if she should go down this path. *Better to get it out into the open.* She continued, "About Sandy, I mean."

Danica gasped and tears sprang to her lashes. She started to say something, then seemed to pause to collect herself. Chase waited patiently, not wanting to push her.

"I-I know she's been gone for three years, but sometimes the grief sneaks up on me still."

"That's not surprising. You were together a very long time." Chase picked her way carefully.

"Yes, we were. It wasn't always wine and roses, but it was a good, solid relationship, and we loved each other very much."

"I imagine the loss is doubly hard when it happens so suddenly."

Danica's tears began to flow more freely, and Chase silently cursed herself. "I'm sorry," she said. "I shouldn't have brought up something so painful."

"It's okay." Danica squeezed her leg. "I'm sorry for losing it. I don't, usually. No matter how much time passes, the fact that I never got to say goodbye to Sandy will always be the thing that weighs most heavily on me."

"There was no closure."

"Right. And because there was no closure, there's no peace." Danica shook her head sadly. "I'm still struggling to reconcile my choices that day."

"Danica," Chase said softly, "I wasn't there and I can't pretend to know everything about what went on, but from all accounts you did exactly what you should've done."

"You can't know that. What if I could've saved her?"

Chase's heart broke at the tortured note in Danica's voice. "Is it realistic to think that you could have?"

"What?" Danica's nostrils flared.

"When I read your account and that of the others who were there, I was curious about how long it took for everything to transpire. So I timed it out." Chase trod carefully. She knew Sandy's death and the events of that day were incredibly touchy subjects, but she hoped what she was about to say might help Danica heal.

"And?" Danica's voice was barely a whisper.

"From a practical perspective," Chase swallowed hard and plowed ahead, "there wasn't enough time once you unburied yourself to locate the rest of your party, unbury the folks on the ground, climb up, and get to Sandy."

"That's where the choices come in," Danica said. She shrugged Chase's arm off, jumped up, and began to pace agitatedly.

"Not really," Chase said quietly. She stayed sitting, understanding that Danica needed her space for this discussion. "If you had gone directly for Sandy instead of the others, even free climbing, which would've been extremely risky…"

Danica whirled around to face Chase. "Are you a climber?"

"No." Chase chuckled. "Not me. I don't like heights. But I wanted to understand what appealed to you so much about the sport."

"You did?" Danica came back to stand in front of Chase.

"Yep, I did." Chase noted the wonder in Danica's question even as the impending darkness made the expression on her face harder to read. It made her smile. "I wanted to know everything about you." She paused before continuing. "Anyway, even if you had free climbed up there, found Sandy, and uncovered her, it would've been too late. And that doesn't take into account the severity of her injuries."

Chase saw Danica shudder and couldn't sit still anymore. She stood up and took Danica in her arms, grateful when Danica didn't resist. "This is too much. I'm sorry."

"No." Danica shook her head against Chase's chest. "It's okay. It's nothing I haven't gone over a thousand times, awake and asleep."

"I'm sure." Chase pulled back, until her arms were only loosely wrapped around Danica. She needed to see Danica's eyes. She feared the impact of her next words but knew this part of the conversation was too important to avoid. "The medical examiner said Sandy might have died instantaneously. Are you discounting that?" Danica stiffened in her arms and her eyes fluttered shut.

"No. It's the one thing that allows me to live with myself."

"I believe he said it was the most likely scenario, didn't he?" Chase asked it gently.

Danica opened her eyes again, and tears spilled out. "Yes, he did."

"But you can't accept that?" Chase wiped a tear away with her thumb.

Danica leaned into Chase. "Intellectually, I can. But my heart has a harder time with it." Her teeth chattered audibly. "I watched my lover die. I was there. And I c-couldn't do a thing about it."

Chase pulled Danica the rest of the way to her and rocked her side to side, rubbing her back. "I know, honey. I know. I can't imagine anything more horrible."

"One minute she was there, and the next she was g-gone." Danica let out a mournful wail.

The sound made Chase's heart bleed. "I know," she cooed. "Let it out." She continued to soothe Danica as she cried. Eventually, the sobs slowed, and Chase leaned back and let go with one hand so that she could dry Danica's tears.

"I'm so sorry," Danica said, her breath coming in great gulps. "It's been a long time since I cried like that. I didn't mean to."

"Please, don't apologize." Chase gave her an encouraging smile. "I'm flattered that you feel comfortable and safe enough with me to do that."

"Trust me," Danica sniffed, "you're one of only two people in the world who's ever seen me cry like that."

"Then I truly am honored."

Danica dropped her forehead to Chase's shoulder. "Now I've ruined your wonderful day by being maudlin."

"On the contrary," Chase said, lifting Danica's chin and forcing eye contact. "You've made my day by showing me a side of yourself very few others get to witness. That means more to me than you can know." Chase hoped her eyes conveyed her sincerity.

"Your compassion and understanding mean more to me than *you* can know," Danica said, smiling tremulously. "You're a very special woman, Chase Crosley."

"So are you, Danica Warren." Chase pressed her lips to Danica's forehead and murmured, "I've never met anyone like you." *And I think I'm falling in love.*

CHAPTER NINE

Danica lay in the dark trying to process her swirling emotions. Even though she hadn't known what to expect, being with Chase was unlike anything she could've imagined. It was comfortable and comforting in a way she'd never experienced, even with Sandy. Yet at the same time, Chase made her heart pound and her body hum.

"Oh, Dani. You're in so much trouble." She turned over onto her stomach and hugged the pillow, and suddenly it was Chase, her body warm and inviting, her arms strong and sure. Danica groaned. She hadn't felt desire for another woman since Sandy's death, and the sensation frightened her.

She rolled back over and took the pillow with her, squeezing it tightly. When Chase had walked her back to the suite, she hadn't pushed her; on the contrary, she'd been gentle and solicitous, clearly giving Danica the space to go at her own pace.

"Can I see you tomorrow?" Chase asked. She was facing Danica, holding both of her hands as they stood outside the door to the suite. If she wanted to come inside, she made no indication of it.

"I'd like that."

"Breakfast and a sail?"

"You have access to a sailboat too?"

"I'm a resourceful girl." Chase winked.

"Yes, you are. Breakfast and a sail sound great."

Chase shifted from foot to foot. "I had a marvelous time today. Thank you."

"I can't remember a day I've enjoyed more," Danica said, and she meant it.

"Well, good night. Sleep well."

Danica's heartbeat sped up as Chase leaned forward. Her lips were soft and no more than a whisper as they made contact with Danica's. The kiss was so brief Danica thought she might have imagined it. What she didn't imagine was her very real yearning for more.

It had been a beautiful end to an emotionally tumultuous day. As Danica's mind continued to click through the details, she remembered her crying jag and blushed. "Smooth, Dani, break down about your dead partner on your first date with another woman." But Chase hadn't seemed the least bit put off. She'd held her and supported her through another layer of grieving, while acknowledging and validating her feelings. *Extraordinary.*

Danica thought again about what she'd seen in Chase's eyes and how she'd felt in Chase's arms. *Home.* The word formed in her mind of its own accord and Danica sucked in a sharp breath. Home. Yes. That was it. Being with Chase was like coming home...for the first time.

But hadn't Sandy been her home? Certainly she'd been *at home* with Sandy, but that wasn't the same thing. Danica stared unseeing at the ceiling. Sandy had always been comfortable and easy to be with. Their relationship was about companionship, shared interests and hobbies, mutual friends, and hectic schedules. They enjoyed spending time together, doing things, and sharing a bed.

Danica's brow furrowed. The connection she felt with Chase was on an entirely different level. She turned on her side, suddenly unable to stay still. Perhaps it wasn't fair to compare the two. After all, when she and Sandy had met they had been barely more than kids. Now, she had life experience and perspective. She'd tasted the bitter pill of loss and grief.

Danica shook her head even as she argued with herself. Those were rationalizations, and she knew it. She closed her eyes, willing sleep to claim her. It was too early to make any snap judgments about Chase's place in her life. There would be time for that later.

≪⊱⊰≫

Chase pulled the covers up and tucked an arm behind her head. She was pleased with herself. The day had gone off just as she had planned. Well, almost as she had planned. The conversation about Sandy's death and Danica's distress had been difficult and heart-wrenching for both of them.

Chase wondered if she'd done the right thing by pursuing the topic. *You didn't start it. It was already there, sitting between you like a living thing.* Still, maybe it was too much, too soon. She shook her head. If they had any chance of moving forward, it would be because they'd been able to put Sandy and the ghost of her relationship with Danica to rest.

Panic suddenly constricted Chase's throat. What if Danica couldn't get past Sandy's death? It had been three years and she still mourned as if the accident had happened the day before. Chase took a deep breath. This was dangerous territory for her. What she felt for Danica was undeniable and growing with every passing second.

If she allowed her feelings to deepen any further and Danica failed to let go of the past, Chase could be hurt. Badly. She squeezed her eyes shut. The way she saw it, there were only two choices—walk away now and save herself from potential heartbreak or go forward and hope that time and love would heal Danica's scars.

Images of Danica from that day played behind Chase's eyes. Danica taking her hand during their walk. The way her face lit up when she smiled. The sun glistening off her tanned skin as beads of water warred with gooseflesh. Her child-like glee when they frolicked in the ocean. The pain and bewilderment in her face when the topic turned to Sandy. The apology in her eyes when she couldn't stem the flow of her tears.

She's struggling, and she trusts you. She left herself completely open and vulnerable. Meet her halfway.

Chase thought about the way the evening had ended, with the feel of Danica's lips against hers, so soft, so warm, so perfect. She groaned, instantly wet. She'd wanted so much more but recognized the need to go slow. Her hand slipped between her legs and she ran a lazy finger through her slick folds. She moaned, imagining Danica's strong hands on her. Oh, yes. It would be worth the wait.

❧↔❧

The ringing of the phone startled Danica out of a light doze. "Hello?"

"Good morning, Dani."

Danica rolled over and checked the clock. "What is it this time, Toni, dear?"

"What do you mean?"

"It's 7:45. By my reckoning, you're usually not functional at this hour of the morning."

"I think my reputation has been taking an unfair beating."

Danica could imagine Toni's pout. "Your reputation is richly deserved."

"Okay, maybe it is. So consider this an attempt to rehabilitate myself."

Danica smiled. "It'll take a whole lot more than one early start for that. Which brings me back to my initial question—to what do I owe the pleasure of your dulcet tones this morning?"

"Believe it or not—"

A knock on the door made Danica's heart skip a beat. No, it couldn't be; it was too early for Chase. "Hold on a sec. Someone's at the door." She put the phone down, threw on a tank top and shorts, and hustled through the suite. "Who is it?"

"Hotel services. Delivery for you, ma'am."

"Deliv…" Danica opened the door a crack, leaving the security chain on. "Holy…" She quickly undid the chain and opened the door wide.

"Where would you like these, ma'am?"

"I…umm…ah. Over there is fine," Danica spluttered, pointing to the coffee table in the living room.

Two bell boys marched in, each carrying two dozen roses in crystal vases. Danica barely remembered to tip them as she gawked at the forty-eight flawless dewy buds, twenty-four red and twenty-four white. She found the card and opened it, a smile splitting her face as she read.

Dear Danica,

Hope these get your day off to a beautiful start. I can't wait to see you today.

Hugs,

Chase

"You're a nut. A thoughtful, romantic, incredibly sweet nut." Warmth permeated Danica right down to the soles of her feet. Only the ringing of her cell phone in the other room brought her back to the present. "Omigod. Toni." She ran to grab the phone, her toes digging into the deep pile of the carpeting.

"Dani? Are you all right?"

"I'm fine."

"You scared the crap out of me, you know that, right?"

"I'm sorry." Danica gave her best hangdog look, although she knew Toni couldn't see it.

"You tell me there's someone at the door and you never come back. I ring your room back and I get a busy signal. What am I supposed to think?"

"I'm sorry, Toni. Really, I am." Danica cradled the cell phone between her neck and shoulder as she hung up the room phone receiver. She waited for Toni's anxiety-fueled diatribe to wind down.

"Okay then. So what was that all about?"

"You won't believe…" Danica halted mid-sentence. If she told Toni about her rendezvous with Chase and the flowers, she'd never hear the end of it. "Just the bellman."

"'Just' the bellman? At a quarter to eight in the morning? What on earth did he want?"

"Nosy, aren't you?" *Let it go, T.*

"Well, yeah."

"Why did you say you called again?"

"Oh, so you're not going to answer me, eh? You know I've got a vivid imagination, right?"

"I'm painfully aware of that, yes."

"And I'm not afraid to use it."

"I know." Danica sat down on the edge of the bed.

"Sure you don't want to share?"

"Positive. Now, was there some reason you were harassing me this morning?"

"Hmph. Yes. For one thing, I really did want to make sure you were enjoying your bonus days at the beach."

"I am. Thank you very much, again, for arranging that."

"You're welcome."

"And the other reason why you're calling?"

"I wanted to go over your schedule for the coming week."

"Oh." Danica didn't want to think about anything except the day she and Chase were about to share. She jumped up and paced to the window overlooking the Gulf.

"You do realize you have to come back from paradise sometime?"

"Of course. I just wish it wasn't so soon." The admission surprised her. She had never been one to shy away from work or to shirk her responsibilities. If anything, she'd always been a bit of a workaholic.

"Everything okay? Maybe I've been over-scheduling you."

The genuine concern in Toni's voice evoked a pang of guilt. "No, no, no. You're doing a great job. I know I don't tell you that often enough."

"You're right about that," Toni jumped on the compliment, her good humor seemingly at least partially restored.

"So what's on tap?" Danica tried to inject a note of enthusiasm into her tone that she didn't feel. A sailboat glided past and Danica smiled involuntarily, knowing that in a few hours she would be out there with Chase.

"A press conference tomorrow afternoon to coincide with the release of your movie on DVD."

"Where? Please don't tell me it's in L.A." She looked up at the bright blue Florida sky dotted with puffy clouds.

"Okay. I won't tell you."

When Toni didn't say anything else, Danica feared the worst. "It is, isn't it?"

"Psych. No, I insisted that there was no way to get you there in time and that if they wanted you to take part, it would have to be an East Coast event."

"I think I love you," Danica said, laughing.

"Be still my heart. Anyway, we only have to get you to New York, and I've already taken care of that. You're on a 10:00 a.m. flight." After a beat, Toni continued, "No, don't thank me for not making you get up at the crack of dawn or, worse yet, leave tonight."

"Okay, I won't."

"Well, if you really want to…"

"Thank you, Toni. What's after New York?" Danica turned away from the window, grabbed a pen, and began writing.

"*Entertainment Tonight* interview immediately following the press conference."

"Joy, joy."

"Mmm-hmm. Then *Inside Edition*, not to be left out."

"Of course not."

"You're booked into the Marriott Marquis tomorrow night."

"Nice."

"Don't get used to it. You're right back out day after tomorrow."

"To?"

"Vegas. Leave your wallet home."

"Yeah, you know what a big gambler I am. What group?"

"I've e-mailed the details to you and FedExed the background info. Should get to you by this afternoon."

"Efficient, as always. Are we done for now?" Danica glanced at the bedside clock. If she didn't get in the shower soon, she wouldn't be ready when Chase arrived.

"Let me guess, the sun's out and you've got a taxing day on the beach planned."

"Something like that."

"Yeah, we're done. Now you want to tell me what the bellman thing was all about?"

"Bye, Toni." Danica disconnected the call. She had things to do. But first, she detoured back into the living room where she spent a few minutes admiring the flowers. The day was off to a promising start.

అఖఏ

"Hi," Chase said when Danica opened the door.

Without a word, Danica moved into Chase's startled arms and kissed her briefly on the mouth. "They're beautiful. I don't know how you managed to arrange that between last night and this morning, but it was a marvelous way to wake up."

Chase struggled to kick her brain into gear as Danica stepped back. "I…" The word came out as a croak, and Chase had to pause to clear her throat. "Let me just say that if it gets me that kind of reaction, I'll send you flowers every day."

Danica blushed. "I'm a sucker for roses."

"Noted." Chase winked. "All set?"

"I think so."

"Great." Chase put her hand on Danica's lower back, pleased that Danica seemed to welcome the contact. Progress. "I hope fresh fruit, cheese, coffee, and pastries are okay with you."

"Sounds perfect."

They walked along the same path they'd taken the previous day, except this time, when they reached the slip, a small skiff awaited them. At the question in Danica's eyes, Chase said, "Our ride is out there." She pointed to a forty-foot Catalina, moored about two hundred yards from where they stood.

༺༻

"Wow," Danica said when they boarded the boat. She peeked below decks and was surprised to find a small galley, a head, and sleeping quarters. "Wow," she repeated. "This is amazing."

"I'm glad you like it," Chase said from her position directly behind Danica.

Danica whipped around and practically ran into Chase. She let out a startled yelp.

"I'm sorry. I didn't mean to scare you."

"You didn't."

Danica's voice was low and soft, and it cut right through Chase. *Speak. Right.* "I guess I'm quieter than I thought. I was sure you heard me coming." She found herself hypnotized by the miniscule gold flecks in Danica's brown eyes.

"No." Danica seemed to be entranced too.

"Umm, how about breakfast before we get underway?" *If you keep looking at me that way, you're going to be on the menu.*

"Sure. What can I do?" Danica asked.

"Sit on the deck and work on your tan until I'm ready." *I can't concentrate with you standing this close.*

"Somehow that doesn't seem an equitable distribution of assignments."

Chase turned her back and busied herself unpacking the large picnic basket she'd brought. "Believe me, when the time comes, I'll find something for you to do."

"Why does that scare me?" Danica joined Chase at the counter and picked up a knife to cut the pineapple, having liberated it from the basket. "Have I told you about my stubborn streak? We do it together."

"Good to know about the stubborn streak. Because, of course, I don't have one of those." She leaned into Danica's shoulder with her arm, tacitly conceding that the preparations would be done jointly.

Once breakfast was finished and the leftover food stowed, Chase asked, "Do you want to help me raise the sails?"

"I don't know that I'm qualified to be a first mate. I have very little sailing experience."

"Nothing to this, I assure you." Chase took Danica's hand and led her back outside to where the mainsail rested neatly furled on the boom. "Here," she said, looking over her shoulder at Danica. "See this switch?"

"Yes."

"When I tell you to, flip it."

Danica laughed. "That's it?"

"Yep. Told you you could handle it."

"Is everything today going to be this simple?"

Everything except keeping my hands off you. "I can't make any promises, but I hope so."

Hours later, they were still out on the ocean, nary a soul in sight. It had been another magical day, and Danica was enjoying the feel of the breeze on her overheated skin. She sat next to Chase as she tacked across the water.

"Oh, look." Danica pointed off the stern. When Chase didn't appear to see what she was looking at, Danica put a hand on either side of her face and turned her in the right direction. Four porpoises jumped in and out of the boat's wake, playing with abandon. "Aren't they incredible?"

"They sure are," Chase agreed. She turned her head back so that she was facing Danica. "I wish I had a camera."

"Why?" Danica wet her lips with the tip of her tongue. The way Chase was looking at her made her skin tingle.

"So that I could capture the expression on your face right now." Chase slowly lifted her hand and covered Danica's with it where it still rested on her cheek.

"Yeah?" Danica was unable to keep the slight breathiness from her tone.

"Mmm-hmm."

Chase's face was inches from hers, and Danica swallowed hard. When their lips touched this time, it wasn't a whisper; it was more like an answered prayer. Danica moved forward, seeking deeper contact. When Chase's tongue traced her lips and gently sought entrance, Danica moaned and yielded eagerly. Nothing in her life had ever felt quite so right.

"Are you okay?" Chase asked softly, pulling back slightly and tracing the curve of Danica's cheek with her fingertip.

"I'm so much more than okay." Danica opened her eyes slowly, not wanting the moment to end.

"I'm glad. I was afraid…"

"Don't be," Danica said, punctuating the point by leaning forward again and kissing Chase thoroughly. Her body felt more alive than it had in years. It was a feeling she intended to cultivate.

CHAPTER TEN

I hate having to go back to reality."

"Tell me about it. I think you've spoiled me for life," Danica said as she and Chase strolled hand in hand on the beach. Their bare feet left deep impressions in the wet sand.

"Then I consider my mission a success."

The sun dipped low in the sky, casting a golden haze over the water. They had the beach all to themselves, and Danica was more relaxed than she could remember being in a long, long time. "Ah, so you admit you had a mission."

"Umm, when you say it that way, I don't know. I think I want to retract that statement."

"Too late now."

"Pretty please?" Chase batted her eyelashes.

"Nothing doing. You got some s'plainin' to do, Ricky."

"I loved *I Love Lucy*!"

"Don't try to change the subject."

"Would I do a thing like that?"

"Apparently," Danica answered dryly.

Chase bent over, picked up a small, flat stone, and skimmed it into the ocean. The expression on her face turned serious. "I didn't know what I wanted, Dani, except that I wanted to be around you…to understand what I was feeling."

"And? Do you understand now?" Danica pulled them up short and faced Chase, noting how natural it was for them still to be holding hands. Unaccountably, that realization made her even more anxious about Chase's answer.

"I think I do." Chase opened her mouth as if to say something else, but no words came out. Her body swayed slightly.

Danica watched as her eyes became unfocused. "Chase?" She tried to keep the alarm out of her voice. Although Chase looked at her, it took her several seconds to respond.

"Yes?"

"Are you okay?" Danica wrapped her arm securely around Chase's waist.

"I'm fine."

"What was that about?" Danica noted that Chase suddenly looked exhausted.

"I-I'm not sure. That's never happened before."

"What's never happened before, exactly?" Danica tightened her grip.

"I don't know how to explain it. It was like I lost track of what we were talking about. My head felt like it was buzzing with a thousand bees."

"Maybe we were out in the sun too long today," Danica offered. Because the moment seemed to have passed, she took her arm from behind Chase's back and entwined their fingers again.

"No. I've had sun stroke before." Chase shook her head. "It wasn't like that." She squeezed Danica's hand. "Anyway, I'm fine now."

Although Chase smiled to lighten the mood, Danica wasn't having any of it. "When's the last time you had a checkup?"

"Relax. I just saw the doctor."

"For a routine physical?" Danica's eyes narrowed. She didn't like the way Chase averted her gaze or the way she appeared to weigh her words.

"Can we sit down for a second?"

"Yes. Of course. Are you sure you're all right? Maybe we should find you a doctor now. I'm sure the resort can make a recommendation."

"No." Chase's eyes widened. "No. Really, it's okay."

"Tell me why you've been seeing a doctor." Although Danica's voice was quiet, the words were a command, not a question. She sat opposite Chase, her back to the ocean. The view no longer mattered to her.

"It's nothing."

"Chase, please." *I'm falling in love with you and I need to know.*

Chase sighed. "I've been having pretty regular headaches and some migraines for a few months." She blew out an explosive breath.

"Okay." Danica drew the word out, sensing that there was more.

"And lately I've been suffering from some wicked and inexplicable mood swings," Chase conceded. "There, now you know as much as I know."

Danica saw the fear in Chase's eyes and her heart lurched. "Thank you for telling me. I'm sure that wasn't easy for you. What does the doctor say?"

"He's still trying to figure it out."

"Okay. When are you scheduled to see him again?"

"Two weeks."

Danica's lips formed a thin, determined line. "That's too far away."

"I'm fi—"

Danica silenced Chase with a glare. "Don't you dare," she warned. "You said this is the first time you've ever gotten disoriented like that?"

"Yes. Look, it could just be a coincidence." Chase's words tripped over each other.

"I don't believe in coincidences like that, and I find it hard to believe that you do, either."

"There's nothing I can do about it right now," Chase said, clearly exasperated.

"You can promise me you'll call your doctor first thing in the morning and get in to see him right away." Danica was equally adamant.

"Danica."

"I mean it, Chase." When Chase didn't immediately answer, Danica changed tactics and pleaded, "For me?"

Chase's posture relaxed. "That's a low blow." She laughed and stroked the backs of Danica's hands with her thumbs. "Very well. Anything for you."

"That's more like it." Danica leaned forward and rewarded Chase with a sweet kiss on the mouth. *Oh, God, please let her be all right.*

❦

"I really am all right," Chase protested grumpily, as Danica ushered her into the suite. In truth, the episode on the beach had wiped her out and left her badly shaken. She resolved to do a bit of Internet research when she got back home. In the meantime, she would relegate her concerns to a remote part of her brain. There would be plenty of time later to think about what was wrong with her. The future was uncertain. She had no idea if, or when, she'd get to see Danica again, and the last thing she wanted was for her health to interfere with their time together.

With effort, Chase shook off her lethargy. "It's our last night." She stood framed in the doorway. "I wanted to take you out to a romantic dinner."

"I find it hard to believe that you're complaining about being invited to a woman's hotel room for room service." Danica stood in the middle of the living room with her hand on her hip.

"I'm finding it hard to believe myself. But context is everything. If, for instance, you were inviting me in here to ravish me... Well, that would be something else entirely." Chase waggled her eyebrows as she moved to Danica and threaded her arms around her.

"Who says I'm not?" Danica's voice was pitched seductively low. She pressed her body against Chase.

Any residual fatigue Chase was feeling disappeared. "Now you're talking." She bent her head and nibbled on Danica's lower lip. *God, even when I can hardly stand you make me crazy.*

"Good," Danica said, playfully pushing Chase back a step. "Since I have your attention, what should we order?"

Chase groaned. "You're maddening, you know that?"

"So I've been told on more than one occasion," Danica agreed amiably. She thrust a menu into Chase's hand.

It took Chase several moments to get her rebellious body back under control. When she'd accomplished that, she made several suggestions for potential entrees and handed the menu back to Danica.

"I'll go place the order. Why don't you sit down until I come back."

"I'm not an invalid," Chase protested.

"Nobody said you were. So just humor me." Danica walked into the bedroom with the menu.

❦

"The food will be he—" Danica stopped talking in mid-sentence. Chase was curled up in a corner of the couch, fast asleep. For several moments, Danica simply stood and watched. In repose, Chase looked so peaceful, so young, so beautiful. Carefully, Danica crept over and swept an errant lock of hair from her face. *I could love you so easily.* She pulled a blanket from the back of the couch and covered Chase with it.

When the food arrived, Danica placed the tray in the suite's refrigerator. She reasoned that it was more important for Chase to get her rest; she could always heat everything up in the microwave later if they got hungry.

Despite the fact that she feared she would wake Chase, Danica cuddled up against her. Chase's arms automatically wrapped around her and pulled her close, and Danica let out a contented sigh.

❦

Chase smelled something spicy sweet. *Danica's perfume.* She cracked one eye open to find Danica asleep, a smile on her face, nestled in the crook of her arm, her head tilted at an awkward angle. *Good Lord, your neck must be killing you.* Chase started to wake her, then stopped. The opportunity to savor the feel of Danica in her embrace a little longer was simply too good to pass up.

Experimentally, Chase turned her head from side to side. No headache. Although she was still a little tired, the overwhelming sense of exhaustion was gone. Relief washed through her. Still, Danica was right; two weeks was a long time to wait. She would call the doctor in the morning and make an appointment right away.

Danica shifted and wrapped her arms more tightly around Chase's midsection, making a sound something akin to a purr. Chase smiled and kissed the top of her head.

"Come on, sleeping beauty. You can't be comfortable like that."

Danica didn't move.

"Danica, sweetheart," Chase whispered in her ear. "Wake up before your neck is permanently locked in that position."

"Mmm. If it is stuck, will you fix it?" Danica mumbled without opening her eyes.

"Absolutely."

"In that case, I think I'll stay like this a while longer." She snuggled closer.

Warmth started at the tips of Chase's toes and traveled throughout her whole body. It wasn't the heat of arousal she'd felt earlier; rather, it was an unmistakable sense of well-being she couldn't ever remember having experienced before. She sent up a small prayer to the Universe that she would always be allowed to feel as she did at that very moment.

"What are you thinking about?" Danica asked from her position beneath Chase's chin.

"I'm thinking about how incredibly right this feels."

"Yes, it does, doesn't it?"

"Why did you ask?"

"Because your heart did a little tumble."

That was me falling irretrievably in love with you. "Hmm, I'm going to have to be careful around you, eh?"

"Why?" The word was muffled slightly, lost between Danica's mouth and Chase's T-shirt.

"Because I won't be able to keep any secrets from you."

"Do you want to? Keep secrets, I mean?" Danica pushed herself up so that she was eye to eye with Chase.

Chase didn't flinch under Danica's penetrating gaze. "No. Not even one. For you, my life is an open book."

"That's good. Honesty is such an important quality for me." Danica laughed at herself. "I know that sounds ridiculous coming from a former politician..."

"But not coming from you," Chase finished for her. "You'll never be what you do, or did, for a living to me, Dani." Chase searched for the right words. "This isn't about *what* you are. The fact that you're a recognizable celebrity isn't what attracted me to you. I hope you believe that." She ran her fingers through Danica's hair.

"I do, Chase. I know it in my heart. I would never have responded to you otherwise. I didn't think I needed anybody in my life before you walked into that auditorium. Now I know that I was wrong."

"Thank you for opening yourself to the possibilities."

"There's something about you...I didn't really have a choice." Danica said the last as though it was a revelation to her.

"No?" Chase continued to stroke Danica's hair.

"I guess that's not right—I mean, we always have choices available to us. What I'm trying to say is that I didn't want to resist whatever that pull was...is," she corrected herself "...for you."

Chase was afraid to breathe, lest she interrupt Danica's words. She stayed stock still.

Danica touched her cheek, then cupped her jaw. "For so long, I've kept everyone at arm's length. You walked through every wall I erected around myself. I'm still trying to figure out how you did that."

"Are you sorry I did?" Chase asked quietly. She felt if she asked the question any louder it would break the spell.

"No," Danica shook her head adamantly. "No, I-I didn't realize how lonely and isolated I'd become. My friend Ted—I call him the Fish man—he's the one who put my feet to the fire and gave me the final shove."

"I think I owe the man a kiss."

Danica laughed. "He'd like that." She brought Chase's hand to her mouth and kissed her palm. "I, on the other hand, won't get off so easily with him. I suspect dinner and possibly dessert and a fine wine will be the minimal required payment."

"I see. He's high maintenance."

"Oh, yes. That he is. But I'll gladly pay the price since it brought you to me."

The shy way Danica looked at her melted Chase's heart.

"I think we should split the cost," Chase offered. "Even so, I'll be forever in his debt." Although she badly wanted to, she swallowed the urge to tell Danica she loved her. *It's too soon. She may not be ready to hear it.* She leaned forward and kissed her tenderly on the mouth instead, hoping the emotion behind the kiss would adequately convey the sentiment.

The kiss was unhurried and thorough, and by the time they pulled apart, they were both breathing heavily. With great self-restraint, Chase disentangled herself and rose from the sofa.

"Where are you going?" Danica's eyes were unfocused, her voice slightly hoarse.

"If I stay here any longer, I'm going to make love to you." Chase took Danica's hands in hers. "When I do that, I want it to be because you're ready and you're sure."

Danica's mouth formed an *o*, although nothing came out.

"So, I'm going to say good night, instead." Chase watched as Danica processed the information, her face registering first surprise, then appreciation.

"I'm not sure you should be alone." Danica's brow furrowed. "How are you feeling?"

"I'm fine now. Really, I am."

"And if anything happens and that changes?"

Danica's concern touched Chase deeply. She bent down and kissed her briefly again. "I promise you that if I'm not, I'll call you right away."

"Okay," Danica agreed reluctantly. She stood and stepped into Chase's arms.

"What time is your plane?" Up until this point, they'd both avoided discussing the inevitable, preferring to live in the magic of the moment.

"Ten," Danica said, turning her head to place her forehead against the side of Chase's neck.

"Mmm. You're out before me." Chase choked the words out. "Okay. I'll bring breakfast at six."

"No." Danica leaned her head back and looked up at Chase. "Let's take a walk on the beach."

"Better yet." Chase kissed Danica one last time. "See you in a few hours. Sleep well."

"You too." Danica followed her to the door and opened it. "Good night, Chase," she said when they were standing on the threshold. "Thank you, again, for a perfect day. And thank you for the beautiful flowers." She sniffed the air appreciatively. "I'm truly spoiled now."

"As you should be, Danica. And I intend to keep seeing that you are." Chase bent once again to Danica's lips before heading for the elevator.

❧

"Where do we go from here?" Danica asked, her voice heavy with uncertainty. She and Chase walked on the beach hand in hand. Storm clouds gathered in the distance, and Danica considered it particularly apropos.

Her thoughts were jumbled and turbulent, and she struggled to make sense of them. There were some things she knew with absolute clarity—her nice, orderly life would never be the same, she was desperately worried about Chase's health, and more than anything else, she wished these couple of days could've lasted forever.

While she felt confident that Chase had enjoyed herself, Danica was uncharacteristically insecure about whether or not it had been more than that for her. She turned expectantly to Chase.

Chase responded, "Do you want the smart-ass answer, where I tell you you've got a ticket for New York and I've got one for Albany?"

"Not quite what I meant," Danica said tightly, her heart sinking.

"I know, honey." Chase kissed her bare shoulder in apology. "Sometimes humor helps me deal with fear."

"What are you afraid of?"

A pair of large pelicans flew directly overhead, apparently on their way to breakfast. Chase watched them intently for a moment.

"I'm scared of a lot of things. I'm afraid that this is all a dream." She gestured with their linked hands and smiled wanly. "I'm afraid that you might not feel the same way I do."

"How's that?" Danica sucked in a deep breath and held it for several beats before letting it out.

Chase stopped walking and pulled Danica to a halt with her. She opened her mouth to speak and closed it again. After another false start, she brought Danica's hand to her mouth and kissed her fingers one at a time.

Danica noticed that Chase's hand was shaking. It didn't make her feel any better.

"I know this may be way too soon. And I understand if you can't go there with me," Chase rushed on. "There's no obligation to respond, I assure you."

Danica's already frazzled nerves went into hyper-drive. The build-up was killing her. "It's okay, Chase. Whatever it is, it's okay. You can tell me."

"I'm falling in love with you," Chase blurted out. As her face turned bright red, she looked at the ground and pushed the sand around with her feet.

Danica let out the breath she'd been holding as a rush of relief flowed through her. Her knees gave way.

"Hey." Chase caught her under the arms and held her up. "Danica? I-I'm sorry. I didn't—"

"Don't," Danica said, caressing Chase's face as tears ran down her own. She had never thought to feel such joy again. She swallowed around the lump in her throat and managed, "I'm falling in love with you too."

"Then..." Chase appeared puzzled.

"I was relieved. That's all. It was just relief." Danica pulled Chase to her, held her tightly, and rocked her. "I was afraid too." As the words flowed, the tension drained from Danica's body. "I wasn't sure what this meant to you. I hoped, but I didn't know for sure."

"It means the world to me, baby. The world."

They clung to each other for several moments before Chase pulled back slightly. When she did, Danica could see that she was crying too. "We're a hell of a pair." She laughed shakily.

"I guess we are."

"How much time do we have?" Danica asked, her voice suddenly husky with desire.

Without a word, Chase led them back toward the resort.

CHAPTER ELEVEN

Danica's heart raced and she was finding it hard to catch her breath. She wanted Chase so much, but it had been more than three years since she'd touched a woman or been touched and more than two decades since she'd been with anyone other than Sandy. A wave of anxiety coursed through her and she squeezed her eyes shut tightly. Now was certainly not the time to be thinking about Sandy. *Oh, God.* Chase swept Danica into her arms and nuzzled her neck, and all thought ceased to exist. *Oh, God!*

"I love you, Danica." Chase framed her face with her hands and stared into her eyes. "I want you so much."

Danica thought she would combust on the spot. Tears pricked her eyes unexpectedly and she trembled.

"Are you okay?" Chase gently stroked Danica's cheek.

The touch was soft and filled with caring, and Danica leaned into it gratefully.

"I'm fine." Danica found her voice with difficulty. "Just a small attack of nerves."

"We don't have to—"

Today is the first day of the rest of your life. Danica silenced Chase with a passionate kiss, imbued with all the emotion that swirled within her.

Chase responded, pulling Danica closer still so that their bodies touched all along their lengths.

Danica's head swam as moisture pooled between her legs. "Make love to me," she whispered breathily.

"Yes." Chase shuddered against her. She ran her hands under Danica's tank top and lifted it over her head.

The brief rush of cool air on Danica's skin was quickly replaced with heat as Chase's hands explored, and her mouth tasted every bit of exposed skin. Danica moaned as Chase removed her bra.

"You taste wonderful," Chase breathed against the side of her breast.

Danica tried to formulate a response. Each touch, each taste, brought her to a place she'd never been before. When Chase took a nipple in her mouth, Danica filled her hands with Chase's hair, urging her on.

"Too many clothes," Danica protested. She lifted her hips in supplication and sighed when Chase removed her shorts and panties. Her fingers found the hem of Chase's T-shirt and tugged.

Chase kissed her way down Danica's body, stroking, sucking, licking, loving her.

Danica wanted to weep for the beauty of the moment. Chase's bare breasts brushed against her stomach and she nearly came. Danica filled her hands with creamy softness and heard a corresponding moan. Her self-control slipped. "Please."

It was both a plea and a prayer, and Chase answered.

Danica soared as she felt the first whisper of tongue against her clit. She was transported when Chase settled between her legs and kissed her center. And when Chase slipped two fingers inside her and matched their motion to the rhythm of her tongue, Danica lost track of everything except the explosion inside her. "Oh, Chase."

"I've got you, baby. I love you, Danica." Chase moved up her body and cradled her as she continued to come around Chase's fingers. "You're so very beautiful." Chase kissed her mouth, and the scent and taste of her own passion sent Danica over the edge a second time.

For several moments they lay like that, entwined in each other, Chase's fingers still inside Danica, as Danica's breathing settled. Chase kissed her again, this time with tender thanks, as she withdrew her fingers.

"Are you okay?"

"Nothing's ever felt like that," Danica was finally able to say. "I love you, Chase." She was overcome by a desperate need to devour, to give life to a passion she hadn't known was inside her.

Without warning, she flipped them over so that she was on top of Chase. Before Chase could react, Danica relieved her of her shorts and panties. She pressed their mounds together, delighting as her clit and Chase's brushed against each other. Chase was wet, her folds slick and soft. Danica supported herself with an arm on either side of Chase as she continued to apply friction, watching in wonder as Chase's face shone with rapture. As Chase came, Danica kissed her, swallowing her cries. The power was intoxicating.

Before Chase had a chance to recover, Danica slipped inside her, bringing her quickly to a second climax.

"Danica, I—"

Danica didn't wait for her to finish the statement. She lowered herself and took Chase into her mouth, licking and sucking, delighting in the smell and taste of her, until Chase cried out once more.

"Please," Chase whimpered. "Come here."

Danica slid up and settled into Chase's embrace. She brushed the hair from Chase's eyes. "Are you happy?" For a brief second, Danica felt shy, which seemed absurd, given the extraordinary passion they'd just shared.

"When I can think and speak again, I'll let you know." Chase smiled and brushed her lips against Danica's hair. "I'm delirious. No one has ever been able to turn me on like that. Multiple orgasms? You're amazing."

"I could say the same about you." Danica kissed Chase's collarbone, relieved that Chase hadn't been repulsed by the frenzied nature of her lovemaking. "I love you."

"I love you too," Chase murmured.

Danica felt Chase's heartbeat slow to a more normal rate, and she smiled. *I did that.* She snuggled closer and closed her eyes. *I want to stay like this forever.*

❧❧

For a long time, Chase lay watching the rise and fall of Danica's chest, marveling at the perfection of her body and the wonder of the lovemaking they'd shared. It had been unlike anything she'd ever experienced—more tender, more passionate, more powerful.

It wasn't about the sex, she realized upon consideration. The magic was a result of the inexplicable connection they seemed to have with each other. Warmth permeated her body from head to toe. She'd found her home and nothing had ever felt so good. No matter that they were about to go in separate directions. They would find a way to be together; she was sure of it.

"Dani?" Chase kissed Danica's shoulder. "Honey? Wake up. We've got to get you showered and out of here."

Danica groaned in protest and snuggled closer. She threw her leg across Chase's body to hold her in position.

Chase's nostrils flared and she sucked in a quick breath. With difficulty, she wrestled her libido under control. "Nice try, sexy girl, but it's not going to work."

"Oh no?" Danica's voice was deep and smooth as honey.

The timbre of it sent a shiver down Chase's spine. "Nope."

"Sounds like a challenge to me." With a small shift of her hips, Danica insinuated her thigh between Chase's legs.

The glint in Danica's eye told Chase she was in trouble.

"I like a good challenge," Danica continued. She bit down on Chase's earlobe.

All of Chase's blood flowed directly to her center. Still, she fought valiantly to keep her wits about her. "Ah-ah. I won't be responsible for you missing your flight." She chewed her lip to keep from crying out as Danica's fingers found her nipples.

"That's very noble of you, love. I'm touched, truly I am, but at the moment, I'm rather tied up." Danica rose up so that she was above Chase. Slowly, she lowered herself until her breast was directly in line with Chase's mouth, hovering just out of reach. "Still want me to hit the showers?"

Chase whimpered but managed to nod.

"Really?" Danica purred as she rocked her thigh against Chase's slick folds.

"God," Chase squeaked. "Yes."

"Yes, what?" Danica asked playfully. "Yes, you want me to shower, or yes keep doing what I'm doing?"

Chase could hardly think, as there was no oxygen flowing to her brain. "Umm."

"I'm sorry, I didn't catch that." Danica lowered herself still farther until the tip of her nipple grazed Chase's lips. Before Chase could capture it in her mouth, Danica pushed herself up again, out of reach.

"This is so unfair." Chase pleaded for mercy with her eyes.

"Life's unfair, doll." Danica slid down the length of Chase's damp body and pressed her tongue against Chase's swollen clit.

"Argh." Chase didn't know whether to laugh or cry when the pressure disappeared.

"I'd like to stay and play, but somebody insists I need a shower." Danica made a move as if to get up.

"You...I...You." Chase was incoherent with need.

"Tell me you don't want me to go."

The look of desire on Danica's face left Chase completely undone. "I. Don't. Want. You. To. Go." She ground the words out between panting breaths, all the while trying in vain to raise her hips to Danica's tantalizing mouth.

"I didn't think so," Danica said smugly. She buried herself in Chase's wetness and feasted.

For Chase, the world narrowed down to one glorious moment, one incredible woman. Willingly, she surrendered.

≈≈≈

The water was as hot as Danica could tolerate. She stood for several moments, letting the shower spray buffet her. The pinpricks of the water warred with the tingling of her nerve endings. Every fiber of her being seemed to be on heightened alert.

"Hi." Chase slipped in behind her and wrapped her arms around Danica's waist. "Is this a private party, or can anyone join?"

Danica turned and kissed the corner of her mouth. "I thought you were the one who said I was in a rush."

"I did. But then I got to thinking about you, all alone in this big shower, and it seemed a shame to waste the water."

"Ah, so you're thinking about the environment."

"Exactly." Chase nibbled the side of Danica's neck, and Danica closed her eyes in sensual pleasure.

"I really do have to hustle," she said apologetically.

"I know." Chase relented. "I just hate the thought of you leaving."

Danica turned fully in Chase's arms. "I know. I do too." She searched Chase's face. "How do you feel?"

"A gorgeous woman spent the last few hours ravishing my body. I feel pretty darn good." Chase smiled.

"I'm glad to hear that, but that's not what I meant."

"I know it's not." Chase kissed Danica briefly on the top of the head. "I'm fine."

"Promise me you'll call the doctor before I leave this hotel room."

"I'll do it later."

"No, Chase." Danica put Chase's hand on her chest. "Do you feel my heart galloping? That's because I'm worried about you. I won't be able to go until I know it's taken care of."

"Okay." Chase gave in. "I promise you. I'll do it while you're getting dressed."

Relief washed through Danica. "Thank you." She cupped Chase's cheek. "I can't stand the thought of anything hurting you."

"I feel the same way about you."

"Good. Then you know why I'm being such a pain in the ass."

"Yes, I do." Chase leaned down and kissed Danica as the spray washed over both of them.

After several beats, Danica gently pushed Chase away. "Let me finish or I'll never get out of here."

Several minutes later, Danica was dry and putting on her clothes. She peeked into the bedroom and saw Chase pick up the phone. She nodded to herself in satisfaction. When she'd finished dressing, she joined Chase, who had also dressed and moved to the living room sofa.

"Everything okay?" Danica asked.

"Mmm-hmm. I have an appointment for tomorrow morning at ten."

"Thank you," Danica said with feeling. "You have to take care of yourself, Chase. I need you." She bent over and kissed Chase on the mouth, worry fueling her sense of urgency.

126

"I'll always be here for you, Danica. Always," Chase said, her voice rough with emotion. She stood up. "Let me go with you to the airport."

"No," Danica said. "I don't want to say goodbye that way. It's better if we do it here." She could see that Chase was about to object. "Please, honey. There's no reason for you to sit around at the airport when your flight isn't for hours yet. I'd rather think of you walking on the beach for both of us."

"When will I see you again?" Chase placed her hands on Danica's hips and pulled her close.

"Soon. I promise. We'll find a way." Danica leaned up for a kiss.

"I know we will," Chase said against Danica's mouth.

"Goodbye, love. Until soon." Danica reluctantly pulled away.

"Until soon," Chase agreed.

Danica was already formulating a plan before the door closed behind her.

≈≈≈

Danica relaxed into the luxurious comfort of the limousine's backseat. As a tear leaked out, she closed her eyes and pondered how it was possible that in a few short days Chase had become the center of her universe. She was less than twenty yards from the resort and already she missed her terribly. The feeling was at once wonderful and terrifying.

She was debating whether or not to send Chase a text message, telling her she missed her and loved her, when the phone buzzed in her hand. "Hello?"

"Hey, sweetie. I'm waiting for my report, and you know patience was never my strong suit."

"Hi, Fish man."

"Well, don't sound so disappointed. A girl could get a complex, ya know."

Danica laughed in spite of herself. "You know I always love to hear from you, Ted."

"Please tell me I'm interrupting something."

Danica looked out the window as the palm trees whizzed past. "Not at the moment. I'm on my way to the airport."

"And? Tell me, tell me, and don't spare the details."

"For the record, you're worse than a girl." Danica smiled into the phone.

"Fine. Just give already. I'm not getting any younger. My heart can't stand the suspense."

"You were so right."

"Yeah?" Ted asked excitedly.

"Oh, yeah."

"You had a good time?"

"Oh, yeah."

"Please, I'm begging you here. You're killing me."

Danica considered tormenting Ted further but decided to take pity on him. "She's incredible. Smart, fun, beautiful, sexy. Do you want me to keep going?"

"Hell yeah, woman." The glee was clear in Ted's voice. "Was she great in bed?"

"Theodore Fisher," Danica said disapprovingly.

"What?"

"You're a shameless pervert, that's what."

"And your point is?"

"You're incorrigible."

"So are you going to tell me?"

"No, I'm not going to tell you."

"Ah-ha!"

"Ah-ha, what?"

"You slept with her." Ted was clearly proud of himself.

"I didn't say that."

"You didn't deny it. And besides, I haven't heard you sound this relaxed and happy in forever, girlfriend."

Danica nodded, even though she knew he couldn't see it. "I am."

"I'm thrilled, Dani. Really, I am." Ted's voice was choked with emotion. "Nobody deserves happiness and love more than you do."

"Thanks, Fish man." Danica gripped the phone more tightly and contemplated whether she should confide in him about Chase's health. Before she could make up her mind, he broke into her ruminations.

"Let me guess, there's a 'but' here, right?"

"How did you know?"

"It could be just because the Fish man knows all." Ted paused. "Or it might have been the hitch in your breathing, like you were nervous about something."

"Hmm. I don't think I've been giving you enough credit. Those are some pretty impressive listening skills you've got there."

The car had stopped moving, and Danica peeked through the limo's privacy glass to see why. When she realized that the drawbridge leading into Sarasota was up, she checked her watch. She still had enough time to make the flight if the delay wasn't too lengthy.

"What is it, Dani?" Ted asked.

"Chase has been having some health issues." She chewed her lip to keep her voice from breaking.

"What kind of issues?"

"She's been getting bad headaches and some migraines."

"Lots of folks have those."

"Yes, but she says she's been experiencing some wild mood swings, and yesterday, when we were walking on the beach, something weird happened. Her eyes went unfocused. I asked her something and she couldn't answer me, and her balance was off for a second. When the episode was over, she looked and felt positively exhausted."

"Is she epileptic?"

"What?" Danica stopped gazing at the scene outside.

"Does Chase have any history of epilepsy?"

"Not that I know of, why?" Danica asked warily.

"What you're describing sounds almost like some kind of seizure."

"But she was conscious the whole time, and she knew what I asked her."

"There are different kinds of seizures, Dani." There was silence on the line before Ted added, "Hey, I could be way off base here. I don't know anything about her and I'm just guessing."

"I'm worried, Ted."

"I can hear that, honey. Has she been seeing a doctor?"

"Yes. She had another appointment scheduled for a couple of weeks from now, but I made her move it up to tomorrow."

"That's great. At least she'll get checked out, and maybe you'll have some answers soon."

"What—" Danica cleared her throat. "What if it's something really bad?" She let out a sob. "Ted, I can't lose someone I love again. I just can't." Her lips trembled, and she leaned her forehead against the cool limousine window.

"Hey, Dani. You're getting way ahead of yourself. We don't know anything yet. Let's wait until we've got a reason to get worked up, okay? It's probably something simple and easily solved." After a beat, Ted said, "Did you say 'love'?"

Danica laughed through her tears. "Yeah, I did."

"Yowzah. That's huge."

"Yeah, it is."

"That's wonderful. I'm so happy for you."

Danica found a Kleenex, dabbed at her eyes, and blew her nose. She sat up straighter, as if gathering her strength. "I'm going to stand beside her every step of the way. No matter what it is."

"I know you will."

"Starting with tomorrow's appointment." The plan she had begun to formulate when she was leaving the resort took shape, and her voice became animated. "I have to be in Vegas, but not until tomorrow night or the morning of the day after." She worked through the details of the schedule out loud. "I could move my flight so that it's later, and I could fly to Albany tomorrow morning from New York, so that I'm there in time for the appointment."

"Do you know who her doctor is?"

"No. I'll have to find another way." Danica thought for a moment. "I could rent a car and pick her up at her house." After a second, she said, "Shit."

"What?"

"I don't have her home address. Damn."

"Don't worry, honey. Is she listed?"

"I don't know. I never asked her."

"I suppose you were a little too busy to discuss such trivial details, eh? Oops. There I go being a pervert again."

"What am I going to do, Fish man?"

"What's her last name?"

"C-r-o-s-l-e-y."

"Give me a sec, please. I'll be right back."

The drawbridge had returned to its normal position, and the car began to move again while Danica waited for Ted.

"Got it."

"What?"

"Chase's home address, silly."

"How'd you do that?"

"Try 4-1-1, honey. It's a great invention."

"I think I love you," Danica said as she wrote down the address Ted recited for her.

"You're not worried that she might not want you there?"

"I'm going to be there. That's all there is to it." Danica's tone brooked no argument.

"Okay then."

"By the way," Danica said, pausing for dramatic effect, "she was fantastic in bed. And now I've really got to run, Fish man. We're almost at the airport." She was glad he couldn't see her blush.

"Good luck, Dani. Let me know how everything turns out."

"I will, Ted. And thank you again. You're a great friend."

"Well, of course I am, dear. Don't say it like it's such a surprise."

Ted's laughter was the last thing Danica heard before she hung up the phone.

CHAPTER TWELVE

Chase smiled and shook her head as she listened to the last message on her home answering machine. Tisha had called six times in less than three days. Chase had to give her points for persistence; her messages had been increasingly amusing and creative.

She picked up her home phone and started to dial Tisha's number from memory. Her fingers paused at the fourth digit when her mind went blank. She slammed the phone down. It was a number she had called at least three times a week for six years. She closed her eyes and squeezed the bridge of her nose as tears of frustration and fear fell.

Her cell phone rang and she glanced down at the readout. Calm and relief trumped the fear. "Hi. How did you know I needed to hear your voice?"

"I'm psychic that way," Danica said warmly. "I just wanted to make sure you got home okay."

"I did, thanks." Chase plopped down in a chair.

"What's the matter?"

"Nothing."

"I can hear it in your voice, Chase," Danica said quietly. "What is it?"

"Stupid stuff. A phone number I've been dialing for years from memory that I just blanked on." Chase wondered at how easy it was to share things with Danica that she wouldn't have told anyone else.

"Aw, honey. It's okay. I forget numbers like that sometimes too."

"I know. It's just…" Chase swallowed hard and blinked more tears away.

"Tomorrow. We'll get some answers tomorrow, love."

"Yeah."

"I wish I were there with you."

"I wish you were too. How is it possible that I miss you so much already?"

Danica laughed. "I asked myself the same thing, and I was only twenty yards outside the resort at the time." There was a pause on the line. "I love you, Chase. Whatever this is, we're in it together."

"I love you too." Chase shook off her mood. "Where are you?"

"The Marriott Marquis."

"It's loud."

"Sorry about that. I just finished the press conference and I'm on my way to the next interview."

"How'd it go?"

"Fine. The usual questions. It was good to see Anka Lynch again."

"She played you in the movie, right?"

"Yep."

"She's not as pretty as you are."

"You've lost your mind."

Chase leaned back into the chair and put her hand behind her head. "Nope. Not my mind. Just my heart."

"How is it that you always say the sweetest things?"

"I only tell the truth." Chase could hear Danica grunt as if she'd been jostled. "Dani? You've got security with you, right? You're not wandering around alone, are you?"

"Don't worry. I'm perfectly safe."

"I note that you didn't answer the question." Chase could hear shrieking in the background, and it set her teeth on edge. "Please, honey. Give me a straight answer."

"That's just some kids wanting Anka's autograph. I promise you, nobody's interested in me."

"Dani?"

"There are some rent-a-cops looking large and important. No worries. Nothing will happen to me. I wouldn't let it."

"You better not. I need you."

"I'm right here, Chase. I promise you. I've got to run. I love you. Can I call you later?"

"You'd better."

"It's a date. Bye."

"Goodbye, Dani. Until soon." Chase hit the end key and tapped the phone against her chin. Her lover was in New York City doing publicity and national interviews for the DVD release of a movie based on her memoir. She couldn't imagine that her life could get any more surreal than it was at that moment.

She picked up the home phone and dialed Tisha's number faultlessly, smiling as her fingers found the correct digits.

"Hello?"

"Hey, Tish. It's Chase."

"Well, it's about damn time. Are you back from your mysterious getaway?"

"I'm home, yes." Chase wandered into the kitchen and opened the refrigerator. She found a bottle of water and twisted off the cap.

"Are you ready to come clean?"

"Come clean?" Chase could clearly hear the exasperation in Tisha's voice, but she ignored it. Winding Tisha up was one of her favorite pastimes. "I don't know what you're talking about."

"Chase Crosley, don't make me come over there and torture the truth out of you."

"You and what army?"

"Come on, Chase. Be fair."

Chase smirked. It wasn't often she could make Tisha whine and beg. "And fair would be?"

"Telling me what the heck you've been up to."

"I don't believe that has anything to do with fairness."

"Stop tormenting me for sport."

"Would I do that?" Chase took a swig out of the water bottle.

"Yes. Yes, you would, and you are, and it's not right."

"Oh, please. Give me a break."

"I'll buy you dinner if you spill it."

"Whoa. Now that's desperation. The day you open your wallet, I know you're serious."

"So?"

"So?"

"Argh. Chase."

"Okay, okay." Chase walked to the picture window in her living room and watched a cardinal eat out of one of her bird feeders. "I did go to Florida to meet someone."

"I knew it! Who? Who is she? It is a she, right?"

Chase laughed out loud. "Do you want me to tell you or do you just want to keep peppering me with questions?"

"Zipping my lip. The floor's all yours. Tell me everything."

Chase could hear Tisha's office door closing. For Tisha, that was the equivalent of hanging out a "do not disturb" sign. Chase never gossiped and so rarely talked about her personal life that she imagined Tisha was salivating on the other end of the line.

"You remember the keynote speaker from the CUNA conference?"

There was silence on the other end of the line.

"Tish?"

"I zipped my lip, remember?"

"Very funny. Guess you don't really want to know, after all."

"No! No, no, no. You can't do that."

"I could." Chase paused for effect. "But I won't."

"Yes, of course. Danica Warren. The hottest thing since God invented chili peppers."

"Nice one. Did it take you long to think of that line?"

"Thanks. No. I've got more where that came from."

Chase groaned and shook her head. "Don't bother. Right. Danica Warren."

When Chase didn't say anything more, Tisha ventured, "Yes? What about her?"

Chase let the question hang in the air for a few seconds, knowing it would make Tisha crazy. After counting to five, she relented. "That's who I went to Florida to see."

Chase held the phone away from her ear as Tisha screamed in her ear. "Has anyone ever told you that you scream like a girl?"

"You hooked up with Danica Warren?"

The phrasing sounded vulgar to her ears, and Chase bristled. "Excuse me?"

"I'm sorry." Tisha's tone was contrite. "I didn't mean it that way. Really, I didn't. You just surprised me, that's all."

Chase took a sip of water and remained silent.

"Please, Chase. I shouldn't have said it that way. I know. I'm really, really sorry. Tell me about it?"

Because she knew Tisha was truly penitent, Chase gave in. "She's really special."

"I'm sure she is. I know I was impressed with her."

"She's incredible." Chase couldn't help but grin.

"How did this all come about?"

"I called and e-mailed her agent."

"And you got through to her? Wow. I would've been afraid that some FBI guy would show up at my door and accuse me of stalking."

"The thought did cross my mind. The agent sounded a bit skeptical, but I guess she must've passed my e-mail along, and the next thing I knew, I was on the phone with Danica, inviting myself to Florida."

"Is that where she lives?"

"No, but it was near where my grandparents used to live. She'd just given a speech there and had a couple days layover."

"Lucky for you."

"No kidding." Chase moved back in front of the window and watched the trees rustle in the breeze. She didn't want to share the intimate details of their time together, so she said, "Anyway, they were the best days of my life."

"That sounds serious."

"It is. I'm in love with her, Tish." Saying it out loud to a third party somehow made it more real, and Chase shivered.

"Wow. And the feeling is mutual?"

"Yes."

"Wow again. I know I keep saying that, but you have to admit, Chase, this is very unlike you. You are just about the least impulsive person I know when it comes to relationships and dating."

"I know. But this is different. She's different. I can't explain it in a way that makes rational sense." Chase shrugged, as if Tisha could see the gesture. "It just is."

"Are you sure, honey? That's awfully fast."

"Positive." Chase didn't even hesitate.

"Okay. That's good enough for me. So what's next?"

"I don't know." Chase sighed heavily. "Right now, she's in New York doing a series of interviews. Today's the release of her movie on DVD. Tomorrow, she's got to go to Vegas for her next appearance."

"Oh, Chase. This has to seem a bit surreal, even to you, doesn't it?"

"Yeah, I was just thinking that a little while ago."

"Is she ever home? And where is home, anyway?"

"She tries to get home at least once a month for a week."

"That's not much time."

"I know."

"You didn't say where home is."

Chase considered. She didn't want to breach Danica's privacy. "Not too far away."

"That's cool, at least."

Chase was grateful that Tisha didn't push her on the subject. "It's something. We still have a lot to figure out obviously. But honestly, the only thing that matters to me right now is being with her."

"When do I get to meet her?"

"I don't even know when I get to see her next, never mind introducing her to my friends."

"Well, I don't care who she is, if she wants to be part of your life, she has to pass inspection."

"You just want to ogle her."

"Duh. Of course." Tisha laughed.

"Can't say I blame you. Oh, before I forget. I moved my doctor's appointment up. It's tomorrow."

"Why?" Tisha's voice rose an octave.

Chase hated to worry her, but she knew from experience that if she didn't tell Tisha, the lecture she'd get later would make her hair curl. "Some weird episode the other day."

"What kind of weird?"

"I don't know. Disorienting, tiring, confusing. Anyway, I just wanted to let you know."

"You need someone to go with you?"

"Thanks, Tish, but no. I'll be all right."

"You're going to call me afterward and let me know, right?"

"I suppose the correct answer to that question is yes?"

"Naturally."

"Then, yes, I'll call you afterward."

"I'm worried about you, Chase."

"Don't be. I'm sure everything will check out fine."

"Does Danica know?"

"Yes. She was there when it happened, and she's the one who pushed me to move up the appointment."

"I do believe I like that woman already."

"That's a relief, I was worried. Not! I'll talk to you tomorrow."

"Bye, Chase. And congratulations. You deserve every happiness."

"Thanks, Tish. I appreciate it. Bye."

◈◈◈

Danica looked out the window of the Amtrak train and watched the Hudson River fly by. She'd heard the note of fear in Chase's voice when she'd called her at bedtime, and it had been like an arrow through her heart. The earliest plane wasn't early enough, so she'd decided to go to Penn Station and grab the earliest train to Albany instead.

She looked at her watch and weighed the possibilities. 7:13 a.m. If she called Toni, she'd be waking her up. Toni before her first cup of coffee was a dangerous proposition. On the other hand, if she waited until later to tell Toni she'd changed her itinerary, Toni would go ballistic. *Be brave.* Danica dialed.

"H'lo." A groggy, muffled voice answered on the fourth ring.

Danica was tempted to hang up without saying anything. She took a deep breath. "Hi, sunshine."

"Danica? What the…what's wrong?"

Danica could hear the covers rustling and imagined Toni sitting up and throwing her legs over the edge of the bed to get her blood flowing. "There's been a slight change in my itinerary, and I wanted to let you know about it."

"How slight?" Toni asked, sounding wary. "Would that be 'slight' as in your plane is an hour late, or 'slight' as in you're canceling the engagement and I have to do damage control?"

Oh, yeah. Toni was definitely waking up. "Something in between. I'm going to need a different flight from a different city, but I don't know yet whether I need it for later today or early tomorrow morning."

Toni was quiet on the other end of the phone for a few seconds. "Where are you? It sounds like you're in a factory."

"Actually, I'm on a train. To Albany."

"Because, why?" After a beat, Toni added, "Never mind. That's none of my business."

Toni was right, it wasn't her business, but if, as Danica hoped, Chase was going to be a fixture in her life for the long term, she would need Toni's help. "There are some things you should know, T."

"Okay." Toni drew out the word. "Are you all right, Dani?"

"Yes. Fantastic, in fact." Danica squared her shoulders and plowed ahead. "Do you remember when I forgot about you on the phone in the hotel room in Florida the other day?"

"A girl doesn't forget being forgotten, dear."

Danica winced. "Yeah. Sorry about that. It was a flower delivery."

"Huh? What was a flower delivery?"

"The reason I forgot about you. It was the bellman with four dozen roses."

"Ah. That'd make me forget you too."

"They were from Chase." Danica's skin tingled at the memory.

"Who?"

"Chase." When Toni didn't respond, Danica continued, "The woman from the *60 Minutes* piece. The one who e-mailed and called you before you'd had your coffee."

"Oh," Toni said, giving the word several syllables. "Something you want to tell me?"

"In fact, there is." Danica smiled into the phone. "I know this will sound patently absurd on the face of it, T, but I'm in love."

There was a squeak on the other end of the line.

"T? Are you still there?"

"I...I'm still here, Dani. What the hell's going on?"

"I just told you—"

"I know what you said, but I don't understand."

"I'm not sure I understand it myself. I just know how I feel. She's everything I ever dreamed I could want."

"Dani, I know it must feel great to be wooed by someone after being alone for so long…"

"It's not that. Toni, this is the real thing."

"How do you know?"

Although she was still watching the scenery pass outside the train window, it was Chase's face Danica saw. "I think of her and my heart skips a beat. I see her and it's like I've known her all my life. I hear her voice and I get goose bumps. She holds me and I feel like I've finally come home." Danica's voice quavered with emotion.

"Sounds like the real thing to me," Toni said into the ensuing silence. "I take it she's in Albany and that's why you're going there instead of Vegas?"

"Yes, and this is where I need your help."

"Let me guess. You can't live without her for a day and you need me to move Vegas to Albany, New York."

Danica laughed. "Not quite that dramatic. And I wasn't aware you were that powerful. Wow. That's impressive."

"I'm an impressive gal."

"It's…I…Chase…" Danica swallowed a sob.

"What is it, Dani? What's the matter?"

Danica struggled for control. "She's sick. At least that's what it looks like."

"What kind of sick?"

"I don't know yet. She's been having migraines, short-term memory loss, mood swings, and the other day she had some kind of episode where she got dizzy and became unfocused."

"What can I do to help?"

Danica was more grateful than words could say for Toni's obvious concern and willingness to assist. "She's got a doctor's appointment this morning. I…I couldn't let her go alone."

"Understood. What time is the appointment?"

"Ten o'clock."

"Let's see."

Danica could hear the clicking keys of a keyboard. It was a comforting sound.

"If the appointment lasts two hours and you need some time with Chase afterward, I could get you on a 4:00 p.m. plane that wouldn't get you to Vegas too late."

"And if I need more time?" Danica closed her eyes. *If she's not okay...*

"We'll get you more time. Hmm...the speech isn't until 2:30 tomorrow afternoon. I could get you a 7:10 flight tomorrow morning that would get you in a little more than two hours before the speech."

"Okay. How long do I have before I have to make a decision?"

"I don't know, maybe three hours before the flight."

"I'll try not to leave it hanging that long."

"You do whatever you need to do. I'll take care of the travel arrangements and anything else to do with your appearance. And if in the end you need to cancel the speech, I'll find a way to make that right too."

"I've never missed an engagement yet. I won't do that, Toni. I promise you."

"I know. But if something comes up..."

"I'll go and come back." Danica could hear more clicking keys.

"I can't get you back until the next day sometime around 6:00 p.m."

"We'll cross that bridge when we get to it. Okay. We're pulling into the station now."

"Keep me posted, Dani. And don't worry about anything on this end. I've got you covered."

"I know you do. Thank you, T, for understanding and for taking such good care of me."

"I'm here for you. And if Chase is that important in your life, I'm here for her too."

"Thanks. That means a lot to me."

"You'd better get going before I get all mushy on you."

Danica laughed. "Yeah, Heaven forbid. Bye, T. I'll call you later."

The train pulled to a stop and Danica grabbed her suitcase. She rolled her shoulders in an effort to loosen tight muscles. *I'm coming, Chase. I promise you won't be alone in this.*

CHAPTER THIRTEEN

Chase rounded the corner at the end of her block. She was jogging, listening to her iPod and rocking out to Coldplay. As the house came into sight, she skidded to a halt and blinked her eyes, certain she was seeing things. *Feet. Move. Right.* She sprinted the last one hundred yards, pulled the ear buds out of her ears, scooped Danica up into her arms, and kissed her hard on the mouth.

"What..." Chase couldn't catch her breath. "What are you doing here?" She took in Danica's appearance—faded low-rise jeans, a cotton v-neck sweater, and a worn leather jacket to ward off the early morning chill. No one had ever looked more beautiful. Without waiting for an answer, Chase kissed her again.

Danica closed her eyes and leaned into the kiss. "Hi," she said, almost shyly, when they broke apart for air.

"Hi," Chase said, a wide grin splitting her face. "I can't believe you're here."

"You've got a doctor's appointment this morning." Danica shifted from one foot to the other. "I couldn't...I didn't want you to be alone."

She looked up at Chase from under long lashes, and Chase's heart skipped a beat. "Nobody's ever..." Unable to finish the sentence, she took Danica in her arms and held her close. "Thank you," she said with feeling. The fear that had kept her up all night, threatening to swamp her, faded into the background.

"You'll never have to do this alone, Chase. Not as long as I'm alive."

It was only the strength of Danica's arms that kept Chase from melting on the spot. They stood like that for several minutes, until Chase remembered where they were.

"I'm an idiot. Come inside." She fished a house key out of her iPod case and unlocked the front door, stepping aside to let Danica precede her into the house with her suitcase.

"You've got a beautiful home," Danica said, pivoting in place to take in the cathedral ceiling, the winding staircase, the soft, pleasing colors on the walls, and the hardwood floors.

"Thanks. It's comfortable." A thousand questions buzzed in Chase's head, like how Danica had found her, but her body was cooling, and she was suddenly chilled. She watched as Danica's intelligent eyes scanned her surroundings, struck again by how right it felt to be with her. "I love you, Dani."

Danica turned to face Chase and grasped both her hands. "I love you too. With all my heart."

The intensity in Danica's eyes might have scared her if she wasn't so desperately in love. "Umm, I have to shower. Please, make yourself at home."

"Mind if I come with you?"

All the blood in Chase's body flowed south. "Nuh-uh," she squeaked.

In the bedroom, Danica stripped slowly out of her clothes. Chase stood transfixed, watching Danica's fabulous hands undo the button and the zipper on the jeans, remove them, then lift the sweater over her head in one smooth motion. Chase licked her lips unconsciously.

"Aren't you going to get undressed?" Danica asked coyly.

"Uh-huh." Chase continued to stand and stare.

"Sometime today?" Danica laughed knowingly and came to stand in front of Chase. She slid two fingers under the waistband of Chase's shorts and lightly traced the skin on Chase's abdomen.

Chase wasn't sure she could breathe, never mind move. Danica strolled around her, her fingers continuing on their path around the waistband.

"Let me help you," she breathed against Chase's neck, as she pulled the shorts and her underwear down. "Step."

Chase obeyed, stepping out of the garments.

"Lift," Danica commanded, and Chase raised her arms so that Danica could remove her tank top. She ducked automatically so that Danica could reach over her head.

"Let's go." Danica gave Chase a gentle shove toward the bathroom, then paused to remove her own bra and panties.

Chase closed her eyes as Danica soaped every inch of her body. Her hands were so strong, so sure. She shuddered.

"You're not cold, are you?" Danica purred.

"N-no."

"Good. Because I might be forced to warm you up if you were."

"In that case, I'm freezing," Chase said, waggling her eyebrows.

"Liar."

"Guilty."

Danica moved behind Chase and rinsed the soap from her body with the handheld showerhead. When she reached Chase's crotch, she cupped her, then slid two fingers inside.

"God. That feels so good."

"Mmm. I'm not sure I've been thorough enough. I might've missed a spot." Danica moved against Chase's back, her mound rubbing against Chase's buttocks.

Chase's nostrils flared and her legs shook as she tried desperately to stay standing. "You're killing me."

"God, I hope not," Danica said, slipping her fingers deeper inside and turning them.

Chase felt the orgasm building and simply let herself go, the waves of pleasure and water washing over her simultaneously. When she was capable, she turned around and pulled Danica into a tight hug. "I love you so much."

"And I love you. Whatever happens today, Chase, that won't change. I need you to know that."

Chase's throat constricted and she tried to swallow. A rush of tears overflowed her eyes and streamed down her cheeks. She wanted to speak, to say thank you, to explain what Danica's steadfastness meant to her, but she couldn't.

"I know, baby," Danica said, as if reading her mind. She held her and rocked her. "I know. It's going to be okay. You're going to be okay."

❧

They were almost to the doctor's office. Neither of them had uttered a syllable since they'd climbed into Chase's car. Chase held tightly to Danica's left hand with her right as she steered with the other.

Danica could see the tension in Chase's jaw and feel the anxiety in her grip. She was glad she'd come. *Time to take her mind off things.* "Aren't you the least bit curious how I came to be on your doorstep this morning?" Danica turned slightly in the seat to face Chase. "I'm actually pretty proud of my ingenuity."

"As a matter of fact, yes, I am curious. I thought about it earlier, but then someone," Chase glanced at Danica meaningfully, "distracted me."

Danica smirked. "You say that like it was a bad thing."

"Oh, no. It was a very, very good thing."

The timbre of Chase's voice sent a shiver through Danica. If they'd had more time, she would've made love to Chase again. The truth was, she couldn't get enough of her. Being with her was so different from being with Sandy. With Sandy, there'd never been that sense of desperate need, as if she'd die if she couldn't have her.

"So, how did you find your way to my doorstep this morning, oh clever one?"

Chase's question yanked Danica back from her ruminations. "First, there was the small matter of finding out where you live. Thank you, by the way, for being listed. You made it pretty easy."

"Glad I could accommodate you, but I'm not sure that makes me feel all that secure."

"I agree. Might I recommend un-listing yourself?"

"I'll get right on that. Continue, please."

"Then I looked for a flight that could get me here early enough. When I couldn't find one that suited my needs, I resorted to Amtrak."

"That was smart."

"Mmm-hmm. From there, it was a simple thing to catch a cab to your house."

"You're pretty pleased with yourself." Chase gave her a small smile and turned her attention back to the traffic.

"Shouldn't I be?"

146

"Absolutely." Chase glanced back at her, a crease appearing in her brow. "What about your schedule, Dani?"

Danica appreciated Chase's obvious concern. "No worries. I have plenty of time to get to Vegas before my speech tomorrow."

"You're running yourself ragged."

"I've got plenty of stamina, or didn't you notice that this morning?"

Chase squeezed her hand. "Believe me, I noticed and I was grateful. I'm just worried about you, that's all."

"You needn't worry. I'm fine."

Chase turned into a parking space and cut the engine. "Well, this is it."

Danica cupped her cheek. "I'm going to be right beside you the whole way, Chase. I promise you. We'll do this together."

"I don't know what I'd do without you. How'd you become so indispensable in such a short period of time?"

"I could ask you the same question." Danica squeezed Chase's shoulder as they walked side by side. "Can I come in with you or would you rather I wait outside?"

"I want you with me." Chase put her arm around Danica's shoulder and gave her a brief one-armed hug. "Please." She opened the door and motioned for Danica to proceed.

❧

"Hi, Chase."

"Hi, Doctor Frankel."

"I see you brought reinforcements this time." The doctor walked the rest of the way into the examination room and closed the door behind him.

"Doctor Frankel, this is my partner, Danica Warren." Chase smiled warmly at Danica. The word "partner" sounded so good in the same sentence as Danica.

"Danica, Doctor Hugo Frankel."

"I see things are looking up for you, Chase. I'm glad. Nice to meet you, Danica." The doctor held out a hand to her.

"You too, Doctor. Chase tells me you're the best."

Doctor Frankel raised an eyebrow. "Now I'm nervous. That's a lot to live up to, especially coming from someone of your stature."

Danica blushed. "Chase means the world to me."

"I guess it's a good thing I don't suffer from performance anxiety, eh?"

"Good thing."

Danica smiled engagingly at the doctor, and Chase was amazed again at her easy ability to charm everyone she met.

"So, Chase." The doctor sat down on a rolling stool and wheeled it over to the counter where he'd put her file. He spent a minute or two reviewing the contents before turning around to address her. "You're early. I see here that you weren't supposed to be in for another two weeks. What brings you here today? Are the headaches getting worse?"

"They're about the same. It was something new...weird."

The doctor was instantly alert and all business. "Describe it."

Chase described for the doctor what had happened on the beach. When she was finished, he took out his penlight.

"Look here, please." He pointed at a spot past his ear and shone the light first in her left eye, repeating the process with her right. "Follow my finger." He moved it in front of her face so that her eyes tracked it.

"What did you have for breakfast yesterday, Chase?"

Chase chewed her lip in concentration. "I don't remember."

"She didn't have breakfast yesterday," Danica mumbled.

Chase looked at Danica's crestfallen expression and whispered in her ear. "I haven't forgotten our lovemaking, sweetheart. I never could." She was rewarded with a tremulous smile.

"Okay," Doctor Frankel said, oblivious to the side conversation. "Who's the last person you talked to on your cell phone?

Chase thought hard. "It must've been Danica. Or it could've been my friend, Tisha."

"Check your call log," the doctor instructed.

Chase accessed her call log. It was Lena. She had called her to tell her she'd be late to work.

"It's all right, Chase," Doctor Frankel said kindly. "We're going to get to the bottom of this."

"I hope..." Chase felt a buzzing in her ears. "I hope..."

"Chase?"

She could hear the voice, but the word didn't make any sense to her. "I hope…"

"Chase, say this sentence." Chase tried, but she couldn't understand. The doctor pointed at a piece of paper, and she stared hard at the print.

"One out of many…" As suddenly as it had come, the buzzing stopped. She looked first at the doctor, then at Danica. "It's over." She wiped her palm on her pants and looked to the doctor. "What was that?"

"What did it feel like to you?" Doctor Frankel asked.

"I don't know. Like I could hear your voice, but I couldn't make out what you were saying."

"Can you read this now?" Doctor Frankel handed her the piece of paper again.

"Ten out of every twenty women suffer from this condition."

"Good." The doctor scribbled some notes in Chase's file.

"What's going on?" Danica asked. Her voice trembled.

The doctor finished writing his note and swiveled around to face both women. "What you just witnessed and what Chase felt on the beach appear to be epileptic seizures. Her repetition of words and lack of comprehension just now seem to indicate she's suffering from some form of aphasia."

"English, please," Danica said, moving away from the seat against the wall where she'd been observing and coming to sit next to Chase. She took Chase's hand and gripped it tightly. "She wasn't epileptic before, and she hasn't described feeling anything like what just happened at any other time. What does this all mean?"

"I have a hunch, but I want to be sure before I say anything more. Chase, I'm sending you downstairs for an MRI right now. I'll call ahead and make the arrangements."

"Now?" Chase was astonished.

"The sooner we have an accurate diagnosis, the sooner we can do something about it."

"I take it you believe me now that this isn't psychologically based."

"You may well be right about that. I never said I didn't believe you. But I'm a scientist, and I need proof."

"And you're satisfied now that you have that?" Danica asked.

149

"I'll be satisfied once we get these tests done and get to the bottom of this." The doctor closed the file folder.

"I'd like to know what you think it could be." Chase ran her thumb over the back of Danica's hand. "You're a noted neurologist, I'm sure you've seen plenty of cases similar to mine. What's your professional opinion?" Chase's voice was tight but steady. She was very conscious of Danica sitting beside her, a shell-shocked expression on her face. It was important to Chase to show strength in front of her.

"I don't want to be premature or irresponsible, Chase. I want the tests done immediately so that we can know with exact precision what we're dealing with and how to proceed. I'm going to go make the arrangements. I'll be right back."

When he'd gone, Chase fell against Danica's shoulder and cried. "I'm sorry. I should be stronger."

"You don't have to be strong with me, Chase." Danica wrapped her arm protectively around Chase's shoulder and wiped her tears away. "It's okay to be afraid. I'm afraid too. But we're tough girls and we'll get through this together. You heard Doctor Frankel. He's not positive what this is. An MRI will give us better information."

"I know you're right," Chase said, sitting up. "It's...I just found you. I've finally got everything I want and now..."

"Don't you dare give up, Chase Crosley." Danica's voice shook. "This is only part of our journey. That's all. Whatever this is, we can beat it. Together." Danica wiped one of her own tears away.

"Together," Chase repeated. "I love the sound of that."

"And I love you, period. Don't you forget that."

"Never."

❧

Danica sat in the waiting room while Chase underwent the MRI. Tension made the muscles in her back tighten painfully and a bout of nausea left her doubled over. She'd watched helplessly as Sandy died; she didn't think she could stand to lose Chase too.

Please, God, don't let this be anything serious. We just found each other. Don't take this away from us.

Danica put her head in her hands and wept. She cried for Sandy who'd died too young, she cried for Chase and what she was going through, and she cried for herself. With Chase, she'd discovered something she'd never expected to find, a depth of love she'd thought only existed in theory or hyperbole.

I can't lose this. I can't lose her.

"Danica?"

A hand on her shoulder made her jump. She straightened up and wiped her eyes on the sleeve of her sweater. "Yes?" Danica looked into the wizened face of the elderly nurse who had checked in Chase earlier.

"I don't want to intrude, but I thought you might like some water." The nurse gave her a kindly smile. "It's going to be a little while."

"Thank you." Danica accepted the plastic cup from the nurse.

"Listen, I know this must be scary for you, as well as Chase. It's a lot to take in. The MRI is great because it gives such clear pictures. And Doctor Frankel is the best there is. Whatever the results are, he'll know what to do."

"That's good to know." Danica took a sip of water and fought the bile back down. "I guess you must see this sort of thing all the time, huh?"

"Goes with the territory, I'm afraid. The best advice I can give you is to stay positive, wait for the results before you start thinking the worst, and trust that God has a plan for you."

Danica was not a religious person, but she found the notion comforting just the same. "Sounds like sage advice. Thanks again." She flexed her shoulders to relieve some of the tension in her back.

"You're welcome." The nurse inclined her head toward a door leading to a good-sized courtyard. "It's a nice day out there...maybe you should enjoy it for a minute or two. If Chase gets done early, I'll come out and get you. But it should be at least another half hour."

"That's a good idea. Thanks." When Danica reached the door, she turned back around. "You'll come get me if Chase finishes before I come back in?"

"Scout's honor," the nurse said, winking.

"Okay then." Danica opened the door and stepped out into the sunshine. The courtyard was ringed by beds of roses. Comfortable-looking wooden benches dotted the perimeter and several sculptures stood sentinel over well-manicured lawns. The smell of freshly cut grass and fragrant flowers helped to calm Danica's raw nerves. She inhaled deeply and strolled along a walkway between the roses and the grass.

Everything around her seemed so normal and so peaceful; it was hard to imagine anything bad could happen to them today. Then she circled around so that she was facing the doors to the MRI suite and reality came crashing back upon her. It was time to make some decisions.

Danica put on her wireless headset, pulled out her phone, and dialed Toni's number.

"What's the news?"

"Hi, T."

"I don't like the way you said that. What's going on?"

"I…" Danica paused to compose herself. "Chase is undergoing some testing right now. I don't know how much longer it will be." She bit her lip. "I can't leave her this way."

"Understood. What can I do?"

"Book me on tomorrow's flight."

"Done."

"I hate to do it. You know I don't like the idea of cutting the timing so close. If the plane is delayed at all…"

"I'll personally go and do a tap dance in your place."

Danica smiled for the first time in what felt like hours. "Wow. It'd almost be worth being late just to see that."

"If you were late, you wouldn't see it."

"You have a point there." Danica's eyes widened as she spied the nurse coming toward her. "Listen, I have to go."

"Okay. I'll e-mail you the new itinerary."

"Thanks, T. You're the best."

"You want me to make it a roundtrip back to Albany?"

"If there's any way to make that work, I'd love it."

"Consider it done. And Dani?"

"Hmm?"

"I hope everything turns out okay."

"Thanks, T. Me too. Me too." Danica headed for the door. She couldn't wait to hold Chase in her arms again and make the world go away.

CHAPTER FOURTEEN

Chase lay with her head pillowed against Danica's shoulder, her arm thrown across Danica's abdomen. Although it was the middle of the night, sleep would not come. They had not talked much on the way home after the MRI. There wasn't much to say. The test itself had been long and tedious. Doctor Frankel had asked for the results to be expedited, which could mean that Chase would hear within a day or two.

Danica stirred and snugged her arm tighter around Chase's waist. Chase turned and kissed her collarbone. Danica had insisted on staying the night rather than flying to Las Vegas, and although Chase had argued that she should go, she was secretly relieved that Danica had steadfastly refused to budge.

They had walked to a nearby park and spent the afternoon sitting on a bench. They watched some ducks splash in the pond, their peaceful swim disrupted by an enthusiastic golden retriever whose antics made Danica and Chase laugh.

Since neither one of them had been hungry for lunch, they ate an early dinner while snuggled together on the sofa, some part of their bodies always in contact. There was nothing sexual about the touches; both of them needed the comfort and reassurance of the other one's solid presence.

Danica moaned against Chase's ear and her hands twitched. Her breathing quickened, and she began to thrash and struggle. Chase rubbed circles on Danica's stomach in a soothing motion and whispered to her.

"You're okay, baby. I'm right here. Shh."

Danica didn't respond. Her agitation increased until suddenly she let out an animal cry and shot bolt upright, dislodging Chase.

"Whoa. Danica. Dani." Chase scrambled to sit up. She dodged a flailing arm and wrapped Danica in a tight embrace. Danica's chest heaved, her heart hammered against Chase's body, and her skin was clammy. When she opened her eyes, they were wild with terror. "Honey, please. You're safe. I've got you. Dani, come back to me."

Danica began to shake violently. She buried her face in Chase's chest and clung to her.

"Shh. It's nothing, love. Just a dream." Chase rocked Danica and kissed the top of her head.

"I...I'm s-sorry." Danica's teeth chattered. "I c-can't help it."

Chase leaned her head back so she could make out Danica's silhouetted face in the dim glow of the night-light shining from the bathroom. "There's nothing to be sorry for, Dani." After a moment more, Chase asked, "Want to talk about it?"

Danica nodded slightly. "It's always the same thing. I see Sandy up on that rock. I shout for her to get down, the avalanche is coming." She shuddered. "She turns and looks directly at me, but she doesn't move. Then there's a tremendous crack—like the loudest clap of thunder you've ever heard—and she's gone. She's just...gone." Danica crawled into Chase's lap. "I felt so helpless. There was no time to say goodbye." A sob escaped Danica's lips.

"I know, baby. I know." Chase ran her fingers through Danica's disheveled hair. *Now you may lose somebody else you love, and there's nothing you can do about it. Oh, Dani. How can I do this to you?* Chase clenched her jaw.

"I'm sorry." Danica sat up a little straighter. "I woke you."

"No. I was already awake. It's all right."

"Why were you up?" Danica asked, moving forward so that her torso touched Chase's stomach and her knees were bent against the headboard.

Chase shrugged. "Just couldn't sleep."

Danica swept a lock of hair from Chase's face and trailed her fingers down Chase's cheek. "Thinking too much?"

"I guess."

"Want to talk about it?"

"There's nothing to say, is there?"

"Oh, Chase." Danica's voice was thick with emotion.

"I can't change what is, Dani."

"No. You can't. But we don't know yet what it is. Maybe it's something simple and easily corrected. Some kind of virus or infection you can take antibiotics for."

"Yeah. Maybe." Chase knew neither one of them believed that, but she allowed Danica the comfort of the illusion because it was easier than talking about the alternatives.

Danica leaned forward and kissed her softly on the mouth. "I love you."

"I love you too, sweetheart. Very much."

"Anything I can do to help you sleep?" Danica pushed subtly forward against Chase's stomach.

"Argh. That's not fair."

"You're just easy," Danica said, running her tongue along Chase's jaw.

This time when they made love, it was gentle, reverent, and full of tenderness. Afterward, they drifted off to sleep in each other's arms.

༄

"I'll be back before you know it." Danica gripped Chase's hand tightly as they stood outside the Albany International Airport. The sun was barely peeking over the horizon, and they both turned toward it, as if by silent agreement. More than any other symbol, the rising and setting of the sun was theirs, reminding them of those first beautiful sunrises and sunsets spent together.

Chase turned into Danica's arms and clung desperately to the feeling of calm serenity that only came when they were together this way. She closed her eyes and breathed in the scent of Danica's shampoo mixed with her perfume, imprinting the smells on her brain. "I love you, Dani. I'll always love you."

"I love you too, sweetheart. Until soon."

Chase reluctantly let Danica go with a last heartfelt kiss.

Danica looked back as she walked away and waved once before the automatic doors closed, obscuring Chase's view.

Chase shoved her hands in her pockets and walked around the car to the driver's side. Without thinking about what she was doing, she got in the car and drove to a parking area from which she could watch Danica's plane take off. As she waited, she followed the progress of the sunrise, wondering how many more such visions she and Danica would get to share. She hugged herself and bit her lip to keep from crying. It seemed to her that she had been doing far too much of that lately.

Her thoughts turned to Danica's nightmare. After three years, Danica was still suffering, still haunted. If Chase's problem turned out to be serious, how would Danica be able to cope? Was it fair to put her through that?

A plane taxied down the runway and Chase checked her watch. The timing made it likely that it was Danica's flight. Even though she knew it was futile, Chase scanned the windows for Danica's face. She continued to follow the plane's path long after it had left the ground, shivering as a feeling of desperate loneliness settled in her heart.

∽∾

When she arrived home, Chase went straight to the bedroom to strip off her clothes. A quick shower and she could be at work early. Since she'd never made it into the office the day before, and she'd taken those few days off for the Florida excursion, she was anxious to get in and return to her workaholic-like routine.

She looked at the bed with its rumpled sheets and imagined Danica lying there, her body still warm and glowing from their lovemaking. Moisture pooled between Chase's legs even as her heart lurched at the knowledge that Danica already was hundreds of miles away.

Chase set about getting ready for work. It wouldn't do to dwell on things she couldn't change.

Within forty-five minutes, she was on her way to the office. Her cell phone rang and she put on her headset. "Hello?"

"You were supposed to call me after your appointment yesterday. Good thing I wasn't holding my breath."

"Good morning to you too, Tish."

"Well, what did the doctor say? I was worried about you."

"I'm sorry. Danica showed up to go to the doctor with me, and I guess I got distracted."

"I shouldn't let you off the hook, but I suppose that's a reasonable excuse."

"Gee, thanks." Chase honked at a car that was drifting dangerously close to her lane.

"So Danica showed up, huh? How cool is that?"

Chase smiled broadly. "Very cool, indeed."

"I thought you told me she was off making appearances or something."

"She was. She rearranged her schedule to be here in time for the appointment yesterday morning, and she stayed until this morning, even though she has to give a speech in Vegas this afternoon."

"She's a keeper, eh?"

"She's very, very special."

"You really love her?"

"More than I can say."

"I'm glad, Chase. Now tell me what the doctor said before I come through the phone and wring your neck."

Chase stopped for a red light. "He sent me for an MRI right from his office."

"Why?" Tisha's voice rose in alarm.

"I had a weird episode in his office and he didn't like what he saw."

"What kind of 'episode'?"

"He called it aphasia."

"What's that?"

The light turned green and Chase proceeded into the intersection. "It's when speech gets mixed up and you can't process the words being said to you or you say the wrong words when you mean something else."

"I never noticed you doing that."

"It never happened before yesterday."

"What about that thing on the beach?"

"Epileptic seizure."

"You're not epileptic."

"I wasn't," Chase corrected around the lump in her throat. She pulled into the office parking lot and struggled to keep her composure.

"Chase, are you going to be okay?"

Because she could hear that Tisha was upset, Chase squashed the urge to cut her off.

"Sure I am," she said as brightly as she could.

"You wouldn't lie to me, would you?"

"Why Tisha, I'm appalled." Chase put the window down so she could get some air and turned the car off.

"I note that you didn't answer the question, but I'll let it pass for now. When do you get the results?"

"I'm not sure. Today or tomorrow, I think."

"What can I do?"

Chase was touched by Tisha's concern. "You're a good friend, you know that?"

"Yep. Now what can I do for you?"

"Nothing, thanks."

"Danica's in Vegas?"

"She's on her way there even as we speak."

"When's she coming back?"

"She's planning on taking the first available flight after her speech, which means tomorrow morning. She should be here around dinnertime tomorrow night."

"Where's she going after that, and when?"

"We didn't get that far, Tish. Why all the questions?"

"I just want to make sure you're not alone, that's all."

"I'm fine. Honest."

"Will you call me as soon as you know anything, please?"

Chase remained silent.

"Promise me?"

"I can't promise you that or I'll get in trouble again."

"Chase, I'm serious."

"So am I, Tish." Chase closed the window, opened the door, picked up her briefcase, and got out of the car. "I have to go. I'm at the office."

"Will you at least give me Danica's phone number?"

"Why?" Chase juggled her keys and the briefcase as she opened the building's front door.

"In case I don't hear from you."

Chase's anger flared at the implication that she couldn't be trusted to speak for herself. She had no intention of giving Tisha Danica's phone number, but she wasn't in the mood for an argument.

"I don't want to do that without asking her first, okay?"

"I'm not exactly a stalker, Chase," Tisha said, clearly offended.

"I know that. I just want to respect her privacy. Let me ask her and I'll get back to you. I've got to go. I'll talk to you later. Bye, Tish."

Chase sat down at her desk and took a deep breath. Maybe she could lose herself in her work. If not, it was going to be a very long day.

≈৩৩≈

Danica was standing on the stage, but her mind was thousands of miles away. She finished her presentation and went backstage.

"That was a great speech, Ms. Warren."

"Thank you." Danica tried to remember the name of the public relations person who'd been dogging her since her arrival less than an hour before her scheduled appearance time. The woman had done everything but go to the bathroom with her and walk out on stage. Where normally such attention wouldn't have bothered her, at the moment all Danica wanted was a second to herself.

"We need to get you to Meeting Room Three for the autograph session, Ms. Warren."

"Yes. I appreciate that. Can you just give me a moment, please?" Danica knew her tone sounded annoyed, but her nerves were frayed to the breaking point. She clenched her teeth and counted to three. "I'm sorry. I just need to check on something. I promise, I'll be right with you."

"Of course." The woman's voice shook and Danica felt a stab of guilt.

"Thank you." Danica fumbled in her bag for her cell phone and checked for messages. Ted had called wanting to know how she was doing, but there was nothing from Chase. She resisted a strong impulse to call her. *You'll only make her more anxious than she already is.*

Danica looked up to see the PR person sulking a short distance away. *Show time, Dani. Let's get this over with.* She approached the woman and pasted on a bright smile. "All set."

"That's great. Everyone is so anxious to get your autograph. Come right this way and I'll…"

Danica tuned the woman out as she made her way to the room where she would spend the next hour or so greeting her public and signing her name. She would call Chase as soon as she was done.

❧❧

"Chase, Doctor Frankel is on the phone," Lena said, sticking her head in Chase's office.

Chase's stomach did a flip and she swallowed hard. "Okay. Thanks." She waited for Lena to go back to her desk before she picked up the phone. With her finger poised over the button next to the blinking light, she inhaled deeply and exhaled slowly. *Whatever it is, it's better to know than not.* Chase pushed the button.

"Chase Crosley."

"Hi, Chase. This is Megan, the nurse in Doctor Frankel's office."

"Hello."

"Doctor Frankel asked me to tell you that the results of your MRI are back. He wants you to come in as soon as possible."

"W-what are they?"

"I'm not at liberty to say. All Doctor Frankel has authorized me to tell you is that the findings were abnormal and he wants to see you tomorrow, if you can make it."

All the blood rushed to Chase's head and she heard a roaring in her ears. The phone slipped from her hand and she fumbled to catch it.

"Chase? What time can you be here? I have a 9:30 a.m. and an 11:15 a.m."

"The earlier one," Chase heard herself say, as if from somewhere far away.

"Okay. We'll see you at 9:30 tomorrow morning."

"Bye," Chase said automatically. She dropped the receiver into the cradle and sat staring straight ahead at nothing.

"Chase, is everything okay?" Lena stood in the doorway.

Chase looked at her assistant without really seeing her.

"Chase?"

"Hmm?"

"I asked if everything is okay."

"Mmm-hmm." Chase blinked and tried to get her brain to kick into gear. "I have an appointment tomorrow morning, so I won't be in until later."

"Okay. Is something wrong?"

"Hmm?" Chase felt a sudden urge to flee, to run, to be outside. "I've got to go." She stood up quickly, gathered her keys and briefcase, and bolted past Lena.

လလ

Danica punched in Chase's cell phone number and listened to the ring in her headset. She was on her way up to her hotel room after the autograph session, which had run half an hour over schedule. The call went to voicemail and Danica frowned. She scrolled through her call log until she found the phone number for Chase's office. It seemed like a million years since Danica had made that first tentative phone call following Chase's initial e-mail.

The phone rang four times before a mechanical voice asked Danica if she wanted to leave a message for Lena, Chase's assistant. Danica hung up and checked her watch. *Damn.* With the time difference, it was after 5:00 p.m. on the East Coast. She thought about calling Chase's home number, but she decided against it for the moment. She would try the cell again later.

She unlocked the door to her room and threw her bag on the bed. Within minutes, she had changed into her running gear and was headed back out the door. If she didn't get rid of some of her nervous energy, she was going to jump out of her skin.

With the help of the concierge, she chose a route that took her away from the famous Vegas Strip and up into the desert foothills. As she turned the corner away from civilization, she dialed Ted's number.

"Hello."

"Hi, Fish man."

"Dani girl. How the heck are you?" He paused. "*Where* the heck are you and why are you heavy breathing in my ear? Not that I don't appreciate a good obscene phone call every once in a while, but…"

"Very funny. I'm in Vegas, and I'm running at the moment."

"Oh, virtual exercise. I love it. It so beats the real thing."

"So glad I could help. I'll run an extra mile for you." Danica sidestepped a large boulder and followed the sign for the trailhead as the concierge had directed. The temperature was in the mid-eighties and Danica's muscles warmed quickly, allowing her to set a fast pace.

"Did you get to Albany in time, honey?"

"Yes. Thank you again for all your help."

"That's what friends are for, sugar. How'd it go? Was she surprised? Glad to see you?"

"She was definitely surprised, and I think pleasantly so."

"You think?"

"Okay, she swept me off my feet, whisked me inside, and we made mad, passionate love."

"Oh. I like that version better."

"I figured you would." The trail turned sharply to the left, and Danica nearly went off into some scrub. "Oof."

"You okay?"

"Yeah. Guess I'm having a little trouble walking and chewing gum. Or, in this case, running and talking to you."

"Be careful out there, please."

"I'm trying."

"So what did the doctor say? Did you go with her?"

"I did." Danica cleared her throat, which had suddenly gone dry. "She had an episode in his office and he sent her for an MRI on the spot."

"The same kind of episode she had on the beach?"

"No. This one had to do with speech recognition." Danica found it difficult to talk about the incident without getting choked up. She clenched her jaw and quickened her pace even more.

"What did the doc think caused it?"

"He wouldn't say. Wants to wait for the test results."

"When do those come back?"

"Today or tomorrow."

"Are you overdoing it, Dani? You're breathing like a freight train."

"I'm scared, Ted." Her voice broke. "Guess I'm trying to outrun my fear."

"Aw, sugar. If only it were that easy. I wish I were there. I'd give you a big hug."

"I wish you were here too. I could use one of those."

"What are you most afraid of?"

"I'm afraid I'll lose her. What if I lose her?" Danica's hands balled into fists and she dug her nails into her palms.

"You're too far down the road, Dani," Ted said quietly. "It's not time to think about that yet. You don't even know what the results of the MRI are. Keep the faith. One step at a time."

"I want to. I really do. It's just..." Danica stopped running, bent over, and rested her hands on her thighs as she caught her breath. She was one block from the hotel.

"It's hard, I know." Ted finished the sentence for her. "Have you heard from her today?"

"No. I tried to call her a couple of times and got her voicemail."

"That doesn't necessarily mean anything. She could be out doing something."

"You're right. I'd just feel a lot better if I could get hold of her."

"She'll turn up before the night is over. Mark my words."

"I hope you're right."

"Where's your next stop?"

Danica started walking toward the hotel to cool down. "I'm going back there as soon as I can. First thing tomorrow." After a beat, she said, "Maybe I shouldn't wait for tomorrow. Maybe I should try to charter a plane tonight."

"Overkill, sugar."

"You think I'm overreacting."

"I think you're in love," Ted said fondly. "Everything will be all right. You'll see. Like I said, keep the faith. And remember, I'm here for you."

"Thanks, Fish man. You have no idea how much that means to me. Bye." Danica disconnected the call. It had been an hour since she'd tried Chase. She tapped the phone against her palm and pursed her lips. After several false starts, she dialed Chase's number again.

❧

Chase sat on the sofa in the dark, nursing a glass of white wine. She felt numb, as though she'd spent all her emotions. Her eyes were swollen from crying and her face was blotchy.

The cell phone buzzed on the end table next to her, and she reached over to pick it up. Danica. Again. Chase's heart jumped guiltily. It was the fourth time Danica had rung her on the cell. She'd tried the home phone three other times. Chase knew she must be frantic.

She fought the urge to answer the call and lose herself in the solace she knew only Danica could provide. *I don't know how to tell you, Dani. You'd be more crazed if you knew the test came back abnormal. I don't know what to say. Nothing can make this right.* Tears she'd thought she no longer had to give poured forth from Chase's eyes, leaving new streaks down her face. With trembling fingers, she pushed the off button on the phone.

CHAPTER FIFTEEN

Danica dialed Chase's cell phone number one more time as she boarded the plane. The phone didn't even ring before sending her to voicemail. She rubbed her overtired eyes. She'd spent most of the night pacing around the hotel room, unable to sleep. By the time she'd worked herself into enough of a frenzy to call to charter a private plane, there was none available until morning.

Heaviness sat in the pit of her stomach, and she checked her watch one more time. Chase's office should be open; she dialed that number.

"Chase Crosley's office."

"Hello, this is Danica Warren."

"Oh, hi. I'm Lena, Chase's admin. You talked to me once before."

"I remember. Listen, I've been trying to get hold of Chase without any success since yesterday afternoon. Is she in?"

"No, I'm sorry. She won't be in this morning..."

Danica sensed that there was more to the end of the sentence, but Lena was professional enough not to say too much. "Lena, this is important. Do you know where she is?" Danica counted to five as she waited for Lena to decide whether or not to confide in her. If she could've reached through the phone to shake the information out of her, Danica would have done so.

The pilot came on the loudspeaker and welcomed the passengers. Danica cursed silently, knowing that the flight attendant would give the instruction momentarily to turn off all electronic devices, including cell phones.

"Lena, please. My plane is about to take off and I have to turn this phone off. I'm really worried about Chase."

"Okay. She's got a doctor's appointment this morning."

"W-what?" Danica felt her stomach drop out.

"She got a call yesterday afternoon. When I asked her if she was all right, she told me she had an appointment this morning and that she wouldn't be in until later. Then she took off like a bat out of hell. I haven't heard from her since."

Danica struggled to think clearly. "But she said she would be coming back to the office?"

"Sort of. But not exactly. She was a little vague. Like I said, she was acting kind of strange. Like she was distracted."

"Did she tell you what time the appointment was?"

"Miss, you'll have to turn off that cell phone now." A flight attendant with a shrewish expression stood over Danica.

"One second, please."

"Ma'am."

"I heard you," Danica snapped. The flight attendant held her ground. "Lena, I'm desperate here."

"No, she didn't say."

"If she calls or comes back to the office, please, please tell her to call me. Here's my number." Danica recited her phone number for Lena. "Tell her..." Danica's voice cracked and she was unable to finish the sentence out loud. *Tell her I love her.* She powered off the phone and sat with it clenched tightly in a shaking hand.

The results of the MRI were in and Chase had been summoned back for an immediate follow-up appointment. That couldn't be good. Not only that, but she had rushed out of her office and wasn't taking Danica's phone calls. *Oh, God, Chase. What's going on? What did they tell you?* Danica banged her head back into the headrest in despair and frustration. It would be almost eight hours before she would touch down in Albany. Eight hours was a lifetime.

❧

"Hello, Chase. How are you feeling?" The nurse bustled around efficiently. She grasped Chase's wrist to take her pulse, then secured the blood pressure cuff and took her blood pressure.

"Fine, thank you."

"Where's your friend today?"

Chase's heart stuttered. "Working."

"That's too bad. She was awfully nice."

"Yes, she is." *And I miss her terribly.*

"Well, Doctor Frankel will be in shortly. Just relax."

"Easy for you to say," Chase mumbled as the nurse exited and closed the door behind her. Chase jumped off the examination table and paced around the small room. Danica would be in the air by now. If she'd tried the office, she might already know about the doctor's appointment. *I'm sorry, Dani. I didn't know what else to do.*

The door opened, startling Chase. Doctor Frankel stepped into the room without looking up; he was reading her chart, and he carried a large manila envelope under one arm.

Chase hopped back up on the exam table and waited.

"Hi, Chase. I'm always glad to see you. I just wish it weren't this soon." Finally, the doctor closed the file and looked over at her, a surprised expression on his face. "You came alone."

Chase's heart tripped a second time. "Yes. Danica's out of town on business."

"I'm sorry to hear that. Will she be back soon?"

It was all Chase could do not to scream out loud. What did it matter to them that Danica hadn't accompanied her this time? Instead, she ground her teeth together and prayed for patience. "Yes."

"That's good. At times like these, it's always good to have the support of loved ones."

All the blood rushed to Chase's head. "Times like...what? Doctor Frankel, please tell me what's wrong with me."

Instead of answering her immediately, Doctor Frankel walked to the X-ray box on the wall and flipped the switch. He removed a series of films from the large manila envelope and put them on the viewer. Then he turned to face Chase.

"To put it in English, you have a cluster of abnormal blood vessels. Technically, it's called a cavernous angioma, and it's located in your left posterior temporal lobe. The low-grade headaches, the migraines, the mood swings, the seizures, and aphasia—those symptoms are all consistent with what we call a CCM, a Cerebral Cavernous Malformation."

The air rushed out of Chase's lungs. A tumor. A brain tumor. A death sentence. Her elbow gave way where it had been supporting her weight against the examination table. She might have fallen over if Doctor Frankel hadn't leaped forward and caught her.

"I'm going to die."

"Not if I can help it, Chase." He ducked until they were eye to eye. "There are things that we can do. A CCM is not necessarily a death sentence."

Chase barely heard the words over the noise in her head. She had a growth on her brain. "But I could die?" A sob escaped her lips. She had just really started living.

"Look here," Doctor Frankel said, walking back to the films. "This raspberry-shaped area right here." He pointed to a spot approximately an inch to an inch and a half in diameter. "That's what we're talking about."

Chase squinted to see the spot to which Doctor Frankel was referring. "What did you call it again?" Suddenly, she was freezing. She hugged herself for warmth and focused on the doctor's words; she would need as much information as she could get.

"It's a cavernous angioma, also known as a Cerebral Cavernous Malformation, or CCM."

Chase nodded and took a deep breath. Her teeth chattered and she clenched her jaw shut; then she straightened her back and looked the doctor in the eye. "Tell me about it."

"All right." Doctor Frankel pulled his stool up next to where Chase was sitting. "Unlike regular blood vessels, the bubble-like caverns that make up a CCM are leaky. Sometimes these vessels leak within the walls of the angioma. That can cause the CCM to grow and press on other surrounding areas of the brain. Sometimes the walls of the angioma are sufficiently weak so that a hemorrhage occurs, meaning there's a bleed into other nearby healthy brain tissue."

Chase heard the word "hemorrhage" and felt the blood drain from her face. *Stay focused.* "Am I in danger of that happening?"

Doctor Frankel put a hand on her knee. "It already has. I believe that's what caused your seizure and the aphasia."

Chase's fingers and face began to tingle as she hyperventilated. Her brain was bleeding.

The doctor stood, walked back to the viewer, and pointed at a darkened area adjacent to the raspberry-shaped growth. "This picture shows a bleed."

"I see," Chase said in a monotone.

Doctor Frankel turned toward her again, his face full of compassion. "Chase, this doesn't mean you're in any imminent danger. Sometimes these things only bleed once and never again."

She shivered uncontrollably and interlaced her fingers to keep them from shaking. "How often is that true?"

"It's hard to say."

"So it could happen again."

"Yes. Which is why I want to monitor you very closely."

"That's it?" Chase's voice rose in pitch. "I could die and you want to 'monitor' me?"

"Let me finish." Doctor Frankel's tone remained level. "There are a number of ways to treat this, and I want to be sure that we proceed as conservatively as we reasonably can. I'm going to prescribe for you an anticonvulsant that you can start taking right away. That should help with the seizure activity. Also, it's critical for you to avoid things like aspirin and Advil. You can take Tylenol, though."

"Will the drugs do anything except stop the symptoms? Will they reduce the tumor?"

"First, it's not a tumor. It's a mass, but not every mass is a tumor. And second, no, the drugs are only meant to allay the symptoms. But it's very important to keep the seizures from becoming intractable, or untreatable, by medication. Since you've only had one or two seizures that we know of, we stand a good chance of controlling them with medication."

"Then what?"

"For now, I want to watch and see if the drugs work. I'll want to do a follow-up MRI in a few weeks to see if there have been any changes. The fact that you were asymptomatic, then suddenly began showing signs of the CCM could be significant. I want to follow that carefully."

"In other words, you think it's spreading rapidly."

"I don't know that, Chase. I need something to compare these images to." He came back to stand in front of her. "I'm going to do everything I can for you. As I said, we have options available to us. This is by no means a death sentence—not at all."

"What are the percentages?"

"I don't know off the top of my head, but I can tell you that the mortality rate is low." Doctor Frankel put his hand on Chase's shoulder. "I need you to do something for me. I need you to try to keep your stress level as low as possible."

Chase laughed bitterly.

"Look, I know that's a ridiculous thing to say, but the lower your stress level, the less likelihood of your blood pressure going up. That means a reduced chance of another hemorrhage."

"I'll do my best." Chase bit her lip. "You said we had other options. What are they?"

"Surgery."

"Brain surgery?" Chase's head swam.

"We can go in and resect the lesion if it's accessible. But I would never enter into brain surgery lightly, Chase. One step at a time, okay?"

"Okay."

"I know you're going to have more questions. I'm here to answer them. And if anything changes—if your headaches get worse, if you have another migraine, if you have another seizure—I want you to call and tell me that."

"Okay. Thank you, Doctor Frankel." Chase got down from the table and walked out the door on shaky legs.

"Chase?" The doctor followed her out. "Will someone be able to stay with you tonight? Will Danica be back? This is a lot to digest. I'd feel better if I knew you weren't going to be alone."

Chase's heart jumped into her throat at the mention of Danica's name. *Oh, babe.* She couldn't imagine how she could break the news to her. "I'll be fine, thanks. I appreciate your concern," she answered the doctor mechanically.

She walked through the reception area and out the doors into the parking lot. When she reached her car, Chase simply got in and sat behind the steering wheel without turning on the ignition. Her whole body shook violently. She had a brain tumor. Her life would never be the same.

The wheels of Danica's plane had barely skimmed the runway in Baltimore before she turned her phone back on and dialed Chase's cell. The call went directly to voicemail and Danica growled in frustration. Immediately, she punched in the office number she'd rung earlier.

"Chase Crosley's office."

"Hello, Lena?"

"Yes. Who's calling, please?"

"This is Danica Warren again. Is Chase there?"

After a slight hesitation, Lena said, "No. She never came in today."

Danica's pulse pounded in her ears. "Did she call?"

"No, she didn't, which is really odd because Chase is always fanatical about checking in when she's out of the office."

Cold dread spread its tentacles throughout Danica's veins. "Okay. Well, if you hear from her..."

"You'll be the first to know. Oh, before you go, Tisha asked me to give you her cell phone number. She wants you to call her."

"Tisha?"

"She said to tell you she met you in D.C. She's Chase's best friend."

"Give me the number, please," Danica said, as she fumbled for a piece of paper and a pen in her bag. She dialed as she hustled toward the gate for the flight to Albany.

"Hello."

"Is this Tisha?"

"Speaking."

"Hi, Tisha. This is Danica Warren."

"Oh, Danica. Am I glad to hear from you. Thanks for calling."

"Where's Chase?" Danica was too anxious to adhere to social niceties.

"You don't know? Shit."

"Excuse me?" Danica sidestepped a child sprawled in the middle of the floor in the gate area.

"I hoped you'd be able to tell me what's going on," Tisha said.

"I would if I had any idea myself. I've been trying to reach Chase since yesterday afternoon. I've tried her at home, on her cell, and at the office. No luck."

"I've done the same. Where are you?" Tisha asked.

"Sorry. I know it's loud. I'm at BWI waiting for my flight to Albany."

"Ah. Chase told me you were coming back today. Listen, why don't I pick you up at the airport, and we can work on figuring this thing out?"

"That would be great," Danica said. *Except that I wish you were Chase.*

"What time do you arrive?"

Danica gave Tisha the details and hung up. She called Chase's home number once more to no avail. Danica banged her fist into her other palm. *Where are you, Chase? Why don't you answer me?* She sat down heavily to await her flight. Whatever had happened, she was convinced it wasn't good.

Chase rolled her suitcase into the hotel room, closed the door behind her, and leaned heavily against it. *Now what?* She was completely numb. Her decision to take off was based on a desire to get away, to disappear. She needed time to think, time to ponder the meaning of her life. It was no surprise that she had picked this particular place for her getaway.

She pushed off from the door and walked to the window. It overlooked the beach, which just then was aglow with the last light of day. If she strained hard enough, she could almost imagine Danica walking along the shore, her hair windblown and her bare feet leaving deep impressions in the wet sand.

Chase bit back a sob. She would've given anything to turn back the clock to those unforgettable moments when life was no more complicated than falling in love.

On an impulse, she threw on a pair of shorts and a T-shirt and hustled down to the beach. Suddenly, she needed to feel the sand, to see the water, to experience the sunset. She ran along the shore until her lungs burned, as if by running she could catch up with the setting sun. When she could run no more, she threw herself down and picked up a fistful of sand. She watched as the tiny grains slipped through her fingers, much as she imagined her own time slipping away.

Hours passed, darkness fell, and still Chase sat on the cooling sand, unable to bring herself to get up and go inside. Her mind was blank save for the knowledge that there was something in her brain that didn't belong, something that could kill her. Eventually, she went in search of a lounge chair. She wanted to sleep with the soothing sounds of the ocean in her ears. Tomorrow. She would think about everything tomorrow.

⋘⋙

Danica scanned the crowd outside the security area. Although she'd signed a book for Tisha in D.C., she had no recollection of what the woman looked like.

"Danica, over here!"

Danica followed the sound and the raised hand that bobbed up and down in the crowd until someone materialized at her elbow.

"Hi, I'm Tisha."

"Danica." As they walked toward the parking garage, Danica asked, "Any word?"

"Nothing. I've called everyone I can think of. I went to the house. Nobody knows anything." Tisha threw her hands up.

"I'm sure the doctor's office wouldn't tell us anything, and besides, they're closed by now." Danica scrubbed her face in frustration.

They reached Tisha's car. "Where to? You must be starving."

"Can't say that I've got much of an appetite at this point," Danica said.

"Still, you probably should eat something. When's the last time you ate?"

"I don't remember. It doesn't matter." Danica fought a feeling of futility.

"Hey," Tisha said, reaching over from the driver's seat to pat Danica on the arm. "We'll find her. Or she'll turn up. Everything will be all right."

"You ought to put a little more conviction in your voice when you give that pep talk next time," Danica said kindly.

"Maybe, but I still mean it." Tisha took her eyes off the road for a second to glance at Danica. "Chase loves you so much. She'll know you're worried. She'll be back."

"I hope so." Danica looked at the impending darkness and thought about Chase out there somewhere, alone. Her heart contracted painfully. *Please, baby, come home to me.*

"How about if I take you directly to Chase's house, then go get some takeout for both of us? Would that make you feel better?"

"Yes, thanks." Danica picked at a cuticle. "Is it that obvious?"

"That you're jumping out of your skin with worry?" Tisha turned on her blinker and made a left turn.

"Yeah."

"It sure is, and I have to tell you, that gets you points in my book. Chase is my best friend, Danica. I've known her for six years. I'd run through fire for her, and I know she'd do the same for me. If I may speak frankly, the girlfriend thing hasn't worked out all that well for her in the past. She's been hurt really badly. I'd hate to see that happen again."

"Since you've been so candid, I'll be equally blunt. I love Chase with all my heart. The speed with which we fell in love boggles my mind. I've never felt about anyone what I feel for her, not with that level of intensity and desperation. I don't know how it happened or why. I only know it's real and it's true, and the thought of losing her..." Danica's voice caught and she buried her face in her hands.

"Chase is a fighter, Danica. She's tough and she's courageous. I know you are too. You'll get through this. I know you both will." Tisha pulled into Chase's driveway. "Here we are."

Danica dried her eyes with a Kleenex Tisha offered her. "Thanks."

Tisha used the key Chase had given her and let them in. The house was just as it was when Danica had left the day before. She peeked in the bedroom; a closet door was ajar, but otherwise everything was in place.

She went into the bathroom and noticed that Chase's toothbrush was gone. A foray into the garage revealed that the car was still there. She looked for a set of keys but found none.

Tisha met Danica on the way into the kitchen. "Find anything?"

"Car but no keys and no toothbrush. You?" Danica asked.

"No note and lots of messages on the answering machine. Should we listen?"

Danica frowned. "I don't want to violate Chase's privacy."

"What if there's something on there from the doctor's office?"

"Hmm..." Danica considered. "The doctor's office would never leave something of a personal nature on the machine."

"True. Damn. Where the hell are you, Chase? Get back here before I wring your neck."

"Hey, that's my girlfriend you're talking about." Danica paused. "If there's any neck wringing to be done, I'll be the one to do it." She sank heavily onto a stool at the breakfast bar. Without looking, she took out her phone and hit redial. "You've got to be kidding me!" She followed the sound to the bedroom, where she found Chase's cell phone ringing on the nightstand. "Oh, baby. What were you thinking?"

Danica picked up the phone and held it tenuously. It was the only clue she had and she was loath to use it. Looking through the list of calls Chase had made and received violated Danica's strongly held beliefs about privacy. But if Chase was in trouble, it might be the only way she could track her. Surely privacy took a backseat to safety and well-being.

"You have to do it," Tisha said from the doorway.

"What?"

Tisha pointed to the phone Danica held in her hand. "You have to check her call log."

Danica still hesitated.

Tisha took a step toward her. "When we find her, I'll be the first one to testify that you didn't want to do it. Heck, I'll go a step farther and tell her I made you do it."

"That won't be necessary." Danica sighed and powered on the phone, scrolling through the list of Chase's recent incoming, outgoing, and missed calls. There were the many calls she'd made, several from Tisha. "Who's Jane?"

Tisha crossed the room and looked over Danica's shoulder. "Ah, Jane is another friend of Chase's and an employee. She's sort of Chase's second in command. I've already talked to her. She doesn't know anything, either. She hasn't spoken to Chase in two days."

"Damn." Danica continued to scroll through the entries until she'd gone back to the last time she'd actually talked to Chase. She blew out a frustrated breath. "There's nothing here."

"Should we listen to the messages on her home phone?" Tisha asked.

"I don't want to do that if we don't have to. Let's check her caller ID. If there are any calls in the last day or two that seem important, we'll listen to the messages."

"Fair enough."

They went to Chase's kitchen and scrolled through the calls on the readout there. They identified calls from Jane, Lena, Danica, and Tisha.

"Damn it all to hell, Chase," Tisha exclaimed, slapping her palm on the kitchen counter.

"It was worth a try," Danica said dispiritedly. She spun in a circle with no clear idea what she was looking for.

"It's getting late. I don't think there's much more we can do tonight."

"This is crazy." Danica shook her head. "Does Chase own a second home anywhere?"

"No."

"Does she have a favorite hangout? Someplace she would go if she were upset?" Danica paced around the kitchen's breakfast bar.

"If she does, she's never told me about it."

"How about relatives? Would she go see family?"

"Unlikely."

The way Tisha said it, so definitively, aroused Danica's curiosity, and she made a note to ask Chase about it. She felt foolish that she was ignorant of so many things about Chase. For the moment, though, she had more important things to think about. "Does she have a favorite vacation spot?"

"Chase doesn't take many vacations. Going to Florida to meet you was the first time she's gone away in months."

"In other words, we've got nothing," Danica said, feeling the fight seep out of her.

"Tomorrow's another day, Danica. I'll call Jane first thing, and the three of us will put our heads together."

"Okay," Danica said, her voice cracking. "Until tomorrow then. Thanks for all your help."

Tisha paused at the front door. "Maybe I should stay with you."

"No. I'll be okay. Maybe Chase will try to call you at home. You should go."

"Here's the key to the house. If you need anything, you have my cell number, right?"

"Yes, thanks. And thanks for everything."

"Hey, I forgot to feed you."

"I'm not hungry," Danica said.

"Well, I'll come by first thing in the morning, okay?"

"Fine. Thanks, Tisha. You're a good friend. Chase is lucky to have you."

"And to have you. Hang in there."

Danica nodded. She was out of words.

CHAPTER SIXTEEN

When Chase awoke, it was the middle of the night. Her back was spasming from the position she'd slept in. The air had cooled and the ocean breeze had turned into a strong wind. Tentatively, she stretched out her legs and flexed her back. Pain shot through her lower torso, but she persevered until it subsided and she was able to stand.

That was a stupid idea. You're too old for anything except a mattress, Crosley. Slowly, she made her way back to the resort, where she crawled into bed.

When next she awoke, the sun was high in the sky and daylight streamed through the window. She groaned and rolled over. Her stomach growled, reminding her that she hadn't eaten since before the doctor's appointment the previous morning.

The clock read 10:42 a.m. She tried to remember if she'd called Lena to check in after she'd left the doctor's office. *Shit.* Lena and Jane would be wondering what the hell was going on. Tisha would be calling out the National Guard, and Danica...Chase grabbed a nearby pillow and pulled it over her head. She didn't want to imagine what Danica might be feeling or thinking. What would she be feeling in Danica's place? She'd be out of her mind with worry and fear. *Good going, Chase.*

She sat up, reached for the pillow that had fallen away, and hugged it to her chest with one arm. Reluctantly, she picked up the phone and dialed her office, praying that the call would go to Lena's voicemail.

"Chase Crosley's office."

Chase closed her eyes tightly. *Figures.* She fought a fleeting urge to hang up.

"Hello? Chase Crosley's office."

"Hi, Lena."

"Chase? Is that you? Where are you? My God, all hell is breaking loose here. Everybody's worried sick about you."

A stab of guilt penetrated Chase's defenses. "I'm sorry."

"Are you okay? Where are you?"

"I want you to tell Jane that she's in charge until further notice." Chase deliberately ignored Lena's questions. "Anything that comes up should go to her."

"For how long? Do you want me to transfer you to her?"

"No." Chase's pulse quickened. Lena was far easier to evade than Jane. "You give her the message. I've got to go."

"Chase. Wait! Danica Warren's been calling everywhere looking for you. She's really worried. Tisha too. And Jane. And me. At least tell me where you are."

"I've got to go." Chase choked out the words around the lump in her throat. "Bye." She could still hear Lena asking her questions as she returned the receiver to the cradle. A tear tracked down her cheek. *There's nothing anyone can do. I've got a ticking time bomb in my head.*

She thought about Danica, frantically trying to find her, and her stomach turned over. *I'm so sorry, Dani. I wish I could change reality, but I can't. I can hurt you now or devastate you later. It's better this way.*

Bile rose up in her throat and Chase barely made it to the bathroom in time to throw up. When she was done, she ran a cool washcloth over her face and brushed her teeth. The prescription she had filled before she left Albany was sitting on the bathroom sink. She stared at the bottle for a long time before shaking out two pills and washing them down with water.

The bed beckoned her, and once again she fell into it and closed her eyes. It was easier to sleep than to feel.

❧

Danica grabbed a fistful of her own hair and tugged. "No, thank you very much. I understand. Right. Privacy regulations are for the patient's benefit. I agree. You have a good day too." She slammed the phone down and swiveled around in Chase's home office chair. "Argh," she screamed in frustration.

"What, what is it?" Tisha burst through the door, out of breath.

"Nothing. Not a damn thing."

"Another dead end?"

"Yeah. That was the imaging place where Chase had the MRI. That makes the doctor's office, the imaging place, and her pharmacy. Nobody will give me the time of day."

"You called her pharmacy?" Tisha was clearly surprised.

"What can I say? I'm desperate." Danica's fingers were trembling, so she clasped her hands together to keep Tisha from seeing. "She had a prescription bottle for cough syrup in the medicine cabinet. I just thought if the doctor had prescribed her medication...I don't know what I thought." She bit her lip.

Tisha moved forward and put a hand on her shoulder. "There's bound to be something soon."

The sound of a car in the driveway had both women running for the front door.

"Well, this is quite a welcoming committee." Jane emerged from her car and walked up the path to the front door. "Hi," she said, holding out her hand to Danica. "I'm Jane."

"Danica."

"I know. I saw you speak in D.C. I'm sorry we have to meet like this. I would've preferred that it was over drinks and dinner with you and Chase."

Danica's heart turned over at the mention of Chase's name, just as it had each time she'd said it or heard it said in the past twenty-four hours or more.

"What's the word?" Tisha asked into the awkward silence.

"She called."

"What?"

"She did?"

"Easy," Jane said. "It's nothing more than a crumb."

"Come inside and tell us everything." Tisha latched onto Jane's sleeve.

They sat at the breakfast bar, which had become command central.

"She called Lena at around 10:45 this morning."

"Where is she?" Danica asked. Her whole body vibrated with tension.

Jane threw up her hands and let them drop to her side. "Lena asked her several times. She wouldn't say. In fact, she wouldn't answer any questions at all and wouldn't let Lena transfer her to me."

"Damn it," Tisha swore.

"All she said was that she wanted Lena to tell me that I was in charge until further notice and that any issue that came up was mine to solve."

"That's it?"

"That's it."

"Where did she call from?" Danica's voice was tight.

"Nothing there, either. According to Lena, the readout simply said 'blocked call.'"

"God damn it!" Danica jumped up and began to pace. She whirled around to face Jane. "Was it quiet where she was or noisy?"

"Quiet."

"How'd she sound?" Danica leaned her forehead against a window that overlooked the backyard. There were birds feasting at the bird feeder, but she barely noticed.

"Lena said she was subdued. And when Lena told her that we all had been worried sick about her, she got a little choked up and said she had to go."

"Did Lena tell her I was looking for her?"

"Yes. She told her you'd called many times and that you were very worried."

Danica closed her eyes against a stab of pain that pierced the center of her heart. Chase knew that she was trying to find her, and she didn't care. No, Danica reminded herself. It wasn't that she didn't care. Lena had said she'd gotten choked up. It was that it didn't matter enough to her to make her reach out. Danica wasn't sure which was worse.

She turned around in time to see a look of sympathy pass between Tisha and Jane. They knew the truth too. The burning ache in the center of her chest blossomed out to envelop her entire body. "I'm going to go for a run. I'll be back." She fled out the front door, shedding her sweatshirt on the doorstep. If it was possible to outrun a shattered heart, she would do it.

≈୨୧∽

Chase breathed hard as she paddled the rented kayak against the current. The pounding of her heart from exertion reminded her that she was alive. The challenge of navigating the ocean swells required all her concentration, a circumstance for which she was grateful. She was still too shell-shocked to process the myriad emotions swirling inside her. Two things she knew for certain— she could die and she missed Danica more than she thought humanly possible.

As she crested a particularly big swell, a pair of porpoises appeared fifteen yards off the bow of the kayak. They flipped in the air, landing back in the water with a huge splash. The sight made Chase smile until, unbidden, she flashed on an image of Danica's face, lit up with joy at the sight of the porpoises off the stern of the sailboat.

The paddle slipped through Chase's fingers, and she barely caught it before it was lost to the sea. Her body shook uncontrollably, nearly capsizing her. She pulled the paddle into the boat and wrapped her arms around herself, tucked her hands under her armpits, and rocked herself, unmindful of the kayak's increased instability. *Dani, I love you so much. How am I going to...I can't do this without you. I thought we had a whole lifetime together. Now...*

A great wail burst forth from Chase as she bent in two, her forehead touching her knees. *No. No. No. I don't know what to do. Help me. I don't know what to do.*

Chase had no idea how much time had passed before she stopped shaking. She felt weak and wrung out. When she looked up, she realized she'd drifted on the ocean current far from the resort. With effort, she wrestled the kayak around and headed back toward shore. As she dragged the kayak onto the beach, an idea occurred to her. Jack. Jack could help her. The thought provided her the first glimmer of hope in days.

≈୨୧∽

Sweat dripped from Danica's hair down her face and into the shelf of her tank top's built-in bra. She shook her head to keep the perspiration from stinging her eyes. When she checked her watch, she was astounded to see that she'd been running for nearly an hour. It had been a long time since she'd run ten miles at a stretch. Her lungs burned and her legs ached, but neither was as painful as the hole in her heart. She sat down on Chase's front stoop and wiped her face with the bottom of her shirt. On her run, she'd reviewed the time she and Chase had spent together. There was no question in her mind that Chase loved her every bit as much as she loved Chase. It was incomprehensible to her that Chase would simply walk away without even saying a word.

The Chase she loved was warm, solicitous, and caring. The Chase she loved would never have abandoned her. She would've understood how torn up Danica would be at being shut out. She would've known that Danica needed to be there for her.

Danica swallowed hard as another sharp stab punctured her heart. She wondered if she could've misjudged Chase so badly. What had she done wrong to make Chase run?

"Danica?"

Danica looked up at Tisha, her vision blurred by the tears that pooled in her eyes.

Without saying a word, Tisha squatted down and gave Danica a hug.

The two women stayed like that for a long time. Finally, Danica wiped her nose and said, "Your legs are going to kill you tomorrow."

Tisha laughed. "That's okay. I'll get over it."

"Thanks for the shoulder. I'm usually a lot tougher than that."

"We all have our moments. In this case, I'm relieved to know you're not made of stone." Tisha stood gingerly, stretched, and sat down next to Danica.

"What did I do wrong?" Danica's lower lip trembled and her eyes filled with tears again.

"Oh, honey. You didn't do anything wrong."

"I must've done something wrong or Chase wouldn't have run away. Maybe I wasn't supportive enough, or—"

"Don't do this to yourself," Tisha interrupted her. "The fact that Chase ran away isn't about you, Danica. It's about Chase and who she is."

"What do you mean?"

"Chase is a very solitary person. She's used to being self-reliant. She's also very private and tends not to share much about herself. Her first reaction is to hunker down and regroup."

"But she's been so open with me up until now. That's part of what I don't understand." Danica slapped her thighs in frustration. After a few seconds, she said, "You think that's what she's doing? Regrouping?"

"It's tough to say without knowing what the doctor told her, but if it was bad news, then yes. She'd take time to process it before talking about it with anybody else."

"Even me." Danica picked at a nonexistent cuticle.

"Yes. Even you," Tisha said sympathetically.

"But I promised that whatever the diagnosis was, we'd go through it together. She seemed to want that too."

"And I'm sure part of her does. She'll come to her senses, I hope."

"If I could just see her, talk to her, I could tell her…" Danica's voice, already hoarse from crying, broke, and she stopped speaking.

"You'll get the chance, Danica. She loves you too much. You love each other too much. She can't ignore that."

"She's doing a pretty good job of it at the moment."

"Give her a little more time. She'll come around."

"What if she doesn't?" Danica whispered the question.

❦

Chase sat on the edge of the chair in Jack's waiting room. Idly, she flipped through a magazine in which she had no interest.

After several minutes, Jack emerged from her office. She glanced meaningfully at Chase's suitcase, then at Chase. "Planning on moving in? Something I should know?"

Chase stood and followed Jack into the office, pulling the suitcase behind her. "I came directly from the airport. I just got in."

"From?"

"Florida."

"I'm flattered. You left the beach to see me. That must be a first." Jack settled into her chair and gestured for Chase to sit too.

"You said it was urgent. What's going on? Last time I saw you, I didn't get the sense you planned on making a return visit."

"I need your help." Now that she was here, she wasn't sure how to begin.

"I'm listening."

Chase's stomach lurched wildly and she thought she might be sick. "I'm lost," she mumbled.

"Tell me about it, Chase." Jack sat up straighter.

"I...I'm so mixed up. I don't know what to do. Everything's a mess."

"Can you be more specific? Last time you were here, you were struggling with a health issue."

Chase nodded tightly without looking up.

"Has that resolved itself?"

Chase's lips started to tremble and she pursed them. Her hands were shaking, so she pressed her fingertips together. "No. I'm really sick."

"Oh? How so?" Jack's voice was gentle.

"I have a growth in my brain. It's some kind of malformation, and it's already hemorrhaged."

"I'm sorry, Chase. What does the doctor say?"

"He says he wants to monitor it for now. He put me on antiseizure drugs."

"You sound like you're not sure that's the right course of action."

"I don't know." Chase got up and walked to a bookshelf. She stared at the titles, although she didn't see them. "He's the expert. He should know best, right?"

"Presumably. Do you trust him?"

"He's a business acquaintance and one of the foremost neurologists in the country."

"Okay."

"It's just..." Chase pivoted to face Jack. "It's not his head, you know? What if he's wrong? What if something happens tomorrow? I could die." She whispered the last word.

"We're all going to die, Chase."

"Yes, but most of us have better odds," Chase said bitterly.

"Is he saying that's a likely outcome for what you have?"

"No. He says folks can live with this. That it's most likely benign."

"So I'll ask you again. You don't trust him?"

"No, I do trust him, I guess." Chase blew out an exasperated breath. She returned to her chair but stood behind it with her arms resting on the back of it. "I thought I had my whole life in front of me."

"You may yet."

"For once, everything was going right. I fell madly in love. Danica and I were making plans for our future—"

"Whoa, back up there a minute." Jack nearly jumped out of her chair. "Danica Warren?"

"Yeah." Chase's stomach turned over again at the sound of Danica's name.

"So you went for it, eh?" Jack smirked.

"Yep, I did."

"Good for you. Apparently that worked for you."

"Oh, yeah. I can't even begin to tell you...we're crazy about each other." Tears welled in Chase's eyes.

"How does she feel about the health news?"

Chase shifted from one foot to the other and ran her fingers over the back of the chair. "She doesn't know," she said quietly.

"She doesn't know?" Jack asked incredulously. "How is that? You just told me that you're planning a life together."

"I haven't told her." Chase's voice was barely above a whisper.

"When did you get the diagnosis?"

"A couple of days ago."

"You've known for a couple of days that you had a mass in your brain, and you haven't told your girlfriend? The woman you profess to love?" Jack's voice got progressively louder as she finished the question.

"I—"

"Why haven't you told her? Are you afraid that she won't be there for you? Is she the type of woman who would cut and run?"

"No. Danica would be here if I let her. She wants to go through this together." Chase shoved the chair forward in agitation, indignant at the implication that Danica didn't care.

"How do you know that?"

"She came all the way back here to go to the preliminary doctor's appointment and the MRI with me, then flew to Las Vegas for an engagement and back again to be with me for when I got the results." Chase straightened up defiantly.

"So how is it she doesn't know what's going on?" Jack picked up a pen and clicked it open and closed.

"I had the follow-up appointment while she was on her way back from Vegas. I took off when I got the bad news. That was before she got to Albany, and I haven't answered her calls."

"How many times has she called?"

"I don't know," Chase mumbled. "At least ten that I know of. I left my cell phone at home, so I don't know how many more times she tried me after I left. I know she tried the house, the cell, and my office."

Jack stood up and leaned on the back of her chair so that she and Chase were eye to eye. "Help me out here if I'm misunderstanding. You say you and Danica are in love. She went to the doctor with you and supported you when you needed her. She traveled all the way across the country to face the music with you, and you ran off to Florida without so much as letting her know what happened."

"Yes," Chase admitted. "That's it."

"Did she know where you went?"

"No. Nobody did."

"I see." Jack leaned forward against the chair. "What are you running from, Chase?"

"What?" Chase's head snapped up. "I needed time to think."

"And you couldn't do that with Danica around?"

Chase bit her lip. "She's better off if I hurt her now instead of devastating her later."

"Oh, so this is a noble gesture?"

"I..."

"Excuse me for speaking plainly, Chase, but that's complete and utter bullshit. So what's the real reason you ran away?"

"It's not bullshit," Chase said heatedly. "I don't want to put her through this. She's already lost one lover tragically."

"And you're...what...ensuring that she loses another?"

"No. It's not like that."

"It isn't? You've blown her off. Shut her out. Don't you think it would've been important to ask her what she wanted? Whether she wanted to stick around and go through this? You've made a unilateral decision for her and given her no say in the matter. Does that strike you as being fair?"

"She's too nice to walk away."

"Good thing for her you're not."

"What!" Chase exclaimed on an expelled gust of air. She felt as though she'd been punched in the gut.

"Apparently you thought nothing of walking away and leaving Danica hanging."

"That's not true."

"No?" Jack arched an eyebrow. "How would you characterize it then?"

"I told you—"

"Yeah, I know what you told me. You did it for her own good, yada yada." Jack came out from behind the chair and moved to within three feet of Chase. "I'm going to ask you again," she said, this time modulating her voice. "What are you really running away from, Chase? Are you running away from Danica?"

"I won't have anything to bring to the relationship right now. I have to be selfish and focus on myself. Maybe after this is over, we can try again. Believe me, I love Dani with all my heart. This isn't easy for me." Chase's voice shook with emotion.

"Then what's this really about?"

"I just told you—"

"And I respectfully disagree. It sounds good, but it's a rationalization of the actions you've taken. So what's it really all about, Chase?"

"I don't know." Chase crumbled into her chair.

"I think I might." Jack went back to her chair and sat down. "Remember you told me in our last session about your ex? The one who cheated on you and ripped your heart out?"

"Yes."

"That was horribly painful, wasn't it?"

"Yes," Chase whispered, staring at her hands in her lap.

"How does what you had with her when you were in love and happy compare with what you have with Danica?"

"There's no comparison," Chase said easily. "What I feel with Danica is unlike anything I've ever felt in my life."

"Mmm-hmm. And if you lost her?"

"I'm not following you." Chase's guts churned.

"If losing the ex devastated you, imagine what it would feel like if Danica walked away."

Chase closed her eyes.

"Look, I know you're scared. There's a lot being thrown at you all at once. You've got a serious medical crisis going on, and if that's not enough, you're feeling a depth of emotion for another human being that you've never experienced before while still carrying the scars from the last time you got hurt. Who wouldn't be overwhelmed?"

Chase fidgeted in her chair.

"But don't make Danica pay the price for something she hasn't done, even if you're afraid she might do it down the line somewhere. Love is never a bad thing, Chase. And that kind of all-encompassing, soul-deep love comes once in a lifetime, if you're very, very lucky. It's a gift. Don't waste it and don't be afraid to live for now. Tomorrow will take care of itself." Jack smiled kindly. "It sounds like what Danica is offering you is something most people would kill to have."

"I know." Chase nodded. "She's incredible in every way."

"Then go find her and don't let your fears get the best of you. Love makes you stronger, Chase, and together you'll face whatever medical challenges come your way." Jack stood up and gestured toward the door. "Time's up."

Chase stood and joined her, dragging her suitcase behind. "Thanks, I think."

"I'm sorry if I was a little tough on you, but you needed to hear that."

"I believe that's why I came."

"I think so too. And that makes you very brave, indeed." Jack squeezed Chase's shoulder. "I'll be here if you need me."

"I know."

"And I want to know how you're doing health-wise, so please keep in touch."

"Okay."

"You're tough, Chase. You can beat this."

"I hope you're right."

"I know I am. Good luck to you, and don't be a stranger." Jack held the door for Chase.

"I won't. Who knows, maybe I'll bring Danica with me next time."

"I'll look forward to that."

"Me too," Chase said around the sudden lump in her throat.

CHAPTER SEVENTEEN

Danica walked into the living room of Chase's empty house with her suitcase in hand. She ran her fingertips over the sofa and the end table and picked up the framed picture of her with Chase that had been taken in D.C. Both she and Chase were smiling broadly, their arms around each other. That seemed like a lifetime ago.

"I'll miss you more than I can say. More than you'll ever know." She ran her index finger over Chase's mouth before setting the frame back on the end table. Her legs were leaden as she made her way to the breakfast bar and the piece of paper and pen she'd set there earlier.

"Dear Chase," she began the note. "I don't really know what to say. I always thought I was pretty good at reading people, but either I badly misjudged your feelings for me from the outset or your feelings have changed drastically. I feel like an idiot. It's obvious to me now that you don't love me as I do you, and that hurts me more than I would've thought humanly possible."

Danica set the pen down with a shaky hand and stared straight ahead. There were no words to describe the excruciating ache in her heart or the emptiness in her soul. What could she possibly convey on a tiny piece of paper that could come close to explaining the pain and confusion she felt?

She picked the pen up again and resumed. "Regardless of how you feel about me—or don't feel—I'd really like to know that you're okay. I'd appreciate it if you would at least drop me a line and let me know what's going on with your head. I know this is a lot to ask, but…please. Do this for me."

Danica blinked away more tears and bit her lip to keep it from trembling. *Please, Chase. Please don't shut me out.*

"I will always love you, but it's clear that you don't want me here, so I guess this note is goodbye..." Danica paused with the pen over the page, her vision obliterated by a round of fresh tears. She hadn't thought she had any more to give. She dropped the pen and rested her forehead on the back of her hands, allowing the hopelessness to wash over her. When the tears finally ran out, she picked up the pen again.

"I won't bother you again. Just know that I love you with all my heart. I'm sorry you don't seem to feel the same way. I wish you the best, always. Take good care of yourself, Chase."

Danica glanced up at the ceiling and tried to force air into her suddenly oxygen-starved lungs. It was several minutes before she was able to control her hand enough to sign the note.

Before she could reconsider, she got up, grabbed the suitcase, and headed for the front door and the waiting limousine that would take her home. *One foot in front of the other. You can do it.*

Once safely ensconced in the backseat, she turned on her cell phone and dialed Toni's number. Talking to Toni would be better than dwelling on what she'd just left behind.

"Hello."

"Hi, Toni."

"Danica. What's going on? Did the car get there okay?"

"You did great, T. I can't thank you enough for arranging that. I would've rented a car to drive home."

"And where would you have dropped the car off, the nearest grizzly bear cave? It wasn't practical."

"You're right. I just wasn't thinking."

"No small wonder. How are you feeling today, Dani?"

Danica felt her face flush with embarrassment. "About last night's call. I'm sorry about that."

"Sorry for being human? I can't even imagine how you must feel. If it were me, I'd be curled up in a fetal ball and completely nonfunctional."

That was exactly how Danica felt inside, but she was well-conditioned at going through the motions. Still, for the first time in her life, Danica wasn't sure she could pull it off. Every second, every breath, was a struggle and more than she thought she could bear. The previous night, she had uncharacteristically broken down on the phone with Toni while explaining the situation. She hadn't wanted to make the call, but she had responsibilities, and no matter what else was going on in her life, she wouldn't shirk those duties.

"Dani? Are you there?"

"Yeah. I'm here." Danica cleared her throat and sat up a little straighter. "Did you get a chance to massage the schedule?"

"You're clear for the next two weeks. After that, there are a few events, but none of them will require an overnight."

Danica closed her eyes as relief washed through her. "I have no idea how you did that, but I'm eternally grateful." As they had all day, tears threatened again.

"Easy stuff, I assure you. What do you want me to do about the mid-range schedule?"

The idea of having to carry on, to face people and act as if her whole world wasn't falling apart, was more than Danica could stand. She gazed out the window at the passing trees and spotted a deer on a slope at the edge of some woods. Even the sight of such beauty failed to move her. "I…Don't cancel anything that's already on the docket, but don't schedule anything new without asking me first, okay?"

"Sure thing. I wish there was something more I could do for you. I've got a lot of contacts. I could put out feelers—"

"No." Danica drew in a sharp breath as a bubble of anxiety settled in the pit of her stomach. "No. If she doesn't want to see me, I don't want to push the matter."

"Dani…"

"No. Besides, it'd be like looking for a needle in a haystack." Danica's tone brooked no argument.

"At the risk of pissing you off again, Chase is an idiot."

"I appreciate your righteous indignation on my behalf, T, but it's not going to bring her back." This time the tears did come, and along with it an unimaginable feeling of loneliness. "I've got to go."

"Call and check in later, please, Dani. I'm worried about you."

"Bye, T." Danica pressed the phone to her forehead with trembling fingers before dropping it into her lap. She turned her head and stared sightlessly at the scenery.

∽৩৩

Chase got out of the cab, paid the driver, and paused on the front stoop, gathering her courage. She tried to think where Danica would have gone when she landed. It seemed likely that she would've come to the house, but she wouldn't have had a key. Chase had no idea what she would say if Danica was inside. When she finally walked through the door into the house, she felt sure she was alone. The house was too quiet. Would Danica have stayed in a hotel?

Chase strode into the bedroom. The bed was made. She hadn't made it before she left, had she? Maybe the house wasn't empty after all. "Danica? Are you here? Dani?" Her heartbeat accelerated and she jogged from the bedroom down the hall to the living room, and finally on to the kitchen, where she spotted the note on the breakfast bar.

The kernel of anticipatory joy she'd felt just seconds earlier morphed into a knot of dread as she read the first lines Danica had written. "Oh, God." She reached blindly for the breakfast bar and gripped the edge tightly as her knees buckled.

"No. Dani, no." She shook her head wildly, and although she told herself to breathe, Chase wasn't at all sure she could. The pressure in her chest was unbearable. With difficulty, she stumbled onto the nearest stool as a wave of dizziness swamped her, and the world started to spin in slow motion.

Chase slumped against the solid surface of the counter and waited for the feeling to pass. When it did, she was exhausted and frightened. The new medication was supposed to eliminate seizures, and yet, she'd just had one anyway.

She remembered the doctor's warning about stress but couldn't block out the sickening knowledge that she could die and Danica would never understand how much she really did love her.

She could spend the rest of her life not knowing the truth. Chase swallowed the bile that rose in her throat. *A plan. I need a plan.* Before she could formulate another thought, the phone rang. *Danica.* Eagerly, she snatched it up.

∼ぴ∽

"Hello?"
"Chase? Is that you?"

Chase closed her eyes and fought to hide her disappointment at the sound of Tisha's voice.

"Yes."

"When did you get home?"

"Just a few minutes ago."

"Is Danica still there?"

Chase squirmed on the stool. "You knew she was here?"

"How do you think she got in the house, genius? Magic?"

Chase digested that bit of information. "Of course. You let her in."

"Let her in?" Tisha's voice rose. "I picked her up at the airport...or at least the pieces of her that were intact. Which, incidentally, did not include her heart, thanks to you."

"Tisha..." Chase's breath stalled someplace between her lungs and her mouth at the unexpected onslaught.

"No. I'm sorry, Chase. I want to know what's going on, and I'm worried to death about you, but I have to say what needs to be said first, before I get sidetracked or start feeling sorry for you."

"Tish...Don't..." Chase said weakly.

"That girl loves you more than I ever thought one person could love another. I sat here and watched her heart bleed out with each passing hour, until it was shriveled up to nothing."

Her hand shook so badly, Chase tightened her grip on the phone to keep from dropping it.

"She cried rivers, wondering what in the world she could've done to drive you away."

"God," Chase whispered. *Poor Dani.*

"I had to watch the life drain from her eyes until they were dull and red from crying and lack of sleep." Tisha's voice shook with emotion. "And I couldn't do anything but stand by helplessly as that strong, brave woman was emotionally ripped to shreds. When I left her yesterday, she barely resembled the woman on stage in D.C. or even the woman I picked up from the airport."

"Tisha, stop. Please." Chase didn't think she could hear another word.

"Oh, I'm just getting started."

"Please. I can't..." Chase held her hand out as if to ward off a blow.

"No, Chase. You need to know that there are repercussions for your selfishness."

The word struck Chase like a fist in the gut. "I wasn't being selfish. At least I didn't mean to be. I was a mess."

Tisha continued as if she hadn't heard Chase at all. "I got to know Danica a little bit in the last couple of days, and let me tell you, there's no finer woman in the world. I have no idea what you could've been thinking to leave her hanging that way, but if by chance you are planning to apologize or explain and she doesn't accept it, it'll be what you deserve."

Chase clutched the center of her chest as a sharp pain made her pitch forward. Was she too late? What if she couldn't make it right?

"And if you really don't love her as deeply as she loves you," Tisha continued, apparently oblivious to Chase's distress, "then you're a bigger ass than I thought."

"Are you done?"

"Just one more thing. I love you, and Danica isn't the only one who's been worried sick. If you ever take off like that again, I'll kill you."

"Understood." Chase breathed a sigh of relief that Tisha finally seemed to be winding down.

"Now, what's going on? Where have you been?"

Chase started with her visit to Doctor Frankel and the diagnosis and ended with Danica's note. By the time she finished, her voice was barely above a whisper.

"Oh, Chase. Do you need me to come over?"

"No, thanks. I'm okay."

"How could you think you'd be better off without Danica's support? Or that standing by you would be harder for her than saying goodbye to you?"

"Like I said, I was a mess." Chase bit her lip and swallowed her pride. "There's one piece I haven't told you." She relayed some of the details of her visit to Jack, including Jack's assessment of why Chase really took off.

"She's right, you know. That makes a lot of sense."

"I know. But I'm damaged goods. What if Danica doesn't want to go through all this with me? What if she does it anyway out of pity? I don't think I could survive that. She has the power to destroy me, Tish."

"So you destroyed her first."

"I…"

"God, you underestimate Danica badly. Listen, I got to watch that woman in the worst possible circumstances. She loves you, Chase. And she'll love you regardless of what happens with your head. She doesn't care about that. It's about your heart and soul. Not your head."

"How can you be so sure?"

"It's in her every word and in the things she doesn't say. You should see the look in her eyes when your name is mentioned or how she defends you and explains away your behavior, even when she should be furious. She's the real thing, and you're a fool if you don't let your heart go, overcome your fears, and take a chance."

Chase swallowed around the lump in her throat. Tisha was right. "I need your help."

"If it means you're going to get your head out of your ass and go after Danica, you've got it."

"Do you know where she was going when she left here?"

"I didn't know that she was leaving. She insisted that I go home after dinner last night. She said she felt bad for taking up my time. I got the sense she needed a little space but was too polite to say so. I left and told her I'd call her today to check up on her. That's why I was calling when you answered. I'd tried her cell and didn't get an answer, so I thought I'd take a chance that she'd answer the home phone hoping it was you."

Chase felt another stab of guilt. "How am I going to find her if she isn't answering her cell? Not only that, but I don't want to do this over the phone. I need to see her, to expla…" Chase's voice failed her.

"Maybe she went home," Tisha suggested.

"Did she say what her schedule was? Did she have another engagement coming up?"

"You don't know that?"

"We didn't get that far," Chase admitted.

"Well, she didn't say, and I don't think she was in any shape to make appearances. I don't think she could've walked onto a stage without losing her composure."

Chase clenched her jaw. *Oh, Dani. I'm so sorry. I'd give anything to do all this over again and take away the hurt.* "If she went home, I'm in trouble."

"Why?"

"She never gave me a specific location or address, and I'm sure she's not listed."

"Mmm. What about that agent?"

"Toni? I'm guessing I'm not her favorite person at the moment."

"If she knows what happened, I'm sure you're right about that. Still, she's got to know how much Danica cares for you and that she's worried. I can't imagine it would be in Toni's best interest professionally to deny you access to Danica at this point."

"Here's a discussion I'm not looking forward to."

"Bite the bullet and make the call, Chase. It's your best option."

"Sure you don't want to call for me?"

Tisha laughed. "Are you kidding me? Do I look stupid or suicidal?"

"Just thought I'd try."

"Nice effort. Now stop stalling."

Chase chewed her lip. "Do you think Danica will forgive me?" She asked the question softly, letting all her doubts float to the surface.

"Honestly, I don't know. You did a lot of damage and she's in a world of hurt. But if I were a betting woman, my money would be on her loving you too much not to forgive you."

"That's confidence-inspiring."

"There's only one way to find out. Do you love her, Chase?"

"God, do I. More than life itself."

"Then tell her. You'll be fine."

"Thanks, Tish. I owe you."

"You certainly do, and I plan on collecting."

"Great, something else to look forward to. Bye."

❧

"This is Toni."

"Hi, Toni. It's Chase Crosley."

"Oh."

Chase sighed. Icicles might've been warmer than the tone in Toni's voice. *This is about Danica. Stay focused.* "I'm sure I'm probably your least favorite person right now."

"You've got that right."

Chase clamped down on a surge of irritation. This wasn't any of Toni's business, and she resented having to answer to anyone other than Danica. On the other hand, Danica was Toni's business, literally. On some level then, Chase was glad to know that Toni would protect her heart. "I appreciate that you've got Danica's back."

"Apparently someone has to."

"Look, caustic replies and innuendo aren't going to be helpful here. You and I both want the same thing."

"Do tell."

"We both want Danica to be happy and to make her heart whole."

"And you're just the girl for the job, I suppose."

"As a matter of fact, I am. I screwed up, and I'm the only one who can make it right." Chase took a deep breath and got to the point. "But I can't do that without your help." There it was.

The pause on the line was so long Chase wondered if Toni had put the phone down and walked away.

"First, tell me your intentions. Then we can talk about whether or not I choose to help you."

Chase bit off a growl and instead paced to the window in a bid to find the patience she was rapidly losing. "I need to go to Dani and show her that she has all of my heart and always has. To explain what happened and why. I don't want her to suffer for another second. I would think that's what you would want too. I love her, Toni. With everything I am and everything I will be. She has to know that."

Another lengthy silence ensued.

"Although I'd really like to know why you did what you did if that's the way you feel, that's between you and Dani. The only thing that's important to me is Dani's well-being. If you hurt her again, I swear…"

"You're right. That isn't any of your business." Chase couldn't hold herself back anymore. She had reached the end of her rope.

Dani was the only one who mattered to her. "I can understand you not wanting to go out of your way for me. But this is about Danica and what she wants. Will you help me or not?"

"What is it you need from me?"

Chase closed her eyes and uttered a silent prayer of thanks. "I need to know how to find her. Now. Today." When Toni didn't say anything, Chase asked, "Are you there?"

"I'm here. Be outside your house in half an hour."

"That's it?"

"You want to get to Danica or not?"

"Of course I do."

"Then you'd better get packed. A car will be there to pick you up in...twenty-nine minutes."

"Thank you."

"Thank Danica. If I wasn't sure she'd want to see you, you'd never get near her again."

"That's comforting. Goodbye, Toni. Thanks for your help." Chase hung up the phone and scrubbed her face with her hands. *Well, that was pleasant.*

CHAPTER EIGHTEEN

D anica sat on the front porch and listened to the noises of nature. Birds called to each other in mating rituals as old as time. Squirrels and chipmunks scurried about with acorns and other treasures. Larger animals—deer, bears, and foxes—went about their lives in the woods that surrounded the cabin. The woods and the lake that glistened beyond, usually so vibrant and colorful to Danica's eyes, seemed as dull and lifeless as she felt. Sounds and sights that had always brought her so much comfort offered her no solace on this day.

Her hands trembled in her lap, and she entwined her fingers to still the motion. Her entire body vibrated with the echoes of despair. There was a hollowness in the core of her being that overshadowed anything she had ever felt before, even in the depths of her grief after Sandy died.

A lone tear tracked down her left cheek, and she didn't bother to wipe it away. There had been so many in the past few days, one more simply didn't make a difference. She wondered, yet again, how it was possible that one woman, in such a short time, had come to matter so much to her. And how the loss of that woman could bring her to her knees in a way that nothing in her life up to this moment ever had.

Time, she realized, had nothing to do with it. She could've spent an hour with Chase or a lifetime, and the connection they shared would've been equally compelling. True, she imagined, their love would have deepened and matured over time. Shared experiences would have added additional layers of closeness. But the bond that drew them inexorably together seemed to have been forged almost before they'd ever met. It was as if it had just been waiting for them to find each other, which made losing Chase all the more poignant and painful.

Danica wondered if Chase felt the power of the bond the same way she did. After all, Chase had said as much. If she did feel it, Danica was at a complete loss to understand how she could simply walk away. Such a connection was a rare treasure; to find it only to ignore it or throw it away was inconceivable.

She gazed at the deepening hues of blues and oranges that signified the end of the day in the Adirondacks and suffered another sharp stab in the heart. Sunset—their time of day. It was just another reminder of all she had lost.

The sound of a car moving closer registered vaguely in Danica's consciousness. The fact that she heard it at all was a testament to the fact that she lived in a remote area on a dirt road. The nearest neighbor was more than three miles away.

When she caught a glimpse of the car through the trees heading up her long, uphill driveway, she tensed. So few people knew where she lived, and even fewer ever visited her. Perhaps someone had taken a wrong turn.

As the car approached she looked through the windshield at the driver. *Definitely a wrong turn.* It was a middle-aged, graying man. Danica was half-standing when the back door opened and a woman jumped out. The car hadn't even come to a complete stop.

Danica momentarily froze, then her legs failed. She barely registered that the woman was running toward her. As she started to fall, strong hands grabbed her under the arms and righted her. It took her mind several seconds to catch up to her heart. *Chase.*

She stared into Chase's eyes, trying to discern what was in her heart. What she found there was fear. She was sure her own eyes mirrored the same emotion, although probably for an entirely different reason. Finally, Chase smiled tentatively, and all the warmth and love Danica had come to know suddenly flooded back.

Chase licked her lips in a gesture Danica idly recognized as an indication of nerves. "Can I hold you, Dani?" Her voice was tremulous.

"Please."

Chase wrapped her arms around Danica and pulled their bodies together until there was no space between them.

Danica felt her heart slide into a synchronistic beat with Chase's and she closed her eyes. *Home. Thank God.* Still, her head resisted. "Is this for real, Chase? Why are you here?" She pushed back until there was daylight between them. She couldn't think clearly otherwise.

"I promise you it's for real, sweetheart. I love you so much."

"Excuse me, ladies," the driver broke in. "Can I go now or will you be needing a ride back?" He directed the question to Chase.

She glanced at Danica and raised an eyebrow. "Do you want me to leave?"

Never. "Not unless you want to." Danica bit her lip as a knot of anxiety twisted her stomach.

"I want to stay." Chase took Danica's hands in her own. "If that's what you want."

Danica nodded without looking at the driver.

"Okay, then. I'll be leaving."

Neither woman even glanced in his direction as he got behind the wheel and made a three-point turn to head back down the driveway.

"Are you okay?" Danica asked as the sound of the engine receded. Her head still was spinning and her pulse raced. She wasn't sure what to think or believe just yet. Her heart leapt for joy, but her head urged caution.

"I'm better now." Chase moved closer as if to kiss her.

"Wait." Danica put her hands against Chase's chest and forestalled her forward momentum. "I just…" To Danica's horror, her body began to shake uncontrollably. "I'm not ready." She saw hurt flicker in Chase's eyes, then quickly disappear.

"I see."

"I don't know if you do. I don't know if you can." Danica turned her back to Chase and walked a few steps away. Being close to Chase made it impossible to protect her heart, a truth that scared Danica more than she wanted to admit. "When you were gone…When you didn't take my calls…"

Danica thrust her hands in her pockets to hide the tremor. She whirled around to face Chase as huge tears teetered on her lashes. "I didn't know if you were alive, if you were okay. I was worried sick." A sob pierced her carefully controlled reserve. "Why, Chase? Why would you do that to me?" Danica collapsed on one of the front steps and buried her face in her hands. "What..." She swallowed hard. "What did I do to deserve that? I must've done something to send you away. I just want to know..."

"Stop." Chase's voice shook as she came within two feet of Danica, but Chase didn't make any effort to touch her. "Please, baby. You didn't do anything. I promise you. It was me. I was a fool."

"How could I have mattered to you so little?" Danica rasped, pleading for an answer.

Chase shook her head violently and tears spilled from her eyes. "You're wrong, Dani. You mattered to me too much, I couldn't handle that. I got scared, then confused. I didn't know what to do. I screwed up big-time by running. It took me a little while to figure it out, but I know that now as surely as I know I love you with all my heart." Chase moved tentatively forward and sat down next to Danica on the step.

Danica stayed very still, afraid to move. Afraid to trust.

"Dani, I do love you. Nothing has changed. My feelings for you haven't changed. If anything, I feel more strongly than I did before. I'm still trying to understand it all myself."

"Why did you come back?" Danica gripped the edge of the step until her fingers turned white.

"I came back because no matter how afraid I am of the intensity of the love I feel for you, I can't imagine my life without you. I'm scared to death of being hurt, Dani. What if you walk away? I wouldn't survive." Chase said the last as a desperate whisper.

"But I would if you walked?" A flash of anger bubbled up from Danica's gut. "I've been dying inside for days, but maybe you've been too busy, wherever you were, to consider that." She shook her head. "So running away was...what...a preemptive strike?" She pushed off the step and stalked away, pivoting when she was several feet away.

"We're both scared, Chase. I've never felt anything close to what I feel for you. For God's sake, life isn't a dress rehearsal. We have one shot at this in this lifetime. Do you not feel what I do? How could you..." Danica's voice broke and she covered her face with one hand. She heard Chase approach and stiffened.

"Dani. Please. I'm so, so very sorry. I'm begging you. I know what I did is unforgivable. I have no valid reason for it and I won't make excuses. But please give me another chance. I know you have no reason to trust me, but I swear to you, I won't run again. Whatever comes, we'll face it together…if that's what you want."

"I want to believe you, Chase. I do. But you can't even begin to fathom the damage you've done to my heart. I'll be picking up the pieces for a long time to come."

"So what are you telling me? It's over?" Chase's voice was thick with emotion. "You want me to go away?" Tears sprang to her eyes.

Danica's heart lurched. "No. God, no. Please…" She threw herself into Chase's arms and held on for dear life. "Please," she whispered, burying her hands in Chase's hair. "Please." She let the tears fall, absorbed by the cotton of Chase's shirt. This time she couldn't hide the way her body shook.

"Shh. Shh. It's okay, baby. Dani. Look at me. Look at me." Chase pulled back enough to tilt Danica's head up so that they were looking into each other's eyes. "I love you with everything that I am and everything that I will be. I'd give anything to take back the last few days. I never wanted to hurt you. If I could take that away, I would. But I can't change what I did. I can only change what I will do. And only if you'll let me. Let me in, Dani. Please. I miss you and I need you. Most importantly, I love you more than life itself." Chase kissed Danica's forehead.

Danica leaned into the comforting sensation of Chase's arms. She nodded against Chase's chin. "Yes."

"Yes?" Chase repeated.

"Yes. Yes. I love you, Chase. No matter how badly you hurt me, and you did, the truth is that I love you, and I don't want to imagine my life without you."

Chase gathered Danica closer and rocked her from side to side.

Danica spent a few minutes enjoying the sensation of coming home before she asked into Chase's shoulder, "What happened at the doctor's office?" She felt Chase's heartbeat stop, then resume its rhythm against her ear. "Chase?"

"I don't want to talk about it just yet. Let's just enjoy the moment, okay?"

"What's wrong?" Danica couldn't keep an edge of panic out of her voice.

"It's fine. I just want to be with you right now. Please? I promise I'll tell you everything." Chase nuzzled Danica's ear with her lips.

Danica shivered involuntarily. "Okay, but you're not off the hook."

"Nope. I consider myself hooked," Chase said as she led Danica inside.

ↄↄ

Chase stretched contentedly and snugged Danica closer to her side. She stroked the side of her face and moved wisps of hair away from her eyes. Although Danica shifted slightly, she did not wake. Chase was glad. The dark circles under Danica's eyes spoke eloquently of how difficult the past few days had been for her.

Chase had seen the tears as Danica had made love to her, the shadows in her eyes as she had come, and the desperation as she had held tightly to Chase afterward. More than anything, Chase hoped that time would heal the wounds she had inflicted. She resolved that she would do anything in her power to make it so. "I love you, Dani," she whispered.

"Mmm. Love you too." Danica lifted herself and settled on top of Chase. "You're still a furnace."

"Always."

Danica kissed her collarbone. "Now tell me what the doctor said."

Chase's stomach flipped. "Later. You need more sleep."

"If I sleep more now, I won't sleep through the night. Stop stalling and tell me. The longer you wait, the more anxious I get."

Chase leaned up and kissed Danica quickly on the mouth. "Let's go for a walk." This wasn't a conversation she wanted to have when she was both literally and figuratively exposed.

"It's dark out."

"A moonlight stroll sounds heavenly."

"Okay." Danica pushed herself off Chase.

They dressed in silence and walked outside. Danica grabbed a large flashlight from the front porch, although the moon and stars were bright enough to illuminate their way. She led them down the driveway toward the water. When they reached the bottom of the drive, Danica slipped her hand into Chase's.

The gesture helped calm Chase's nerves. She had no idea how to tell Danica the news.

"Whatever it is, honey, we'll face it together. You and me. I'll never leave you alone, Chase. I won't walk away."

Chase's heart tripped. "Don't make promises, Dani. I want you to make decisions that are best for you, regardless of my condition. Otherwise, I'll always wonder why you stayed."

"You don't ever need to wonder, sweetheart. All I want is to be with you. Nothing changes that." Danica squeezed Chase's hand. "Now tell me, what's going on? What did Doctor Frankel say? What did the MRI show?"

"I..." Chase kicked a small stone on the path and took a deep breath in an effort to steady herself.

Danica let go of her hand and wrapped an arm around her instead. "Together," she said fiercely.

"I have a mass in my brain," Chase said in a rush. She felt Danica stiffen beside her. "It's called a cavernous angioma."

"W-what does that mean, exactly?"

"The way it was explained to me, it's a cluster of abnormal blood vessels in my left temporal lobe."

"Is the mass malignant?"

Chase could feel Danica shivering against her. "Doctor Frankel didn't say that. But it is leaking."

"What?" Danica stopped walking and faced Chase.

"The MRI showed that it hemorrhaged. That's probably what caused the seizure and the episode of aphasia in his office when we were there."

"Why aren't you in the hospital? Why aren't they doing anything about it?"

Chase could feel Danica vibrating. "Easy, honey. Doctor Frankel says lots of people live with this every day. He's put me on some antiseizure drugs and wants to monitor me for now."

"That's it?"

"It may never hemorrhage again."

"But it's causing the seizures and the speech issue and the headaches, I presume?"

"Yes, or so he thinks."

"And he doesn't want to do anything about that? Let's get another opinion."

"Hang on, tiger." Chase had to smile at Danica's desire to fight for her health. "The idea is to see how I do on the medication."

"Have you had a seizure since you've been taking it?"

Chase considered lying but knew that she could never do that with Danica. "Yes," she admitted. "Stress is one of the things that trigger seizure activity. I had an episode earlier today."

"Let me guess, it was when you read my note. That was my fault," Danica said bitterly.

"Dani—"

"Oh, God, I never want to be responsible for making your condition worse."

Danica started to pull away, but Chase held her fast. "It wasn't your fault, baby. I'm the one who screwed up, not you. Please don't take that on yourself." Chase took Danica's face in her hands. "You're the best thing in my life. I love you. You only make me better, stronger. Please know that." She kissed Danica softly on the mouth.

Danica leaned into her. "Where do we go from here?"

"We wait and see, for now."

"Okay. I'm here for you, Chase. I meant what I said. I'll be beside you every step of the way."

"That means the world to me. But if you ever change your mind..."

"You'll be the first to know. It's never going to happen. I'm here to stay."

"I love you." Chase tried to let everything she felt for Danica show through. "Let's go home, shall we?"

"I love you too. And for the record, you're my home, Chase."

❦

Danica woke to the early morning sounds of the country. Birds chirped, nocturnal creatures made way for the day, and daylight critters were getting an early start. Chase was draped across her, her head pillowed on Danica's shoulder.

Despite the early hour, Danica felt well-rested for the first time in what seemed like forever. She smiled against Chase's forehead.

"What're you smiling about at this hour?" Chase asked groggily, cracking one eye open.

"It's a beautiful day, the sun is shining…"

"It's too early for the sun to shine."

"It will be shining," Danica corrected herself, "as soon as it hits the tree line."

"You're entirely too chipper."

"You're cute when you're sleepy." Danica kissed the top of Chase's head.

"Mmph."

Danica leaned in and traced Chase's ear with her tongue. She laughed when Chase squirmed. "You're not waking up, are you?"

"Not a chance," Chase mumbled.

"I didn't think so." Danica nibbled along Chase's jaw line and down her neck, nipping at her pulse point.

Chase turned to give her a better angle.

"Still sleeping, right?"

"Mmm-hmm."

Danica licked along Chase's collarbone and ran her fingertips ever so lightly up the inside of Chase's thigh. She smiled against Chase's skin as Chase shivered and opened her legs to allow access.

"Not yet, sleepyhead. You just go back to bed since you're not awake anyway."

Chase groaned.

Danica rolled Chase the rest of the way onto her back and sucked an erect nipple into her mouth. At the same time, she grazed a fingertip over Chase's clit.

"Oh, God." Chase reached for Danica, who managed to evade her.

"Ah, ah, ah. Sleep, remember?" Danica put pressure on Chase's center by inserting her thigh between Chase's legs and rocking forward.

"You're torturing me."

"If you were sleeping, you wouldn't even notice," Danica said, barely lifting her mouth from Chase's breast to comment.

"Okay, I give. I'm not sleepy anymore. Please, please have mercy."

"Hmm…" Danica pretended to consider. As she looked into Chase's eyes, brilliant in passion, the gravity of Chase's health situation struck her hard in the solar plexus, and all playfulness leached out of her. *I could lose you.* She knew her expression must have changed because Chase sat straight up, dislodging her.

"No, Dani. Don't think about it. Not now."

Instead of answering her, Danica scrambled up and straddled her so that they were both sitting with their legs splayed. Danica framed Chase's face with shaky hands, tears blurring her vision. Without saying a word, she kissed Chase tenderly at first, then with increasing intensity, until they both were gasping for air.

As tears ran down her face, Danica explored Chase's body with her hands, her fingertips lovingly outlining Chase's shoulders, collarbones, arms, breasts, and abdomen. *You can't leave me. You can't. Not now.* She could feel Chase's body responding to her, and it only served to fuel her desperate hunger, her need for that physical connection.

Danica took Chase's mouth again, her tongue stroking Chase's, demanding supremacy. Her hand found Chase's hot center, and she entered her slowly, carefully, until she was deep inside, her fingers slick with Chase's passion, Chase's muscles closing around her. Her thumb circled Chase's clit in rhythm with her thrusts.

Chase's chest began to heave, and Danica put her other hand there so that she could feel Chase's heartbeat. The strength of it brought a fresh round of tears. She released Chase's mouth and said against her lips, "I want to watch you come." Then she leaned back just far enough until Chase's face came into focus.

Danica marveled as rapture changed Chase's features, making her eyes go dark and her face flush. "You're so beautiful." Her eyes widened in surprise when she felt Chase penetrate her with two fingers.

"I'm right here, Dani. I'm not going anywhere. Can you feel me? I'm real and I'm strong and I'm yours. And I love you so very, very much."

With one last thrust for each of them, they tumbled together, their eyes locked on each other, blissfully ignoring, for a moment, the uncertainty of their future.

CHAPTER NINETEEN

T his way," Danica said, turning right onto the wooden bridge over the dam.

"It's beautiful out here. The water, the mountains—all of it," Chase said, holding her arms out and pivoting 360 degrees.

"It's my haven from the rest of the world. I bought it just after...I bought it three years ago."

"After Sandy died."

"Yes." Danica felt the reassuring pressure as Chase took her hand.

"It's okay to talk about her, Dani. She was a huge part of your life for a very long time."

"Thank you for understanding."

"Of course. I love you. I'm glad you had someone in your life to love."

"You're unique, you know that?" Danica smiled up at Chase.

"One of a kind, lucky for the rest of the world."

They reached the other side of the dam and followed a path into dense woods.

"Is this the hike you took with the *60 Minutes* guys?"

"Yes. It's a lovely walk, not too strenuous and wide enough to walk side by side."

"Aha. I sense ulterior motives."

Danica laughed. "Yeah. I didn't want you staring at my back for an hour on a narrow trail."

"Oh, but that's where you're misguided, my dear. I could've spent an hour staring at your lovely ass."

"Letch."

"Maybe. Or it could be that you turn me on more than I thought humanly possible." Chase's voice was pitched low. She stopped their progress, swept Danica into her arms, and kissed her longingly.

"Mmm. We'll never get where we're going this way."

"It isn't about the destination. It's about the journey."

"I'd heard that rumor," Danica said, bumping Chase's hip and resuming their forward progress. "But negotiating this trail in the dark is a little more adventure than I want to entertain right now."

"But it's only midday."

"Trust me, we could easily be out here after the sun goes down. With you I seem to lose all track of time."

"I know what you mean. It's as if time loses all relevance when we're together."

They hiked on in silence for several minutes more, enjoying the scenery and the companionship.

"This is the log the *60 Minutes* photographer almost took a backward header over," Danica said, pointing to a massive downed tree that blocked the path ahead.

"He did?"

Danica chuckled. "Yeah. It was a train wreck waiting to happen. He was walking backward, taping, so he didn't see it coming."

"What happened?"

"I saved his bacon."

"Where's the fun in that?"

"I know. I'm such a killjoy. If it had been the reporter, I might've let him fall, but the photographer was a nice enough guy."

They scrambled over the log in unison.

"Not to change the subject, but can we talk about the future?" Chase asked. "At least logistical plans for the near future?"

"Of course," Danica said. The muscles in her back tightened and her jaw tensed. The pain of the past week was still too fresh in her mind and her heart to trust in promises of forever or talk of the future.

"I want to spend as much time with you as possible." Chase rushed on, "I know it's too soon to talk about moving in together and I don't want to push you."

"Mmm," Danica muttered noncommittally.

216

"You've got a killer travel schedule and I'm mostly stuck in an office. How are we going to make this work?"

"We'll make it work because we love each other, Chase. I've got some flexibility—probably more than you do. Toni cleared my schedule for the next couple of weeks at my request. After that, I have a few engagements, but none of them will require an overnight. When I thought..." Danica's voice broke and she cleared her throat. "I've asked her to check with me before she schedules anything after that."

"You cleared your schedule because I hurt you." Chase said it quietly, regretfully.

Danica paused midstep before continuing on. *Honesty is best. Otherwise, this will always be between us.* "I cleared my schedule because I couldn't imagine standing up in front of strangers and having to put on a show when all I wanted to do was curl up in a fetal ball." Danica felt the residual shock as the words hit Chase like a blow.

"I'm sorry. I wish I hadn't..."

"I know, Chase. I don't want you to feel guilty, and I'm not trying to make you uncomfortable. But that's my truth, and I won't sugarcoat it."

"I don't want you to. I'd give anything to change it for you, Dani. I'd...I'd...I'd..." Chase stopped walking.

Danica felt the tremor travel up her arm from where their hands were clasped. She turned to look at Chase. Her eyes were unfocused again and her face was slack. "Chase. Chase," she said urgently. Danica's heart raced. *No. The medication is supposed to make this go away.* She pulled Chase into her arms and held her tightly. "It's okay, love. I'm right here. I've got you. I'll always be here."

"I'm...I'm okay," Chase said after a minute. "I'm okay, honey." She pulled back and wiped a tear from Danica's cheek. "Don't cry. I'm fine."

"Chase, that was bad. It lasted longer than the one on the beach or in the doctor's office."

"I'm fine now."

Danica heard the words, but she also recognized the fear Chase tried to hide. "We have to get you home and back to the doctor."

"I'm..."

"Don't argue with me, Chase Crosley." Danica heard the tremor in her own voice. *I won't lose you. This time I can do something about it.*

"Dani."

"Do you have Doctor Frankel's number programmed into your cell?"

"Yes."

"Give it to me."

"Dani…"

"Chase, please."

Chase unclipped the cell phone from her belt and handed it silently to Danica.

Danica scrolled through the address book until she found what she was looking for.

"Doctor Frankel's office."

"Hi. This is Danica Warren, Chase Crosley's partner."

"What can I do for you?"

"Chase has just had a significant seizure and…"

"Let me see if I can get Doctor Frankel for you."

Danica was on hold for several minutes. She ignored Chase's protest that she was fine.

"This is Doctor Frankel."

"Hello, Doctor Frankel, this is Danica Warren."

Danica explained the situation to him.

"I see. I want Chase here tomorrow morning first thing. I'm ordering another MRI. I'll put a rush on it so we'll have the results before the day is over."

"Should we be worried, Doctor Frankel? Is she in imminent danger? Is there something I should do?"

"Has she been taking her medication regularly?"

"Yes."

"Let's wait until tomorrow and see what we're dealing with before we start worrying. She should be fine for now."

"Okay."

"I'll have someone call you back at this number with a time for the MRI. As soon as we have results, someone will get in touch with you and fit you into the schedule. It should be later tomorrow afternoon."

"Thank you, Doctor."

"You're welcome. I'll see you tomorrow."

Danica hung up the phone and looked at Chase. "Let's go." She headed them back toward the cabin.

❧

Chase took a deep breath and held it. The MRI machine was loud and the music in the headphones they'd supplied her with wasn't nearly enough to drown out the banging, whirring, and clicking. She closed her eyes and conjured up an image of Danica sitting astride her from the previous morning. Warmth suffused her loins and she resisted an urge to squirm. *Better think about something else.*

She replayed the brief discussion they'd had on the hike. It sounded as though Danica was hers for the next week to ten days before she had any obligations. Guilt pierced Chase's bubble of happiness when she reminded herself of the cause for the schedule break.

She squeezed her eyes tightly shut while an unwelcome image of Danica's face, crumpled and distraught as she watched the car approach the cabin, flitted across her mind's eye. Dani's cheeks had been gaunt and her eyes had been hollow. *Oh, Dani. I'm so sorry.* Chase knew that causing Danica that kind of pain would be one of the biggest regrets of her life.

She gasped as a sharp pain stabbed her just above her right eyebrow.

"Please...still, m..."

The voice in the headphones sounded as though it was swaddled in cotton. Chase struggled to understand the words. The buzzing in her head got louder, then faded away. She panted and fought to take a deep breath.

"M...all right?"

Chase opened her eyes. The technician, his expression concerned, hovered over her within her line of sight. Chase was surprised to find that she was outside the tube.

"I'm a seizure. Okay, I think." Chase furrowed her brow. She knew she was speaking words, but she couldn't understand what she was saying. Her nostrils flared, and her fingers and cheeks tingled as she began to hyperventilate.

"Do you need anything? Some water?"

She understood him that time. Chase closed her eyes and fought to control her fear. "No. I'm fine now. I…It's never been that bad before."

"Okay. Well, you're in the right place. Let's find out exactly what's going on in that noggin of yours, shall we?"

Chase recognized that the technician was trying to set her at ease, so she played along. "I'm game if you are."

"Are you sure you're okay to continue right now? Do you want to take a few minutes first?"

"No," Chase said determinedly. "Let's get it over with."

"Right. Here we go. Just signal me, if you can, if you need me to stop again, okay?"

"Okay." Chase gritted her teeth as the machine started its cycle again.

❧

Danica paced outside in the courtyard and looked at her watch for what seemed like the millionth time. She couldn't figure out whether it was her imagination or whether this MRI really was taking much longer than the last. She bit down on her lip and waited as another round of butterflies made her stomach roll.

She huffed out a nervous breath and put on her wireless headset. She couldn't remember when the last time was that she had talked to Ted, but she knew she owed him a call. Perhaps it would help take her mind off the interminable wait.

"Well, sugar. It's about time. Where on earth have you been? I've been dying of curiosity. Tell the Fish man everything."

Danica sighed deeply. "I don't even know where I left you in the story."

"You were either in, or going to, Vegas, then back to Albany. Chase had an MRI and you were waiting for the results."

Danica's heart twisted. That seemed like a lifetime ago.

"God," Ted continued, "I feel like I'm recapping a soap opera. When last we left our heroine…" He laughed at his own joke.

"She's having another MRI right now," Danica said quietly.

"Oh, Dani," Ted's tone turned serious. "I'm sorry. I never would've made a joke if I had known. What happened?"

The concern in Ted's voice broke through Danica's careful composure. It was several minutes before she could talk again. When she'd finished telling him the saga of the past week, she could hear him growling on the other end of the line.

"She's lucky I'm not there, sugar. What was she thinking?"

"Ted, please. Don't. I appreciate the sentiment, but now's not the time." Danica's voice shook. "What happened is between Chase and me. You may not understand it—I'm not completely sure I understand it myself—and I'm sure we'll be struggling with the ramifications for a long time to come. But I love her and I know she loves me. That, and her health, are all that matter to me right now. I can't think about anything else. I..." Danica swallowed hard. "I have to stay focused on whatever's ahead of us."

"Okay, Dani. I hear you," Ted said. "I won't say I'm not worried about you and that I won't continue to feel protective of you, but the last thing I want to do is make this harder for you. Whatever you need from me, you've got it."

Danica let out a breath she didn't know she was holding. "Thanks. I'll take all the help and support I can get."

"I'm here for you, honey. After all, I'm the one who talked you into going for it in the first place."

"I'm glad you did. I wouldn't trade what Chase and I have for the world. Even with the challenges."

"That's my girl. Listen, I've got to run. Please let me know what the doc says, okay? Toodles, sugar."

"Bye, Fish man."

Danica checked her watch again. Chase had been in there for nearly an hour and a half. It was time to find out what was going on.

She walked back through the door to the waiting area where the nice nurse she'd spoken to during Chase's first MRI was standing.

"Excuse me..."

"Oh, hi, dear. I see you couldn't get enough of us last time, eh?" The nurse winked. "I imagine you're wondering what's taking Chase so long, right?"

"Yes, ma'am."

"I was wondering the same thing, so I checked just a few minutes ago. It seems she moved, and that wreaked havoc with some of the images, so they had to start again."

"Moved?"

"Yes. To get good images, the patient has to stay very still. At any rate, the boys in there are being very thorough so that Doctor Frankel can tell exactly what's going on. It'll just be another twenty minutes or so. Do you need some water?"

"No, I'm fine, thank you. And thank you for the update. I appreciate knowing. It helps me worry less."

"Worry's bad for the stress level. We'll do everything we can to keep yours low."

Danica thanked the nurse again and walked through the door back into the sunshine. She thought of Tisha and wondered if Chase had contacted her before coming to the cabin. In all the excitement, she'd forgotten to ask. She thought maybe she should leave the call to Chase, then reconsidered. After all, she and Tisha had been through a war together.

"Hello?"

"Tisha? It's Danica."

"Hey. How are you?"

"I'm…okay. Better than when I saw you last."

"You saw Chase."

"How did you know?" Danica sat down on the bench facing the sun.

"I called the house to check on you and she'd just gotten home."

"Oh. So you did talk to her. I wondered."

"Hmm…I'm not sure talk is how she would classify it. More like I yelled at her for fifteen minutes straight."

"You did?"

"She deserved it."

Danica's stomach twisted. "You didn't yell at her on my behalf, did you?"

"I guess it would depend on your definition of 'on your behalf.' I certainly let her know that she had her head up her ass and that if she didn't want to lose you, she'd better do some explaining."

"Tisha…" Danica felt all the air leave her lungs.

"It had to be said. She needed to hear it."

"Is that why she came back?" Danica asked softly. "Because you told her to?"

"No, Danica. No, no, no. I'm sorry if I made you think that. No, that's not true at all. Chase loves you with all her heart. Don't ever doubt that."

"Now I'll wonder if she would've come back if you hadn't said anything to her."

"She would've come back. I promise you. She'd made up her mind. All I did was reinforce what she had already decided to do. She loves you so very much."

"I love her too."

"I know. So where are you two lovebirds?"

Danica hesitated. It was so hard to talk about Chase being sick. "We're back in town. Chase had another bad seizure. They're doing an MRI now. Doctor Frankel will have the results this afternoon and we'll know more."

"Is she all right?"

"Yes. She's scared, but then, so am I."

"I know you are, but Chase is strong and stubborn. She'll fight."

"Did she tell you what the diagnosis is?"

"Yes. Is there anything I can do?"

"Not yet. But I'm sure Chase is going to need all of our support, whatever the tests show."

"You know I love her. And now you too. I'll be there anytime you need me to be."

"Thanks, Tisha. I'll let you know when we know more." Danica looked up to see Chase coming toward her. She looked somehow fragile. "I've got to go. We'll call you later."

Danica didn't even bother to say goodbye before she hung up and ran to Chase. "What's the matter, honey? You look really done in."

"I had an episode during the test. They had to start over again."

Danica's stomach dropped. "What kind of episode?"

"A seizure, but it was more than that. This time I think I was getting my words mixed up when I was speaking. And I couldn't understand what the tech was telling me."

Danica's heart leapt into her throat. "Did you tell them what you felt?"

"Yes."

"And they didn't bring a doctor in?"

"It wasn't necessary. I was fine after a minute."

"Chase. They should've..."

"Shh," Chase said, putting two fingers to Danica's lips. "Can we please just go home? I'm really worn out and I'd like to lie down."

"Of course. Did they say how soon they'd send the results to Doctor Frankel?"

"As soon as they read them, which should mean in a few hours."

"It can't be too soon, if you ask me," Danica muttered, putting her arm around Chase. She led them back inside and through the building to the front entrance. Chase looked beyond exhausted, and the fact that the episodes seemed to be escalating in intensity and frequency scared Danica more than she wanted to admit, even to herself.

CHAPTER TWENTY

C hase and Danica sat alongside each other in the same examination room where Doctor Frankel had given Chase the news of her diagnosis days earlier. Wordlessly, Danica took Chase's hand and stroked the back of it with her thumb. Chase gave her a smile of appreciation.

The three-hour nap she'd taken in Danica's arms had revived her, and she was feeling a little stronger.

"You okay?" Danica asked.

"Yeah. The nap helped a lot. Thanks."

"For what?"

"For staying with me and holding me, even though I knew you weren't tired."

"Chase, it wasn't a hardship to spend quiet time with you. I love lying with you."

"I hate that I'm so tired most of the time. I used to be able to go forever. Now if I can stay up past ten o'clock, it's a miracle."

"Whatever adjustments we need to make, we'll make them together. If you need to nap, we'll nap. If you need to go to bed earlier, we'll go to bed earlier. Whatever it takes to make you well."

"This isn't your problem. You don't have to stay around—"

Danica withdrew her hand. "Or maybe you're still not sure you want me here." She got up and paced to the opposite side of the small room. "Why did you come back, Chase?"

Chase felt the air rush out of her. "What?" The first part of the word was lost to incredulity.

"Why did you really come back to me?"

"Why would you ask me that? I came back because I love you and because I made a mistake that I'll regret for the rest of my life."

Danica was staring into her eyes as if she was looking inside her for the truth of the statement. Chase tried not to fidget and met her stare.

After several heartbeats, Danica said, "I talked to Tisha earlier today while you were having the MRI."

"Oh?"

"I didn't know if you'd spoken to her, and I thought she would want to know about the MRI. I was going to leave it for you, but..."

"It's okay that you called her, Dani. I didn't have a chance to do it myself and it's great that you two like each other. I want you to be friends."

"She told me that she yelled at you."

Chase's cheeks turned hot and her eyes narrowed as she put two and two together. "You're worried that my conversation with Tisha is why I came back."

Danica nodded slightly. "Should I be?"

"It wouldn't say much for me if I could be that easily influenced, now would it? What, you don't think I have a mind of my own? You think she had to tell me what to do?" Chase knew her anger was out of proportion to the situation. Still, she felt powerless to stop it. "I came back because I love you, Dani. I came back because I want to spend the rest of my life with you. If you don't believe me or that isn't good enough for you, get out now." She pointed toward the door. Her heart was beating wildly.

Chase watched Danica's nostrils flare and her jaw set. She could see the hurt in Danica's eyes, the wound reopened. Chase's anger deflated. "I'm sorry." She took two tentative steps toward her. "I'm sorry, Dani. You didn't deserve that. I don't know what happened there. It's not...it's like I can't control my feelings sometimes. I don't know what to do when it's like that."

Danica crossed her arms over her chest. "What do you want from me, Chase?" Tears filled her eyes but did not spill over. "Do you want me here? Because all I want is to be with you. But not if you don't want me here or even if you're just ambivalent about it. If you don't want me here with all your heart and soul, tell me now and I'll go. You'll never have to worry about me bothering you again."

"I want you by my side more than anything in the world, as selfish as I know that is. I can't promise you a future because for all I know I may only have a present—" Chase swallowed hard and her body began to tremble. She shook her head and took a deep breath to regain her composure. "But whatever time I have left to me, I want to spend it with you, if you'll have me."

"Okay then." Danica closed the distance between them. "I don't ever want to hear you offer me a way out again. I know I can leave, Chase. It's my choice to stay because there's nowhere on earth I'd rather be. Understood?"

Chase nodded and opened her arms for Danica to step into her embrace. She lowered her arms when Danica remained just out of reach.

"When you tell me I can go, Chase, it cheapens what I feel for you. It's disrespectful. It makes me wonder if it would matter to you if I left, and I end up feeling less than confident about how much you really care."

Chase opened her mouth to speak and Danica held up her hand.

"I'm not done yet. Maybe you think it's noble to offer me an escape clause. To me, that's actually the coward's way out. Sticking it out together and holding on to love, hope, and optimism—that's so much harder."

"Please come here, Dani," Chase said thickly.

Danica took the last two steps forward and Chase framed her face with her hands.

"I have so much love and respect for you. I always want you to be proud of me, and I'm so lucky that you feel about me the way you do. I don't ever want to do anything to jeopardize that. If I do, please know that it won't be intentional. I'm sure I'll make more mistakes over time, but I'll always hope that we can work through them. Open dialogue and discussion is the way. I'm not always great at the communication thing, but I promise you I'll give it everything I have."

"That's all I can ask. Thank you for hearing me."

"Thank you for making me listen." Chase leaned forward and touched her lips to Danica's. "I love you, Dani."

"I love you too, Chase. We're both under a lot of pressure, and I know that if I'm scared, you must be terrified. We'll get through this…together…I promise you that."

"With you by my side, I can't lose."

There was a knock on the door just as they resumed their seats.

Doctor Frankel entered the room carrying a large manila envelope. "Hi, Chase. Danica, it's good to see you again."

"Thank you, Doctor Frankel, although if you'll forgive me for saying so, I wish we could stop meeting like this."

"Agreed," the doctor said, laughing. He turned to Chase. "How are you feeling? I'm told you had a bit of a rough time of it during the MRI this morning."

"I'm better now, thanks. A nap helped."

"I'm glad to hear that. Rest is important at this point. How have you been feeling otherwise? Obviously, I'm aware of the seizure that prompted this morning's MRI."

"The mood swings are still a problem." Chase looked guiltily at Danica. "And I'm tired almost all the time. The headaches come and go and I had another seizure a few days ago."

"You're taking the medication regularly as prescribed?" Doctor Frankel asked.

"Yes. I haven't missed a dose. I've set up a reminder system in my PDA."

"That was smart. Good for you. Are the memory problems persisting?"

"Yes."

Doctor Frankel shined a light in Chase's eyes. "Now hold your arms out, hands palms up. Close your eyes…okay, you can open them now." He walked to the counter on which he had placed the manila envelope.

"Are those the images from this morning?" Danica asked.

"Yes."

"I hope they took pretty pictures," Chase joked weakly. Her palms were sweating and she rubbed them on her jeans.

"I'm sure Danica here would agree with me that you couldn't take a bad picture."

"That's for sure," Danica said. She intertwined her fingers with Chase's where they rested on Chase's leg.

Doctor Frankel arranged the images on the light box. When he was done, he turned to face the two women. "These pictures are about as clear as we could possibly get, so I'm confident there's enough information here to make some informed decisions. Also, I've had one of my colleagues, Doctor Jacoby, review the images, as well. Doctor Jacoby is a surgeon, and he's one of the best in the country at dealing with CCMs."

At the sound of the word "surgeon," Chase's stomach did a somersault. Danica's grip on her hand tightened.

"Doctor Jacoby and I agree that this location here," Doctor Frankel pointed to a darkened spot on one of the films, "is a new area of hemorrhagic activity."

"Meaning that the lesion is leaking again?" Danica asked.

"Yes, I'm afraid so." Doctor Frankel pointed to the film next to the one he'd just referenced. "This is the image from the other day. You can see right here," he pointed to the corresponding area, "that there was no leakage in that particular spot previously."

"Is the damage extensive?" Danica asked.

Chase was grateful that Danica was taking the lead in the questioning. It was easier to listen than to participate. She was cold again, so very cold. She clamped her jaw shut to minimize the chattering of her teeth and focused on the discussion buzzing around her.

"The hemorrhage was significant. In conjunction with the other evidence we have, it is my opinion that we should consider surgery to remove the lesion."

Chase felt a rushing in her ears. "Brain surgery," she said dully.

"That's right," Doctor Frankel agreed. "Doctor Jacoby has some of the best outcomes in the country for lesionectomies. I've asked him to come in and speak to you both."

"Wait a minute," Danica said. "Before we get to that, what are our other options? Do we have any?"

"Good question. As you've already witnessed, treatment with only the anticonvulsant medication is not working sufficiently to halt all seizure activity. The fact that Chase has had two hemorrhagic episodes in a relatively short period of time and that her symptoms appear to be escalating is a fair indication that the lesion is not stable."

Doctor Frankel walked away from the light box and sat down on his stool in front of Chase and Danica before he continued.

"Any time there is new hemorrhagic activity, it affects healthy brain tissue around the lesion. Since the growth is in the left posterior temporal lobe, there is a danger that speech and memory functions could be permanently affected if the lesion is not removed."

Chase swayed and was vaguely aware of Danica wrapping an arm around her supportively. *This has to be happening to somebody else.*

"I'm sorry," Doctor Frankel said. "I know none of this is easy to hear. But there is good news. The chances of success with this procedure are quite good."

"If—" Danica cleared her throat. "If there's a danger that speech and memory functions could be permanently affected without the surgery because the lesion is that close to the speech and memory centers, is there also a chance that going into that area surgically could cause permanent damage?"

"I'll let Doctor Jacoby speak to that, but I will say that there is always a minimal risk of what we call eloquent areas being affected. Overall, however, the risk of that happening is less than the risk of another hemorrhage if we don't intervene."

"So you're saying I'm damned if I don't, but I may be damned if I do too?" Chase said.

Danica tightened her grip around Chase's waist and Chase leaned into her.

"Let me get Doctor Jacoby and the four of us will discuss it together, all right?" Doctor Frankel rose and left the room.

"We'll get through this, honey," Danica whispered to Chase fiercely. "Side by side. If we're not happy with the answers we get, we'll get another opinion."

"I chose these guys because they're the best, honey. I agree with you, but I don't want to shop for an answer I want to hear. I want to get the best advice there is, regardless of what it is."

"Me too. But before I let someone cut into that beautiful head of yours, I want to be sure we've got the best possible chance of success."

"Chase Crosley and Danica Warren," Doctor Frankel said as he re-entered the room, "please meet Doctor Jacoby."

A tall, middle-aged man with a shock of red hair and a riot of freckles entered on Doctor Frankel's gesture. His engaging manner was warm but professional.

"It's a pleasure to meet you, ladies." Doctor Jacoby shook each of their hands. "Doctor Frankel is very fond of you. I've taken the liberty of reviewing your records and examining the MRIs done today and last week. What I see is a very clear pattern of symptomatic escalation and increased hemorrhagic activity within the lesion and the surrounding area."

"Is there any way of knowing what exactly is causing the 'escalation,' as you call it?" Danica asked.

It was Doctor Jacoby who spoke. "That's hard to answer with any degree of certainty. But most likely what's happening is that the lesion is increasing in mass. As it does so, it's pushing on the adjacent tissue and structures, which, in turn, is wreaking the havoc we've been seeing in the past week or so."

"The symptoms we're talking about—the seizures, the aphasia, the memory issues, the mood swings—can all of that be reversed by removing the lesion?" Chase asked. *Will I be able to get my life back?*

"Odds are in your favor, I believe."

"You believe? Or you know?" Danica asked pointedly.

"If you're looking for a statistic, fifty to ninety percent of patients are completely seizure-free after the operation. However, there's a possibility that Chase might have to stay on medication for the rest of her life, albeit at lower doses."

"So there's a fifty–fifty chance I'll still have seizures afterward?" Chase asked.

"Speaking strictly statistically, yes," Doctor Jacoby said. "However, if we were to consider that prior to one month ago you'd never had a seizure and the fact that you are somewhat medically controlled at this stage, I think our chances are far better than what the statistics show on paper."

"Doctor Frankel has mentioned to us that additional hemorrhages could have long-term consequences for Chase's speech and memory. Are there percentages for which is more risky, intervening surgically in those sensitive areas or trying to control the condition non-invasively?"

Doctor Jacoby looked at Danica appraisingly. "I can see why Chase wanted to bring you along. Your questions are very astute."

"And your answer is?" Danica persisted.

"I'm obligated to tell you that any time we do something invasive, such as a craniotomy, there is a chance that we can affect brain function. Issues such as the aphasia and the memory loss could persist afterward. Also, there is always a risk of hemorrhage and infection. Such complications are unlikely, but in the brain, they can certainly be life-threatening."

"How likely is that?" Danica gripped the examination table for support.

"Assuming you've done this surgery once or twice," Chase interrupted, "has that ever happened with one of your patients?" She struggled to detach herself from the fact that they were talking about her and her brain function and instead tried to think of the questions she'd ask for someone she loved.

"I've never lost a patient. As for the aphasia and memory loss, I can't say it's never happened. I can say that it's relatively rare and that I feel good about your particular potential for a very positive outcome based on your age, your overall health, and the fact that the lesion, while aggressive, is relatively new."

"How many of these procedures have you done?" Danica asked.

"Hundreds. I average a case like Chase's two or three times a month."

"What's the recovery period like?"

"The surgery itself takes anywhere from four to six hours. The hospital stay, depending on how involved the surgery ends up being, could last anywhere from four days up to a week. Then, if necessary, you might go to rehab for speech therapy. That's not always necessary, but I want to lay out all the possibilities for you so that there are no surprises."

"I appreciate that, Doctor," Chase said. "How fast would all this happen?"

"If I had my druthers, I'd operate on you day after tomorrow."

Chase gasped. "That soon?"

"Yes." Doctor Frankel jumped in. "The sooner we take care of it, Chase, the less damage it can continue to do."

"And if we wanted to get another opinion?" Danica asked.

"If you are at all uncomfortable with what we've discussed, please, by all means, get another opinion," Doctor Jacoby said. "I'm confident that any neurosurgeon with experience with cavernous angiomas will tell you the same thing I've told you. But I want you to be comfortable with your decision. This is brain surgery, and that should never be entered into lightly or without very serious consideration."

"Thank you, Doctor. I have one more question for you." Danica leaned forward. "If it were your daughter or your wife, instead of Chase, would you be recommending the same thing?"

Doctor Jacoby also leaned forward. "Ms. Warren, I treat every patient as if she were my daughter or my wife. That's how seriously I take what I do."

"We'd like some time to discuss this," Chase said.

"In order to schedule it for the day after tomorrow, we'll need to know before the end of the day so that we can book the operating room, secure the team, et cetera. Unfortunately, that only gives you an hour or so," Doctor Frankel said apologetically.

"And if we don't decide by then?" Danica asked.

"I'm afraid my next opening isn't until three weeks from now," Doctor Jacoby said. "That's another reason for the urgency. I don't want to wait that long." He looked directly at Danica. "And, yes, if it were my family member, I'd say the same thing."

"Thank you, Doctor. I didn't mean my question to be insulting."

"No offense taken. On the contrary, I wish more patients and their loved ones asked half the questions you did. Good luck to you, ladies, whatever it is you decide."

The two doctors moved into the hallway. After only a few seconds, Doctor Frankel returned. "I apologize. I know this is an awful lot to take in. And it seems crazy that you should have to make such a momentous decision that quickly. If it's any consolation or comfort to you, let me tell you that, ironically, my daughter had a CCM. I entrusted her care to Doctor Jacoby because he is, in my opinion, the very best there is."

"I'm sorry for your daughter, Doctor Frankel," Danica said. "How long ago was this, and how is your daughter doing?"

"It was three years ago and she's never been happier or more herself. She still takes anticonvulsants in low doses, but other than that, she leads a completely normal life. So you can see, I trust Doctor Jacoby with my life."

"That's good to know," Chase said. "What happens if I wait until his next opening?"

"Chase, that man's schedule is atrocious. I couldn't believe our good fortune that he had an opening so soon. If you wait, it could be that he will be unavailable to do the surgery himself. Not only that, but given the progression of the lesion and the sharp increase in seizure activity and related issues, I would urge you most strongly not to delay."

"Thank you, Doctor. Danica and I would like at least a little while to discuss this. I promise you an answer before your office closes today."

"If there's anything else you need or you have any further questions, don't hesitate to call and ask me."

"We appreciate that. Thank you."

Chase and Danica followed Doctor Frankel out of the examination room and headed for their car in silence.

"There's a little park around the corner. Can we go for a walk?" Chase asked as they approached the car.

"Of course. Anything you want."

Chase took Danica's hand and led her down the block and around the corner. They strolled together into the park and along a tree-lined path.

"You think I should get another opinion?" Chase asked.

"I'm actually less worried about that than I am about the short timeframe," Danica answered.

"I know. Day after tomorrow. I've got so much to do."

"What's your feeling about it, Chase? This is your decision to make."

Chase squeezed Danica's hand. "We're in this together, right?"

"Of course. Side by side."

"Then it's our decision to make, not mine."

"Still…"

"I know. I'm scared to death, but I'm more afraid that we'll wait and I'll have another hemorrhage that will do irreparable harm."

"Do you trust him? Do you feel comfortable with him?" Danica asked.

"I think so. Before I chose Doctor Frankel, I checked out his practice and everyone who was in it. Doctor Jacoby was one of the selling points, in my mind. He's operated on foreign princesses and big-name entertainers. He's got a stellar reputation."

"I liked the man. He didn't sugarcoat anything and he wasn't a pompous ass the way some doctors are. He was relatable, and that's a big plus for me."

They stopped walking and stood facing each other, their hands linked and their eyes locked on one another.

"I think he's my best chance, Dani. I want a future with you that's seizure-free. I want to be whole again."

"Then I say we go for it."

"Side by side, right?"

"Side by side," Danica agreed.

CHAPTER TWENTY-ONE

H i, Fish man."

"You sound mega stressed, sugar."

"You can tell that from a 'hello'?"

"Of course. I am attuned to your every inflection."

"That's just scary."

"Perhaps. So, what's got your pretty knickers in a knot this early in the morning? You do know that it's early morning, right?"

"I do, but thanks for telling me." Danica took a steadying breath. "The surgery is tomorrow."

"Surgery? For Chase, you mean?"

"Yes."

"What kind of surgery exactly?"

"The kind where they cut her head open and..." Danica put her hand over her mouth, unable to finish the sentence.

"Oh, honey. Tell me what happened. No, scratch that. Tell me what time the surgery is and where."

When Danica was able to compose herself sufficiently to talk, she gave Ted the details.

"I'll meet you at the hospital at 7:00 a.m."

"Ted—"

"I mean it, Dani. No arguments, no ifs, ands, or buts."

"It will be a long surgery...four to six hours."

"Good. I'll bring a book. Are you okay for now? Where's Chase?"

"She had a million things to do today, as you can imagine. She went to the office to square things away there, then she had some other business she needed to attend to."

"How's she taking it?"

"She's a little shell-shocked, as you might imagine. I know she's frightened, but she won't talk about it."

"Ah, the stoic kind, eh?"

"She's just very private and not used to sharing her feelings. And it's a lot to take in. I don't think the magnitude of it has really hit her yet."

"And you?" Ted asked gently. "Has it hit you yet?"

"I'm painfully aware of the situation, believe me. But there's something to be said for going on autopilot. I'm trying my hardest not to think too much about anything other than what has to happen today."

"And is that working for you?"

"Not so much, but it sounded good, didn't it?"

Ted laughed. "Yep. You had me fooled."

"Liar."

"What are friends for if not to lie to you in your time of need?"

"Thanks, Fish man. You're a rock, and if I haven't said it lately, thank you. Your friendship means more to me than you know."

"Likewise, sugar. You going to be okay until I see you in the morning?"

"Yep." Danica ignored the sudden pressure in her chest. In truth, she wanted to beg Ted not to leave her alone, not to hang up. She wasn't sure she could stand being alone with her emotions at the moment. Instead, she said, "I'm fine."

"Liar."

That surprised a laugh out of her. "Ex-politician's prerogative. We lie for a living, remember?"

"You told me you were the world's only honest politician. I'm crushed to find out that's not true. Crushed, I tell you."

Danica closed her eyes in gratitude. *I love you, Fish man, for understanding what I need right now.* "Liar."

"Now we're even. And that's twice in one conversation you've questioned my integrity. Not that I'm keeping track. A girl could get a complex."

"Ah, Fish man. It's good to see you haven't lost your flair for the dramatic."

"Hence the term *drama queen*, doll. It was invented for me."

"I should've known."

"Better now?" Ted asked, all playfulness gone.

"Much. How did you know I needed that?" Danica's voice was thick with emotion.

"It's okay to ask for what you need, Dani. Anyone who knows you knows how strong you are. It's a sign of strength to lean when you need to."

Danica began to cry. "I can't tell you how grateful I am that with you I never have to ask. You always seem to know just what I need."

"It's too bad I'm not a lesbian, isn't it? We'd be a perfect match."

"First of all, that's a truly frightening thought. And second of all, I'm already spoken for, and so are you, as I recall."

"Pesky details. Pish posh."

"Goodbye, Fish man."

"See you soon, sweetheart."

❧❦

"The reason I've asked you all here," Chase said, raising her voice so that the folks in the back of the training room could hear, "is that I need to step aside temporarily."

A buzz went through the crowd.

"I..." Chase stopped and cleared her throat. There was no way she would break down in front of her staff. These were 125 of the most dedicated, most hard-working people she knew. She respected them, and they, in turn, respected her.

"I'm going in for brain surgery tomorrow. I could be in the hospital for up to a week, and I'm not sure how long I'll need to recuperate at home after that. Jane will have the title of Acting President and CEO. Anything you need, any decisions that need to be made, Jane will have full authority to carry out all the business of the trade association."

"Chase?" The question came from Alicia, the head of Education and Training.

"Yes?"

"What can we do to support you?"

Tears sprang to Chase's eyes and it was several seconds before she could wrestle her emotions under control. "You can carry on and do the same great job you always do for me. I'm so very proud of all of you." She stopped and collected herself again. "I'll see you all soon, I'm sure."

Afraid that she would lose what little was left of her composure, Chase walked to the door. As she was leaving, the staff began to clap. It started with four or five people and swelled until the applause was deafening. Chase paused, her hand trembling on the doorknob. She turned and waved, then hurried down the hall to her office where she closed the door behind her, leaned against it, and wept.

She cried for the love she felt from the staff and for the knowledge that it could be the last time she ever saw them. She cried because it occurred to her that even if she did see them again, she might not be capable of remembering their names, might not be capable of carrying out the responsibilities of her job, might not be able to communicate verbally.

For so long, her career had been everything to her. These people and this place had formed her identity. All of it was in jeopardy. All of it could be gone tomorrow with the slip of a surgeon's knife. *Don't think about it that way. If you do, you won't be able to get anything done. Let's go.*

Chase blew her nose and dabbed at her eyes. She picked up the box of stuff she had decided to take home with her in case she could work during her recuperation.

A knock at the door stopped her in her tracks. She didn't want to see anyone; she didn't think she could handle it. But there was no way around it.

"Come."

Jane stuck her head in the door. "Hey, boss."

"You're the boss now."

"Only temporarily. You're coming back, Chase. I know you are. You'll get through this and be behind that desk again in no time. I'm only keeping the chair warm for you."

Chase smiled tightly. "We'll see."

"Have faith. We're all rooting for you."

"I can't tell you what that means to me."

"The staff loves you. No one can fill your shoes."

"That's not true. If I didn't think you could do the job, I wouldn't have gone to the board with the recommendation to make you acting president this morning. They agreed with me wholeheartedly and without hesitation. You're going to be great."

"I'd rather not be in a position to have to do this," Jane said.

"I know. But it is what it is." Chase shrugged.

"Well, I know you have a lot to do before tomorrow. I'll come by the hospital and check on you."

"Yeah." Chase moved toward the door. "Do me a favor?"

"Anything."

"Will you and Tish take care of Danica for me?" Tears filled Chase's eyes and flowed over. "She's going to need support, and I'd feel better knowing you guys had her back."

"You've got it. But you're going to take care of her yourself."

"Maybe. But not right away, and maybe..." Chase choked on the thought.

"You're going to be fine, Chase Crosley. But if it will make you feel better, Tish and I will be there for both of you."

"Thanks," Chase said. She gave Jane a quick hug and headed out the door.

❧

Danica was physically and emotionally exhausted. It didn't help that she and Chase had gotten little sleep the night before. As if by silent agreement, they'd talked about nothing of great import, instead enjoying the simplicity of each other's company. Neither of them had wanted to close her eyes. The hours were short and sleeping somehow seemed a poor use of time. There would be plenty of time for that...afterward.

And so, Danica was punching her way through her "to do" list. After the conversation with Ted, she'd gone shopping. She'd known exactly what she'd wanted, but finding it hadn't been as easy as she'd hoped. An errand she'd expected would take her two hours at most had turned into an entire morning's venture.

She couldn't escape the feeling that time was slipping away too fast. All she wanted was to spend every second with Chase, but she understood that Chase had obligations to take care of, just as she had her own agenda.

With Tisha's help, she had arranged for someone to take care of Chase's yard and someone else to clean the house every week.

Then she'd gone grocery shopping and picked up the ingredients for the special dinner she planned to make. With those chores covered, Danica finally sat back and waited for Chase to come home.

∾ৎ৯∾

"Are you sure this is what you want, Chase?"

"Positive."

"It's not unusual for people to make emotional decisions at a time like this—"

"Joe," Chase fixed her estate attorney with an icy glare, "this is *exactly* what I want. Can you get it done in an hour or not?"

"I can do it, it's just—"

"Then please hurry. Time is wasting and I have miles to go before I sleep."

"Okay. Come back in an hour."

"Thank you." Chase stood up and shook the lawyer's hand. He'd been her attorney for fifteen years, and she trusted his judgment and his ability to get the job done right, but theirs had always been a somewhat contentious relationship. Chase found him to be opinionated and condescending, and she had little patience for him. His role, as she saw it, was to carry out her wishes as she expressed them, not to make editorial comments about her choices.

She'd hired Joe originally because, at the time, there had been very few gay estate attorneys who understood the complex legal issues that gays and lesbians face. At this moment, she regretted that she hadn't followed through on her vow to find herself another attorney.

Chase checked her watch. She had fifteen minutes to get to the coffeehouse to meet Tisha.

When she arrived, Tisha was already seated at a small table in the corner. Chase ordered coffee and joined her.

"Hey," Tisha said.

"Hi, yourself. I'm sorry we don't have more time."

"I know you're running around like a lunatic, Chase. I honestly didn't expect you to be able to fit me in."

"I wouldn't have missed…Well, anyway, how are you?"

"I'm good. It's you I'm worried about."

"I'm doing fine." Chase shredded her napkin.

"We have little enough time, please don't spend it feeding me the same line of crap you've been dispensing to everyone else. It's demeaning."

"I'm sorry," Chase said sincerely. "I'm having a hard enough time keeping it together in private. I have no interest in turning into a sniveling fool in public."

"No one would blame you. God, I can't believe how calm you are."

"Trust me, I'm not calm on the inside."

Tisha touched the back of Chase's hand. "I'm sure you're not. Jane told me about your meeting with the staff."

"Word travels quickly, as always."

"Surely you didn't expect her not to call me."

"No, I knew she would. I'm sorry. You know how private I am. I hate that everybody knows my business. I feel like everyone's looking at me as if I'm some charity case, and it's making me crazy." Chase started on a second napkin.

"People care about you. Don't expect them to hide that."

"It's not that, it's just…I wish I could just sneak in there under the radar screen, get it done, and come back out as if nothing happened."

"That's a lovely fantasy, but unfortunately, that's all it is."

"I know." Chase sighed and sipped her coffee. "I'm going to ask you the same thing I asked Jane."

"What's that?"

"I need you to promise me…" Chase closed her eyes momentarily and prayed for composure. "I need you to promise me that you'll take care of Danica for me. Make sure she's okay. She's going to need some good friends." Chase's eyes filled with tears despite her best efforts. The fact that Tisha was crying too, was not helping her.

"You'll be here to take care of Danica yourself, Chase. You're too tough to let a little thing like brain surgery hold you down."

"But if I'm not, or if…"

"You're going to come through this with flying colors," Tisha said, gripping Chase's hand tightly. "I don't want to hear any negative thoughts coming from you."

"I'm trying to be realistic, Tish. What happens if I come out of there and I have no short-term memory? Does that mean I won't remember that I love Danica?" Her voice broke. "Can you imagine what she would feel like?" Tears streamed down Chase's face. "I can't…"

"That won't happen, Chase. It won't," Tisha said fiercely.

"We can't know that. What if I don't even know who she is? And that doesn't begin to address the rest of it. If I end up with permanent speech problems, how will I communicate well enough to be able to work, to hold a regular conversation? What if I'm a vegetable?"

"You won't be. You said yourself that Doctor Jacoby is the best there is. He's done hundreds of these operations. You told me so yourself. It's going to be fine. He's going to take the lesion out and you're going to be good as new. You have to believe that. The power of positive thinking goes a long way. You know that."

"I know." Chase wiped her eyes with a tissue. "But I have all these doubts and fears, and I can't tell Danica because she's already bearing a tremendous burden. She lost one lover as she stood by helplessly. Now she's facing the possibility that she'll lose me too, and just like with Sandy, there isn't a thing she can do about it. Imagine what that must be like for her."

"Danica is stronger than you give her credit for. I think you should talk about your fears with her, Chase. She's your partner. She needs to know how you feel."

"But she's got her own stuff—"

"Your stuff *is* her stuff. Just as her stuff is your stuff. That's the way it works. Not only that, but letting her help you and comfort you will make her feel like there's something she can do…like it isn't all out of her control."

Chase nodded. "Maybe you're right."

"Of course I'm right." Tisha sat back in her chair. "I'm always right."

"Modest too. Listen, there's one more thing. I had Joe change my will and create a healthcare power of attorney and all the other good stuff for me. I'm picking the documents up when I leave here. I just want someone to know that I've done that and where I've put them. Joe has a copy, and I'll have a copy in my files in the house."

"You're not going to need those things."

"At the very least, I'll need the power of attorney so that Danica can be treated like family at the hospital. She'll have control over who can visit me, whether to keep me on life support…"

"I get the idea, Chase. Okay. I know where everything is. When it becomes necessary to find those things fifty or sixty years from now, I'll be sure to take care of it for you."

Chase checked her watch. "I've got to go. I've got to get those documents, and I've got one more stop to make before I get home to Dani."

Both women stood. They embraced silently for several minutes.

"You're going to be fine. Next time I see you, you're going to be cracking jokes. And I'm going to be making fun of your bald head."

"Hey, bald is beautiful."

"I'll let you know when I see you."

"Great. That'll give me something to look forward to."

"I'll see you after the surgery." Tisha's voice was hoarse with emotion.

"I'll see you then. Wear a sign in case I don't recognize you."

"Very funny. I love you, Chase."

"I love you too, Tish."

≈୨୧≈

"Hey, sweetheart. I'm home."

"I'm in here," Danica called from the kitchen.

"Mmm. Something smells delicious."

"It's you." Danica turned from the stove and kissed Chase tenderly, nibbling on her bottom lip and licking the spot she'd nipped.

"Keep that up and I'm going to make you turn off the stove." Chase's voice was deep and filled with longing.

"We'll get to that in due time," Danica said, pushing Chase away from her and onto a stool. "For now, sit and watch."

"Hmm. Watching your cute little butt scurrying around my kitchen. That's a tough one. Don't know how I'll manage."

"I have faith in you. How was your day?" When Chase didn't immediately answer, Danica turned to face her. "Are you okay?" She came around the counter and settled between Chase's legs.

"Yeah. I'm not going to say it was easy. First, I had to tell the staff. Those people have worked for me forever."

"I'm sorry, baby, that must've been awful."

"They gave me a standing ovation." Chase's voice was filled with wonder. "Can you imagine?"

"As a matter of fact, I can. Chase, you're easy to love. I'm sure they're all crazy about you."

"You know what?" Chase asked, pulling Danica closer and running her fingers under Danica's shirt. "I don't want to talk about my day."

"You don't?" Danica lost herself in the lush green of Chase's eyes.

"Nope. I don't. I want to talk about us."

"Okay."

"I know this all seems a little crazy. We've had to compress so much into such a short time."

"It isn't about the time that's passed, Chase. That's not how I measure what we have."

"No?"

"No." Danica shook her head. "I knew the second I saw you that you were meant for me. Time will only deepen that bond. Shared experiences will make our love richer and fuller. But the core of what we have has been in place forever."

"I feel the same way," Chase said thickly. "I love you, Dani. With everything I am. I hate that I'm putting you through all this—"

Danica put two fingers over Chase's lips. "Don't ruin a beautiful sentiment. You didn't do this. You didn't ask for it, don't have control over it, and can't take the credit or the blame for it."

"But I've dragged you into it."

"Did you know about the lesion when you met me?"

"No. I only knew I was having wicked bad headaches."

"Right. You didn't know. You have to let go of that guilt. It's misplaced. You can't blame yourself for seeking your life."

"But I'm so worried about you."

"Don't be. I have complete faith that everything is going to work out fine. That you're going to get your life back and we're going to start on the next chapter of our lives...together. Side by side. I hope you feel the same way."

"Who am I to argue with that kind of faith?" Chase fidgeted on the stool. "I...umm...I got you something," she said shyly.

"You did?" Chase seemed unaccountably nervous to Danica, and she found it endearing.

"Yeah. I hope you don't mind." Chase reached in her pocket and pulled out a small velvet box, which she nearly dropped. "I know it's awfully soon, but this is how I feel, and I wanted you to...aw, heck."

Chase got off the stool and knelt down on one knee. "Danica Warren, you are my everything. I can't wait to spend the rest of my life with you. This is a symbol of my love for you. When this is all over, if everything turns out all right, will you marry me?"

Chase opened the box to reveal a beautiful diamond and platinum band.

Danica swallowed hard. Tears of joy clouded her vision and her heart beat double-time, both at the romance of the gesture and at the knowledge that Chase wanted that kind of commitment. "Yes, Chase. And that's not a dependent yes."

"What does that mean?"

"It means for better or worse I'm going to be right here by your side. It isn't about your head, love. It's about your heart. What we have comes from the heart." Danica reached out and brought Chase's hand to her heart as she covered Chase's with her own hand. "Nothing changes that. Not brain surgery or any other physical obstacle. I'm yours forever."

Chase slipped the ring on Danica's left ring finger and held it up to the light.

"It's beautiful," Danica said. Her heart tripped happily. She pulled Chase to her feet and kissed her, putting everything she felt for her into that one kiss.

"Wow," Chase said when they broke apart breathlessly. "I ought to bring you baubles more often."

"Speaking of which," Danica said, reaching into her pocket. "Great minds seem to think alike, and now you've stolen my thunder." She took Chase's hand. "The depth of my love for you knows no limits. It goes beyond the here and now and exists apart from all boundaries." She opened her hand to reveal a three-carat round-cut diamond solitaire with a diamond baguette on either side. "This ring represents a symbol and a promise—from me to you—of forever."

"It's incredible," Chase said, her voice barely a whisper, her face awestruck. "I can't believe—"

"You should believe, Chase. We both should always believe." Danica closed her eyes as Chase kissed her again. They would eat dinner—Danica would make sure of it since Chase wasn't allowed to eat anything after midnight—but for at least a little while, the food could wait.

CHAPTER TWENTY-TWO

The room was dark save for the natural light of the moon floating in through the skylight over Chase's bed. She ran her fingers lightly over Danica's soft skin as Danica lay in her embrace. A tear tracked down her cheek and she sighed.

"What is it, honey?" Danica asked, raising herself up in an effort to see Chase's face. "Are you okay?"

"What if…What if I can't speak when they're done with me? How will I tell you I love you?"

"You tell me with every look and every gesture you make."

"But what if I can never say the words again?"

"You will. And even if you never said them again, I'd know you felt them. Do you know sign language?"

"A little."

"You know the sign for 'I love you'? The thumb, index finger, and pinky held outward?"

"Yes."

"You can always tell me that way."

Chase nodded and pulled Danica a little closer. "I keep thinking that if there's the slightest mistake, the tiniest slip, it could make the difference between me being whole again and me losing important functions."

"We picked Doctor Jacoby because he doesn't make those kinds of mistakes, remember?"

"Yeah, but sooner or later everybody makes a mistake."

"Not this time." Danica kissed Chase's shoulder. "He's going to be steady as a rock."

"Even if he is, what if the lesion is impinging on my memory center or my speech center? Even if he's perfect, there could be residual damage."

"That's not something we can control, honey. We'll have to leave that in his capable hands and trust that he'll know what to do about it. A surgeon who's done hundreds of these surely must have run into that problem once or twice already and figured out how to solve it."

"Dani..." Chase's voice broke, and she buried her face in Danica's neck.

Danica stroked Chase's hair and whispered soothing words to her. Chase let the words run over her, instead focusing on the melodic sound of Danica's voice.

Finally, she whispered the question she'd been most hesitant to ask. "What if I don't remember you or what we have, Dani? What will you do?" She finished the question on a sob.

"Chase," Danica said, sitting up and pulling Chase with her. She turned the bedside lamp on low. "Look at me."

Chase looked into the mesmerizing gold-flecked eyes she loved so well. Danica smiled at her, and Chase fell in love all over again.

"Your heart will always know me, baby, even if your head doesn't. What we have reaches all the way to our souls. Your soul will always recognize mine, just as mine will always recognize yours."

Chase closed her eyes as Danica kissed her forehead, her eyebrows, her eyelids, and finally her lips.

"Besides, think of the fun we could have falling in love all over again," Danica said.

Chase watched the way her eyes twinkled, the easy smile meant just for her, and knew that Danica was right. If she lost every memory she had of them and woke up thinking she was meeting Danica for the first time, she'd fall in love all over again.

"I don't want to hurt you, Dani. If I don't remember..."

"It won't be because you didn't love me. I know that. And it won't be because I wasn't important to you. It's a physiological thing. It's not emotionally based."

Danica cradled Chase in her arms, and Chase felt utterly safe and protected.

"I won't leave, Chase. Not for that reason or any other. Side by side, remember?"

"I remember."

Danica shifted until their naked upper torsos were in full contact. "I love you, Chase Crosley. I'll always love you. You're a part of me and nothing will change that."

"I love you, Danica Warren. Nothing, not even death, could change that."

Danica gently collected a tear off Chase's eyelashes and replaced it with a kiss. Chase leaned in to the pressure. She sighed as Danica tipped her chin up and kissed her softly on the mouth.

Chase's nostrils flared as silky smooth skin glided over her, leaving gooseflesh in its wake. Skilled fingers traced a path over her awakening nipples, then disappeared, and she groaned. Kisses along her shoulders, collarbone, and throat made her nerves sing, and she felt herself arching into Danica to prolong the contact.

"Your body will always know mine, baby. Just as it does now."

Danica's voice was deep and sensuous, and Chase shuddered at the sound of it next to her ear.

"I love you, Dani."

"I love you too, Chase."

"I want to feel you on top of me. Against me."

Danica hovered over Chase, waiting, suspended by her arms and feet, until Chase was flat on her back. Then slowly, as Chase watched, she lowered herself so that their mounds touched each other.

The first contact made Chase shiver. Danica slid against her, the slickness of her desire leaving a path of heat along the length of Chase's clit. Chase gasped and pulled Danica harder against her. She filled her hands with Danica's firm buttocks, as Danica rocked into her, bringing their clits into full contact.

The feeling was beyond anything Chase had ever experienced. Her soul soared, reached a peak, and soared again. She could feel Danica's soaring with her. It was as if the moment, the sensation, the connection, existed apart from time and space, as if they were outside themselves, their bodies merely the vessels to record the moment.

Chase saw the look of awe on Danica's face and knew that she had felt it too.

"I've never felt anything like that."

"That was our souls touching," Danica said. "More proof that you will always know me, love. You will."

Danica slid her body lower and kissed Chase's center. Her thumb made lazy circles on Chase's clit, and within seconds Chase came again. Before she had a chance to recover, Danica entered her with two fingers, stroking her to the same rhythm that her tongue played on her clit.

"Dani," Chase gasped, as she came for a third time.

"This is what love feels like, Chase. It will always feel like this. Your body will always answer to mine."

"Always," Chase said and reversed their positions. She felt an insatiable need to taste Danica, to feel her, to stroke her. Tears streamed down her face as she watched Danica enraptured as she loved her. "I love you, Dani," she whispered, as Danica came with a cry. "I'll always love you."

"I know, baby, I know." Danica pulled Chase up until they were wrapped so tightly around each other it was impossible to tell where one of them started and the other one ended.

They rocked each other, crying, stroking, and murmuring words of love, until just before daylight.

"I'll never forget you, Dani," Chase said, kissing Danica on the shoulder.

"And I'll always be here, love."

"We have to get up."

"I know."

Still, it was long minutes before they rose and headed to the bathroom to get ready for the day.

"Hi, Chase. I'm Jolie. In this case, I'm known as the barber of Albany Medical Center." She held up electric clippers to make her point.

Chase was already lying on a bed, dressed in a hospital gown with a sheet draped over her. She had an IV port taped to the bend in her right arm and another IV line in the back of her left hand. Danica was sitting on the side of the bed with her, holding her right hand.

Danica watched Chase's eyes widen and assumed it was at the thought of having her head shaved. She nudged her. "Hey, you're going to be just like Demi Moore in *GI Jane*. How cool is that? Very sexy," she purred.

"You think? What if my head is shaped like an egg? I'll look like an idiot."

"Your head is beautiful, and you're going to look very sexy. If you want, I'll let Jolie shear me too."

Chase stared at Danica in horror. "No way. I love your hair."

"It'll grow back," Danica said, shrugging. Her offer wasn't impulsive; she'd been thinking about it since they'd agreed to the surgery. She knew that Chase might feel awkward and self-conscious about how she would look, and although going bald wasn't something she relished, she certainly would do it in solidarity.

"That's a very sweet offer, but I'd rather be able to run my hands through your hair, if you don't mind."

"It's your call, honey."

"Jolie, make me pretty," Chase said, smiling gamely.

"For a pretty woman like you, that's a cinch."

When Jolie was done, Chase asked to see a mirror.

"You look great, sweetheart. No egg heads for you." Danica ran her hand lovingly over Chase's shaved head while Jolie retrieved a hand mirror.

Chase regarded the results critically.

Although she smiled and made a joke, Danica saw the ill-concealed shock in her expression. She leaned over and whispered in Chase's ear. "I really do think it looks sexy on you, love. I can't wait to show you just how sexy." Danica was rewarded with a shiver.

Doctor Jacoby poked his head in the room. "I see we're just about ready. I just stopped by to see how you were feeling."

"Nervous," Chase answered honestly.

"That's to be expected. If you weren't, I'd have to have your head examined."

Both Danica and Chase groaned.

"I know...don't quit my day job," Doctor Jacoby joked. "Seriously, everything looks good. I've talked to the team and prepped them for the procedure. All systems are go. Do you have any questions before I scrub?"

Danica felt Chase tremble beside her and decided a little levity was in order. "What did you have for breakfast, and did you get a good night's sleep?" She winked at him.

"Wheaties, breakfast of champions, of course, and I slept very well. I'm feeling fit as a fiddle. In fact, I could run a marathon today if I had to. Fortunately, all I have to do is brain surgery."

"All," Chase echoed. "You didn't happen to read your horoscope today, did you?"

"Thankfully not. So we're safe there." He came over and squeezed Chase and Danica's joined hands. "I'm going to take great care of you, Chase. As for you," he glanced at Danica, "I'll come out to the waiting room just as soon as I'm finished to give you the good news. Remember, it could be quite a while. That doesn't necessarily mean anything bad. This is a complex procedure and I want to make sure I do everything right."

"I appreciate that, Doctor. Take good care of my girl." Danica felt tears prick her lashes and she willed them not to fall. Once they took Chase away there would be plenty of time to feel. For now, she needed to stay strong.

When Doctor Jacoby was gone, yet another nurse came in. "The anesthesiologist will be in shortly." She looked at her watch. "You've probably got about three to five minutes." She winked at them and left.

Danica's heart skipped a beat, and she could just imagine what Chase's heart was doing. Suddenly, there was so much she wanted to say, and she had no idea where to start. "I love you, Chase. That's forever."

"I love you too, Dani. Together, right?"

"Side by side," Danica said, leaning over to rub her cheek against Chase's cheek. "Feel this?" Danica asked, putting Chase's hand over her heart. "That beats for you alone. I'll be waiting for you."

Chase nodded mutely as tears ran down her face. She bit her lip.

"Don't cry, honey. We're going to fix you so that you and I will have a lifetime together where you're seizure-free and better than ever."

"I know," Chase choked out. "My heart will always know you, right?"

Danica couldn't stop her own tears at how small and uncertain Chase looked and sounded. "Your heart will always, always know me, I promise you," she said with all the conviction she could muster.

Chase looked down at their joined hands. "I guess you'd better take this," she said, reluctantly surrendering her ring.

"I'll keep it safe for you." Danica kissed her fingers.

Chase fingered Danica's ring. "I'm going to marry you," she said determinedly.

"I'm counting on it," Danica said, running her fingertips lightly over Chase's skull. "My sexy girl."

The anesthesiologist knocked and entered. "Okay. Show time. Chase, first I'm going to give you something to make you sleepy. That will only take a minute. Then we're going to wheel you to the operating room, okay?"

"Okay."

As the doctor prepared to put the needle in the IV tube, Chase put a hand on his arm. "One second." Her voice shook and she looked at Danica with desperation. "I love you with all my heart, and I always will. Even if my brain loses you, I'll still love you."

"I know, baby." Danica leaned over and kissed Chase gently on the mouth, conveying with that action the words she was too emotional to say. She gulped and swallowed a sob. "I love you, Chase. Come back to me."

"Side by side." Chase's voice trembled.

"That's right. Side by side. Your heart will always know me."

Chase nodded at the doctor. "Go ahead."

"Until soon, my love," Danica said, gripping Chase's hand tightly.

"Until soon," Chase agreed, squeezing back. Within a few seconds, her eyes started to droop shut.

As two orderlies wheeled Chase away with a nurse alongside monitoring her vital signs, the anesthesiologist paused and touched Danica on the arm. "She's in good hands."

"Thank you. I'm counting on that."

When Chase was completely out of sight, Danica walked down the hall on rubbery legs to the private surgical waiting room. To her surprise, Ted, Toni, Tisha, and Jane were all there.

"It's seven in the morning, don't you all have anything better to do?" she asked as her composure finally slipped the rest of the way. Her whole body shook violently, and she let out a small cry of distress. Chase was gone and she wouldn't know for hours—maybe days or months—if she'd ever really be coming back.

Before Danica could take another step, all four friends rushed forward and enveloped her in a group hug.

ھوپ

Danica didn't know how long she'd been crying or how it was that she came to be sitting. She had a box of Kleenex in her hand that she didn't remember having been given. Ted was kneeling in front of her, Toni and Tisha were seated to either side, and Jane walked over with a cup of water.

"Drink this. You'll feel better."

"Thanks," Danica said hoarsely. Her mouth felt like someone had stuffed wads of cotton in it, so she drank greedily. "Sorry about that, guys."

"Don't be," Toni said. "That was a lot to carry around. You needed to get it out."

"I haven't seen waterworks that impressive since my trip to Niagara Falls in grade school," Ted said. "You go, girl."

"I wish I could promise you that it won't happen again, but I can't guarantee that."

"Nobody expects you to hold it all in, Danica," Tisha said. "Toni's right…it's not healthy."

"I see you've all met," Danica said, regaining some of her emotional equilibrium.

"Yes, we bonded over the coffee machine," Toni said.

"How did you get here? When did you get here?" Danica asked her.

"I took the train up last night. You sounded a little rough on the phone yesterday, and I figured you might need reinforcements."

"Thanks," Danica said, touching Toni on the cheek. "That's way above and beyond."

"This isn't about being your agent, Dani dear. It's about being your friend."

"I know," Danica said sheepishly. She had called Toni while Chase was out running errands the day before and brought her up to speed. She wanted to give Toni as much lead time as possible to cancel or reschedule anything that was on the calendar for the next month or more.

Despite the fact that Danica knew Toni was less than enthralled with Chase's earlier behavior, Toni had been nothing but supportive.

"Anybody for a game of Trivial Pursuit?" Ted asked, pointing to the board game on the table.

"You've got to be kidding," Danica said.

"Nope. It may be my one and only chance to wipe the floor with you. I couldn't pass up the opportunity."

"You're a sick man," Danica said, shaking her head.

"Given. Are you game or what?"

Toni, Tisha, Jane, and Danica all groaned at once.

"What?" Ted asked, feigning innocence.

"That was a terrible pun, that's what," Danica said.

"Can't blame a girl for trying." Ted pretended to pout.

"You're pathetic. Okay. Let's do it." Danica didn't feel like playing a game. She didn't feel like doing anything except running down the hall to the operating room and holding Chase. But she appreciated Ted's effort to take her mind off things, and she didn't want to hurt his feelings.

The game actually turned out to be a good distraction for a while, and despite her obviously wandering mind, Danica still won handily.

"That was just so unfair," Ted said.

"Stop whining," Toni said.

"She won on a constitutional question. That was a slam dunk. Why couldn't it have been a geography question?"

"Let's face it, Fish man, you're never going to beat me," Danica said.

"Gloating will get you nowhere." He sat back and crossed his arms over his chest.

"That wasn't gloating. That was just a fact." Danica checked her watch.

Tisha put a hand on her arm. "The time will pass more quickly if you stop looking at that."

Danica got up and paced. "It's been hours."

"It's been three hours," Jane said. "The doctor said it would be at least four. If they were done already, I'd be worried."

"I suppose. It's just…" Danica put her forehead against the wall. She felt Ted's hand on her shoulder. "Keep the faith, sugar."

"I'm trying," Danica said tremulously. She turned and faced the others. There was a question she'd wanted to ask for a while, and she hadn't known how to approach it.

"Where is Chase's family? Why are they not here?"

Tisha cleared her throat. "I doubt she told them about it."

"Why?" Danica asked.

"Do you know anything about Chase's upbringing?"

"I know that she was very close to her grandfather who lived in Florida, and he's dead. Other than that, I don't know much. She doesn't talk about it."

"I know," Tisha said. "It was a long time before she confided in me. I don't think she ever would've, except that I asked her point blank one day."

"If she doesn't want me to know…"

"I'm sure she'd get around to it, Danica." Tisha took a deep breath. "Her father died in Vietnam near the beginning of the conflict. Chase was barely seven years old."

"That sucks," Ted said.

"Royally," Toni added.

"Yeah, it did. Chase was really close to him. She was definitely a daddy's girl. Her mother took the death hard. She was pregnant at the time, and she miscarried when she got the news."

"God," Jane said. "I never knew any of this. Chase never said a word."

"From what I can gather, her mother couldn't bear to look at Chase because she was the spitting image of her father. So Chase pretty much raised herself, except for the time she spent visiting her grandparents in Florida. Her mother shipped her off there often. As you can imagine, she and her mother don't keep in touch."

"Oh, Chase," Danica murmured. "No wonder you're worried about me leaving you." Danica's heart mourned for the little girl who had, in essence, lost both parents to war.

And now she was fighting a war of her own—a war to survive.

CHAPTER TWENTY-THREE

Danica stopped pacing mid-stride and stood stock still as she watched Doctor Jacoby walk down the hall toward her. She'd been too antsy to stay in the waiting room and so had been wandering the hall outside while the others played cards.

He looked tired, and Danica's heart leapt into her throat. It had been six hours since they had wheeled Chase into the operating room. That was the outside length of time the doctor had said the operation could take, and Danica worried that the length of time corresponded to difficulties encountered during the surgery.

She tried to speak as he came within hearing distance, but nothing came out. Her legs wobbled and she leaned against the nearest wall. "Is she…" Danica finally was able to force out.

"She's okay," Doctor Jacoby said, reaching out and grasping Danica by the shoulder.

Danica closed her eyes tightly and tears leaked out. Her lips trembled uncontrollably, and she put her hand up to cover her mouth. When she opened her eyes again, the doctor was gazing at her kindly.

"I'm not going to tell you it was easy because it wasn't. The lesion was bigger than I originally anticipated. Also, because it was in the posterior-most portion of the left temporal lobe, I was concerned about affecting speech functions."

"And?" Danica asked, her voice shaking.

"I think we're okay. Of course, we'll have to wait and see to be sure. These things are very tricky. It could be days before we really know."

"Her memory?"

"Again, we'll have to wait and see. I was able to resect the entire lesion, and I took a small remaining clot around the CCM. My hope is that I've eliminated the areas that were causing the seizures."

"You got all of it?"

"Yes, I got all of it. I had to detach the upper temporalis muscle attachment from the temporal bone, so I had a wonderful view of the full temporal lobe. There was a little more bleeding than I would've liked because of the length of time we were in there, but I wanted to spend the time to make sure we got everything we needed to get."

Danica's teeth chattered as a chill swept through her. She didn't want to imagine Chase, her head cut open and bleeding, her brain laid bare. "And you're confident that you did? You're positive?"

"As positive as I can be. It will be some time, maybe six months or more, before we'll know exactly where we stand. But I'm confident that it was a good surgery."

"Can I see her?"

"She'll be in the PACU for about an hour, but I think we can sneak you in there for a minute to say hello."

"The PACU?"

"The Post-Anesthesia Care Unit. Come on." He took Danica by the elbow. She was grateful for the support. Her legs still felt like Jell-O.

On the way by the waiting room, she stuck her head in and said, "I'm going to go see Chase for a second." Her voice only shook slightly, and she was grateful.

The room was divided into cubicles. Chase was in the third cubicle to the left. Danica sucked in a sharp breath as she got a good look at her. Her head was encased in a gauze turban and tubes and machines were everywhere. Her eyes were shut.

Danica hesitated at the foot of the bed. *God, baby.*

"It's okay," Doctor Jacoby said gently. "You can hold her hand and talk to her."

Danica slid her hand underneath Chase's so that their palms touched. She lowered her head and kissed the back of Chase's hand. "Hi, love. I'm here."

Chase stirred and her eyes opened a fraction. She mumbled groggily.

Danica didn't understand what she said, but the fact that she was able to speak at all brought tears to her eyes. "I love you, honey."

Chase said something else unintelligible and closed her eyes again.

"We should let her get some rest," Doctor Jacoby said.

"Right." Danica watched Chase for a few seconds more. She looked so fragile. "Together, sweetheart. You're going to be fine." She leaned over and touched her lips to Chase's.

"We'll get her into a room and settled in an hour or so."

Danica took one more look back as the doctor led her out into the hallway.

"How long will she have to stay in the hospital?"

"Four days to a week. I would say we're looking at closer to a full week based on the complicated nature of the procedure and other factors."

"But I can stay with her?"

"That'll depend on hospital policy. I don't have an objection except that you'll both need to get some rest."

"I'll rest better if I can be near her."

"I understand. I'll let the nurses know I have no problem with that arrangement, but I imagine they'll insist on sticking with whatever the hospital rules say."

"Okay." She swallowed hard as the tension of the day caught up with her. "I can't..." She took a moment to compose herself. "Thank you, Doctor Jacoby. For everything." Impulsively, she reached up and hugged him hard.

"You're welcome, Danica. I'll be in to check on Chase later."

"Okay."

He smiled at her. "It's going to be okay."

"Right," she said.

❧ঔ৹

Chase was vaguely aware of activity around her—hushed voices, pressure on her arm, bright lights in her eyes—but she wasn't able to hold on to any of it long enough for it to make sense to her.

She smelled something spicy sweet. The aroma was familiar, but she couldn't place it. A voice whispered something in her ear. The timbre of it made her feel warm inside, although she couldn't make out the words.

Something soft brushed against her cheek. With effort, she opened her eyes. A beautiful woman was leaning over her; she looked familiar, but a name would not come.

The woman's mouth was moving. Chase could hear the sounds, but the words held no meaning for her. The woman caressed her cheek, and Chase smiled at her. "Home," she thought, although she didn't know why. She closed her eyes and surrendered to sleep again.

When next she woke, there was a man in a tie and lab coat standing over her. A doctor.

"Eyes…into…look."

Chase squinted. She understood that he was asking her to do something, but she couldn't make out what it was. He leaned over with a small flashlight and shone it into her eyes. She blinked and pulled back. The pain from the motion was instantaneous and sharp. Chase heard herself cry out.

The beautiful woman was back. Chase could see her out of the corner of her eye. She looked concerned. And tired, Chase thought. She looked so tired. There was a soft touch on her hand and Chase looked down to see that the woman had taken her hand. She smiled at her.

The doctor was standing over her again. His mouth was moving, but Chase only caught a few words intermittently.

"…responding…poorly…days…wait…" He shook his head and moved away.

Chase followed his progress until he disappeared from sight. She turned her head and pain exploded behind her eyes. She cried out again.

"…still…love."

The woman…D?…was crying as she leaned down to whisper in her ear.

"No…tears."

"What?"

Chase slowly raised her arm until she was able to touch D's face with her fingertips. D turned her palm and kissed it and Chase closed her eyes as the pain receded.

⋘⋙

Danica let the hot water sluice over her tight neck and shoulders. Tears flowed freely down her face, as they had every morning since the surgery. She leaned against the wall of the shower stall and prayed that this day would be the one that Chase would come back to her.

It had been three days since the surgery, and although Chase appeared to recognize her face, she had yet to call Danica by name or to respond properly to verbal commands. Danica only needed to look at Doctor Jacoby's expression each day to know that he was deeply concerned.

She turned the water off. Chase was a fighter, and there was still time.

⋘⋙

"Hello?" Danica answered the cell phone with her Bluetooth as she navigated downtown traffic.

"Where are you?"

"Hi, Fish man. On my way to the hospital."

"Did you get any rest last night?"

"Some."

"You're a bad liar, sugar. What's the latest?"

Danica checked her mirrors and moved to the right lane. "I think she understood me for a second yesterday. I was crying and she said 'no tears.' That's appropriate, right?"

"Of course it is. That's great."

"That's the first time she's responded properly to something going on around her."

"That's encouraging. What does the hunky Doctor Jacoby say?"

"You're incorrigible."

"Part of my charm, doll. Well, what does he say?"

"He's very concerned about the extent of the aphasia and the memory gaps. I asked him if it was unusual for those issues to last this long after surgery. He said he wasn't ready to call out an alarm yet, but if it continues much longer..." Danica blinked back tears and gripped the steering wheel more tightly. She needed to face the truth. "If it continues much longer, it could be permanent." She was barely able to whisper the last word.

"She'll turn it around, Dani. Keep the faith."

"I'm trying, Fish man. Really, I am. But..." Danica pulled off the road onto the shoulder and rested her forehead on the wheel.

"Today's a new day. Every day that goes by, her head heals a little more."

"Every day that goes by is one day closer to her not being able to come back."

"You can't think like that, sugar. I know it's hard, but you have to stay positive. She responded to you yesterday, right?"

"Right."

"That's a start."

"Yes, it is." Danica straightened up and wiped her eyes.

"Say it once more with feeling."

"Yes, today is another day," Danica said with more conviction.

"That's my girl."

"I've got to go. I want to be there when visiting hours start."

"They won't change their minds about letting you stay with her?"

"They've been great about letting me stay after hours, but they won't let me stay overnight."

"Okay then. I won't keep you. Chin up, Dani. I'll check in with you later."

"Thanks, Ted."

৵৶

Chase pushed the button to elevate her upper torso. The door opened and she smiled. "Hi."

"Hi."

"When's the last time I told you I loved you?"

"What?"

"I love you, Dani." Chase crooked her finger and beckoned Danica to come closer.

"Did you just say what I heard?" Danica's voice shook and tears filled her eyes as she approached the bed.

"I love you, baby."

"Oh, Chase." Danica reached over and hugged her gently. "Say it again."

Chase breathed in the smell of Danica's shampoo, mixed with the spicy-sweet scent of her perfume. Home. "I love you with all my heart, Danica Warren."

"I love you too, Chase Crosley. So very, very much."

"What's for dinner this morning?"

"Huh?"

"Breakfast? What's on the bill?"

Danica looked at her oddly. "Has Doctor Jacoby been in yet?"

"No."

"Maybe I should see if he's around."

Danica sounded panicked and Chase felt a frisson of fear tickle her spine. "Don't stay."

"You mean 'don't go'?"

"Yes."

"Okay."

"Can you lie with me?" Chase patted the bed beside her. She needed to feel Danica next to her.

"You bet."

Chase shifted to her left to make room, and Danica climbed gingerly onto the bed. "I don't want to hurt you."

Chase wrapped an arm around her. "Just don't jostle my head."

"I'll be very careful."

"I miss you, Dani."

"I've missed you so much."

Danica's voice was shaking again and Chase frowned. "You look exhausted. I don't like it."

"I'm fine."

"They did the surgery, right?"

"Right, honey."

"How long ago?"

"Three days."

"I don't remember—" Chase's stomach dropped. "Three days?"

"It's okay, Chase."

"My head hurts."

"I know."

"Did it work?"

"The surgery?"

"Yes." Chase felt Danica stiffen beside her. "What is it?"

"Nothing. Doctor Jacoby says he got the whole lesion."

"That's good, right?"

"Right."

"So why do you look like you lost your best friend?"

"No," Danica smiled. "I'm good."

"There's something you're not telling me." Chase pulled back a little so that she could see Danica's face better. The motion sent shockwaves of pain through her skull. "Argh."

"Oh, honey. You can't make sudden movements like that."

"I get that now." Chase closed her eyes and waited for the pain to subside. "What's going on, Dani?"

"Well, this is an encouraging sign." Doctor Jacoby said from the doorway. He pulled out a penlight as he approached the bed. "How are you feeling today, Chase?"

"My head feels like someone ran over it in the parking lot."

Doctor Jacoby laughed. "Fantastic."

"That's a good thing?"

"Yep. We call that progress. Do you know where you are?"

"The hospital."

"Good." Doctor Jacoby shined the light in her eyes and Chase blinked hard.

"Who is that lying next to you?"

"Danica."

"Excellent."

"What do you do for a living?"

Chase pursed her lips together. "I don't know." Her stomach sank.

"No problem. Rome wasn't built in a day."

"Was the surgery successful?"

"I was able to remove the entire lesion and a small blood clot around the CCM."

Chase frowned again. "You didn't really answer the question."

"Are you asking me if you'll have any remaining deficits?"

"Yes."

"Let's just say that I take the fact that you understood my question as a very encouraging sign."

"Things seem jumbled sometimes. Like I hear you or Danica talking, but I can't discern the meaning. And I know I'm mixing up some of my words."

"You've still got some residual aphasia and some short-term memory issues."

"Will they be permanent?"

"I can't answer that, Chase. It's early yet."

"When will we know?"

"It's hard to say. I'm sorry. I'm not trying to be deliberately vague. That's just the truth. It's possible that you'll have the same kind of problems you had before the surgery for a short while, then it may resolve itself. Or it could be that these deficits could be permanent. I know that's not what you want to hear."

Chase felt the tension in Danica's body next to her. She rubbed her hand up and down Danica's side. "I need to know the truth. That's all I ask for."

"Who was president of the United States when you were born, Chase?"

"Lyndon B. Johnson."

"What's the last trip you took?"

Chase narrowed her eyes in thought. "I don't know," she whispered.

Danica stroked her arm. "It's okay. It'll get better."

"Maybe," Chase said bitterly.

"How's the pain level?" Doctor Jacoby asked.

"On a scale of one to ten?"

"Sure."

"Twelve."

Doctor Jacoby chuckled and consulted Chase's chart. "Okay. Well, right now I've got you at the maximum dosage of pain meds that I'm comfortable with, so I'm afraid you're going to have to grin and bear it for a bit."

"Gee, thanks."

"Sorry about that." He wrote something in the chart. "Overall, I have to say, today is a good day. You've made significant progress, Chase, and that's really, really good. Don't be discouraged."

When the doctor was gone, Chase closed her eyes.

"Tired?" Danica asked.

"Exhausted. Will you sleep with me for a little while?" Chase was tired, true, but she was more worried about Danica, whose eyes were deeply etched with shadows.

"Of course."

Chase pulled Danica's arm across her and used the electric controls to lower the head of the bed. Rest and time would do them both good.

��

"You aren't supposed to be up and around," Danica said disapprovingly.

Chase took Danica in her arms and kissed her softly on the mouth. "I smelled something good."

"It's dinner, but you don't get any unless you get back in bed." Danica nudged Chase gently. It was so good to have her home. She'd picked Chase up three days earlier. Just to be able to sleep close enough to hear her breathe gave Danica peace of mind.

"I'm bored."

"Tough." Danica put down the knife she'd been using to chop vegetables, turned off the stove, and took Chase by the hand. "Let's go, you. Back to bed." When Chase seemed about to object, Danica added, "Now."

"Slave driver."

Danica put a supportive arm around Chase's waist and led her toward the bedroom. "I can't believe you got up by yourself."

"I told you, I was compelled to follow my nose."

"Next time you pull a stunt like that, you can go to bed without dinner, smart girl."

"You're just cruel."

When they reached the bed, Danica wrapped both arms around Chase to help ease her onto the bed.

"I…"

Chase's eyes went unfocused and Danica felt her tremble in her arms. "Chase?" She got no response. "Chase?" *Oh, God. No.* "Chase?" Danica heard the edge of panic in her own voice. "Come back to me." She pulled Chase tight into her body and supported her weight.

"I...I'm okay."

Danica helped her down onto the bed until she was resting in a comfortable position. "I'm going to call Doctor Jacoby." She didn't wait for Chase to answer her. Her heart hammered in her chest.

"Doctor Jacoby's answering service."

"This is Danica Warren, Chase Crosley's partner. Doctor Jacoby operated on Chase ten days ago. Something's wrong. Can you get him for me right away?"

"I'll reach him for you and have him call you back."

Danica hung up without saying goodbye. She sat on the bed next to Chase and stroked her cheek. Chase looked exhausted. Doctor Jacoby hadn't said anything about further seizure activity. He'd said that he'd gotten the entire lesion and that that should've solved the problem.

"I'm okay, Dani."

"I know, baby." Danica knew her voice was shaking. She couldn't help it. When the phone rang, she snatched it up on the first ring.

"Hello?"

"This is Doctor Jacoby. What's going on?"

"Chase just had a significant seizure."

"Is she conscious?"

"Yes."

"Is she lucid?"

"Yes."

"Okay."

"I didn't think...she wasn't supposed to have any more seizures, right?" Danica asked plaintively.

"That was the plan. But you just don't know. She's been taking her medication regularly?"

"Yes. I've been giving the pills to her myself."

"Okay. Does she appear to be comfortable now?"

"Yes."

"I want to see her in my office first thing in the morning."

"What if she has another seizure?"

"Hang tight, Danica. Keep her comfortable. If she has another seizure, call me back."

"Okay."

When Danica got off the phone and looked over at her, Chase was asleep. Danica lay down next to her and watched her for a long time.

࣯ঌয়ঌ

"How do you feel this morning?"

Chase looked up at Doctor Jacoby. The seizure the previous evening and the trip in the car to get to his office had taken a lot out of her. All she wanted to do was lie down. "Peachy."

"Now how about the truth?"

"I'm exhausted."

"Did last night's seizure feel any different to you than ones you've had previously?"

"No. Was that supposed to happen?" In truth, it had scared the daylights out of her.

"These things are unpredictable, Chase. Do you remember when I told you that fifty to ninety percent of patients who undergo this surgery are seizure-free post-operatively? It was not beyond the realm of possibility that you could have additional seizures, but I had hoped you'd be seizure-free once the lesion and adjacent clot were excised."

"So does this mean I'm part of the other ten to fifty percent? Will I have more seizures? Is there a chance it could be as bad as it was before the surgery?"

"It's possible, although I'd like to hope not." Doctor Jacoby shined the penlight in Chase's eyes. "Mmm-hmm. Now hold your arms out with your palms up. Close your eyes."

Chase followed his instructions.

"Looks good," he said.

"Meaning?" Danica asked.

"Meaning everything looks the way it should this morning."

"Now what happens?"

"We get Chase back home and into bed, let her get some rest, continue to follow the post-surgical protocol, and let time do its bit."

"And if there are more seizures?" Danica asked.

Chase heard the aggravation and tension in her voice. She was still worried about Danica. She hadn't been getting nearly enough sleep and was running herself ragged taking care of her.

"As I said, it's not beyond the realm of possibility," Doctor Jacoby answered. "It will be six months to a year before we know for sure how successful the surgery was."

"So we do nothing in the meantime?"

"No. I'll check Chase's blood to ensure that the drug level is what it should be. If it's low, that might explain the seizure. If the level is low, we can increase the dosage. If it's in the therapeutic range already, all we'll be able to do is wait and hope that this seizure is the last."

Danica tucked Chase into bed and put a fresh glass of water on the night table.

"Dani, come here."

"What?" Danica asked.

Chase could see that she was fighting off tears. "Lie down with me."

"You need to get some rest."

"Yes, and I'll rest much better if you're snuggling with me."

"But—"

"Danica, please." Chase opened her arms and waited for Danica to comply.

She did. "I'm afraid I'll jostle you."

"I know. That's why you keep your distance at night."

"What if I accidentally bump into you?"

"I'm not made of glass, Dani."

"No, but I don't want to hurt you."

"I miss you."

"I miss you too, Chase." Danica's voice broke.

"I'm right here. I know I'm not one hundred percent. I know my short-term memory still sucks and I get mixed up with speech occasionally, but we have to give it time."

"I know. I just want so badly for everything to be perfect."

"And I thought I had a problem being patient. You make me seem like patience itself."

"Very funny."

"Come here." Chase gestured to her lap and indicated that she wanted Danica to straddle her.

"I'm too heavy. I'll hurt you."

"Honey, I won't break. Please."

Danica slowly lowered herself until she was sitting astride Chase. They were nose to nose.

Danica was looking down, and Chase frowned. "Look at me, baby."

Danica reluctantly looked up. There were tears in her eyes.

"What is this about, really?"

"I talked you into the surgery. I was convinced it could fix everything and you could have your life back. What if I was wrong? What if I put you through all that for nothing? I risked your life and almost lost you and—"

"Whoa." Chase put two fingers under Danica's chin and urged her forward until their mouths were fused together. Gently, carefully, she explored Danica's mouth. She pulled back slightly until their lips were a whisper apart. "You're my hero, you know that?"

"I am? Why?"

"Because you always, always, believe in the best possible outcome. So many people see insurmountable obstacles and give up. Not you. You fight to the end and never accept anything less than total success."

"And in the two instances where it mattered most, I failed miserably."

"Danica Warren, that is not true. Sometimes fate has a different plan. You did everything humanly possible to save Sandy. It wasn't meant to be. And as for me, let's set the record straight."

When Danica would've looked away, Chase stopped her.

"First of all, you didn't push me into anything. I wouldn't have let you. I decided to have the surgery because it was the right thing to do. It offered the best hope of a positive outcome, and I grabbed it because I would rather have died than not have a full life and a future with you."

"Chase."

"No, Dani. That's the truth. It was my choice and I'm not sorry. Second, I know you're tired. I know you've put your life on hold to take care of me—"

"There's no place I'd rather be. You are my life. I'm here because I love you."

"I know, honey. Let me finish. I know you're here for me because you love me, and I can't tell you how grateful I am. My point is that you're running on empty, and it's easy to get discouraged. But the truth is you're looking at this all wrong."

"How so?"

"The point of the surgery was to give me the best possible chance at a normal life. Without the operation, that would've been impossible. I made it through, the lesion is gone, at the very least I'm no worse off than I was before, and the results aren't clear yet. I may still get everything we wanted for me, and, best of all, my brain hasn't lost the one thing that's most important to me—you."

"Oh."

"I love you, Dani. Whatever happens in the end, I made it through because I had you waiting for me. You gave me the courage to live and take a risk. You were my strength."

"In many ways, you saved my life. For the first time ever, I knew there was someone I could count on. Someone who would never leave me to face a challenge by myself."

"Never," Danica said. "Together. Side by side."

"I know. I'm counting on it. Above all else, I know that no matter how tough life gets, no matter what else happens, I have someone who will always love me just the same and fight for me."

"Always, Chase."

Chase shrugged. "That's all that matters, Dani. Everything else is gravy. We have each other, and whatever fate has in store for us, together we'll make it the best life it can be."

"I promise you, we will."

"And I promise you, we will. Together we can do anything."

"Yes, we can."

EPILOGUE

Danica and Chase walked hand in hand along the beach—the same beach where they first had fallen in love a year earlier. The sun was slipping toward the horizon and they stopped to admire the brilliant hues of red, orange, and deep blue.

"Are you happy?" Chase asked.

"Very," Danica answered. "Are you really enjoying being on tour with me full time? I know you're making my life and Toni's so much easier."

"Oh, yes. The separations were too long. I missed you terribly, and I love the challenge of managing the road show."

"And I worried about you, endlessly. There's only one thing more I could wish for—" Danica was interrupted by the ringing of her cell phone.

"Hello?"

"Is this Chase Crosley?"

"No. This is her partner, Danica. Who is this?"

"This is Doctor Jacoby's office. Sorry to be calling so late, but I'm just catching up on my 'to call' list."

"That's fine."

"Is Chase there? Can I speak to her?"

Danica's stomach did a flip. "She's right here. Hold on." She handed the phone to Chase and said a silent prayer.

"Hello? This is Chase."

Danica watched Chase's face.

"Yes. Okay. I see. Very well. Thank you. Yes, I appreciate your working late so that I could have the news. Okay. Right. Have a good night."

Chase hung up the phone.

"Well?" Danica tried to read something—anything—from Chase's expression, but it was impossible.

Chase turned to face her and took both her hands. For long seconds, Chase seemed to be searching for something in her eyes.

Danica swallowed hard but withstood the scrutiny.

"The MRI says I'm perfectly fine. No evidence of a lesion, no residual clotting, nothing at all. I'm completely clear."

Danica whooped with joy.

"There's more. Because I haven't had any seizures except that one shortly after the surgery, Doctor Jacoby wants to transition me completely off the anticonvulsants. He's confident I'm seizure-free and that I'll remain so."

"Oh, baby." Danica's eyes shone with unshed tears.

"And since I haven't had any episodes of aphasia or instances of short-term memory problems, he's prepared to pronounce the surgery a complete success. I'm in the clear."

"Chase." Danica's voice was choked with emotion.

"I love you, Dani. You are my present and my future. And a long future it will be."

"I love you, Chase." Danica held up their joined hands and watched their rings sparkle in the waning light of the sunset. "The first light of day and the last golden ray of sunshine. I want to spend every sunrise and sunset with you."

"My sun rises and sets with you, Dani, and there's no other way I want to live."

Chase leaned forward and captured Danica's mouth. The kiss was slow, tender, sweet, passionate, and filled with the promise of forever.

They only broke apart long enough to watch the last bit of orange disappear below the horizon, secure in the knowledge that it was a sight they would enjoy together for many years to come.

The End

Visual Epilogue™

    I hope you've enjoyed spending some quality time with Chase and Danica. I'm sure you've heard the expression, "A picture is worth a thousand words"—it is when it's taken by the extraordinary photographer Judy Francesconi.

    When I look at this beautiful Francesconi photograph, I see Chase and Danica brought to life before my very eyes. I wanted to share that vision with you. If you look closely at the front cover of *Heartsong*, you will find both of these women. It is fitting that although they started their journey apart, Chase and Danica end it together, united by a love so profound that nothing can tear it asunder.

    Enjoy.

Lynn Ames

    I am a hopeful romantic, and that fact is evident in my images. They reflect my belief in the power of honoring the love you share with someone, and in the power of that love conquering all. I prefer stories that have a happy ending! That is why I love *Heartsong* and why I reread it and revisit the characters time and again.

JUDY FRANCESCONI

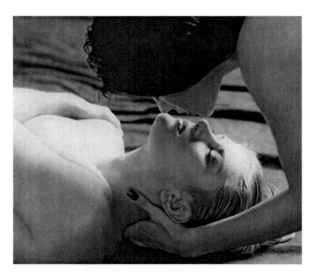

About the Author

A former press secretary to the New York state Senate minority leader, an award-winning former broadcast journalist, a former public information officer for the nation's third-largest prison system, and a former editor of a national art magazine, Lynn Ames is a nationally recognized speaker and CEO of a public relations firm with a particular expertise in image, crisis communications planning, and crisis management.

Ms. Ames's works include the best-selling novels *The Price of Fame* (which was short-listed for the Golden Crown Literary Society's inaugural award for best lesbian romance), *The Cost of Commitment, The Value of Valor* (winner of the 2007 Arizona Book Award), *One ~ Love* (formerly *The Flip Side of Desire*; nominated for a 2007 Goldie Award for Best Popular Fiction), *Heartsong* (a finalist for the Golden Crown Literary Society's award for best lesbian romance), and *Outsiders.*

More about the author, including contact information, other writings, news about other original upcoming works, pictures of locations mentioned in this novel, links to resources related to issues raised in this book, author and character interviews, and purchasing assistance can be found at www.lynnames.com.

You can purchase other Phoenix Rising Press books online at www.phoenixrisingpress.com or at your local bookstore.

Published by
Phoenix Rising Press
Phoenix, AZ

Visit us on the Web: **www.phoenixrisingpress.com**

LaVergne, TN USA
18 January 2011
212878LV00004B/58/P